Praise for R. G. Belsky
The Kennedy Connection

"Engrossing thriller . . . a terrific story."

—*Kirkus Reviews* (starred review)

"Deserves to be short-listed for the year-end best of lists."

—*BookReporter*

"Fascinating character study . . . a roller coaster ride that veers back to 1963 and forward to the present."

—*The Huffington Post*

"Unexpectedly clever twists."

—*Library Journal*

"Must-read . . . a great tabloid yarn."

—*New York Post*

"Had me from the opening line."

—*Star-Ledger*

"I loved *The Kennedy Connection*!"

—Jan Burke

"Gil Malloy for President!"

—Donald Bain

"This is a very clever murder mystery . . . could not put it down."

—*Men Reading Books*

"Intriguing . . . will appeal to those who just can't leave the grassy knoll alone."

—*Booklist*

"Shrewd doses of competition, conspiracy, and corruption fuel this intriguing media thriller."

—Julie Kramer,
national bestselling author of *Delivering Death*

"Who better to tell the story of a newsman in disgrace—than a man from the New York tabloids, where disgrace was a badge of honor. Belsky has the newsman's gift. He tells his story well."

—Jimmy Breslin

"If you love your mysteries with historical references and a modern twist, you are gonna love this page-turner!"

—*Bless Their Hearts* book blog

"In Gil Malloy, Belsky has created a character who you'll want to spend time with."

—Matthew Klein, author of *No Way Back*

"Great read."

—Bill Reynolds, *Providence Journal*

"*The Kennedy Connection* begs to be finished from the first page to the last. Be prepared to stay at home all day with this book in hand!"

—Briana Goodchild, reviewer, Killer Nashville

Shooting for the Stars

"I read it in two sittings."

—Sandra Brown, *New York Times* bestselling author

"Smart, juicy . . . highly satisfying."

—*Publishers Weekly*

"Belsky is a tantalizing, devilish, mesmerizing writer."

—Killer Nashville

"What shines brightest here is Belsky's talent for keeping the pace steady and fast so that every round of inquiries produces more satisfyingly tawdry revelations."

—*Kirkus Reviews*

"This wisecracking but suprisingly sensitive and self-aware crime solver will appeal to fans of Robert Crais's Elvis Cole novels and Harlan Coben's early Myron Bolitar mysteries."

—*Booklist*

"Completely entertaining. And he nails the voice of his wonderfully authentic reporter Gil Malloy. Loved it."

—Hank Phillippi Ryan,
Agatha award–winning author of *Truth Be Told*

"Great story. . . . A highly readable book."

—*Men Reading Books*

"A fast-paced, fun read with twists around every corner."

—Julia Dahl, author of *Invisible City*

"Belsky has created yet another entertaining Gil Malloy thriller. . . . Malloy's personality makes it comical, shrewd, and engaging, a truly enjoyable read."

—*Mysterious Galaxy Bookstore*

"This book is journalism at its best. . . . There is not a dull moment throughout this book as it is laden with mystery and suspense."

—*Night Owl Reviews*

BLONDE ICE

A Gil Malloy Novel

R. G. Belsky

ATRIA PAPERBACK

New York   London   Toronto   Sydney   New Delhi

ATRIA PAPERBACK
An Imprint of Simon & Schuster, Inc.
1230 Avenue of the Americas
New York, NY 10020

First Atria Paperback edition October 2016

ATRIA PAPERBACK and colophon are trademarks of Simon & Schuster, Inc.

For information about special discounts for bulk purchases, please contact Simon & Schuster Special Sales at 1-866-506-1949 or business@simonandschuster.com.

The Simon & Schuster Speakers Bureau can bring authors to your live event. For more information or to book an event, contact the Simon & Schuster Speakers Bureau at 1-866-248-3049 or visit our website at www.simonspeakers.com.

Manufactured in the United States of America

10 9 8 7 6 5 4 3 2 1

Library of Congress Cataloging-in-Publication Data has been applied for.

ISBN 978-1-5011-2978-0
ISBN 978-1-5011-2979-7 (ebook)

"The female of the species is more deadly than the male."

—*Rudyard Kipling*

"She's so cold, she's so cold . . . I'm so hot for her, and she's so cold."

—*The Rolling Stones*

PART ONE

LIVE FROM NEW YORK

CHAPTER 1

THE best thing about being a newspaper reporter is working on a big story. A big story is what it's all about in the news business. It gets your adrenaline flowing. It makes you remember why you wanted to be a reporter in the first place. It makes you forget about all the problems in your life. A big story always makes everything better.

I did not have a big story.

Gil Malloy, the hotshot reporter, did not have anything to report.

It was 9 a.m., and I was sitting in the newsroom with my feet up on my desk, sipping black coffee and pondering this dilemma—along with trying to remember exactly why I had ordered that last tequila the night before—when the phone rang.

"There's someone here to see you, Malloy," said Zeena, the receptionist outside the *New York Daily News* offices.

"Who is it?"

"A woman."

"What's her name?"

"She didn't say."

"What does she want?"

"She says she has a news story."

"What kind of a news story?"

"She didn't tell me."

Zeena was a practitioner of the minimalist school of receptionists. She never gave you anything more than she had to. Getting information from her was like interrogating a prisoner at Gitmo.

"Have her talk to one of the other reporters," I said.

"She asked for you."

"I don't do walk-in news tipsters."

"Why not?"

"I'm a TV star now, remember?"

"Okay."

"Anything else?"

"Stacy was looking for you before you came in."

Stacy Albright was the city editor of the *Daily News*.

"Any idea what she wanted?"

"No."

"Where is she now?"

"Beats me."

"Good job, Zeena," I said.

After I hung up, I checked my voicemail just in case the Pulitzer people had called, Hillary Clinton wanted to do an exclusive sitdown interview, or Bob Woodward was looking for any reporting tips from me. There was a series of messages. All of them from the same person. Peggy Kerwin.

I listened to them one after another. The basic highlights were that she really wanted to see me again, she thought we hit it off as a great team, and—if you read between the lines of what she was saying—she hoped to be the mother of my babies.

Now I remembered why I'd had that last tequila.

To try to forget about Peggy Kerwin.

Peggy Kerwin was the worst kind of date. Nice woman, decent looking, good job. But she was completely boring. She talked about working at some big accounting firm, about her family, about her life and dreams and world peace and a zillion other things during the entire damn evening. By after-dinner drinks, she'd made my Top 10 list of all-time worst dates. Hence, that final tequila.

Marilyn Staley, the *Daily News* managing editor, walked over to my desk. Marilyn was in her fifties, had a husband and two kids in Westchester, and was my city editor at the *News* for many years. Then she got fired when the paper went through a big youth movement—stressing a digital-first strategy, enhanced social media presence, and total demographic makeover—that they decided she was too old to be a part of. They told her she didn't understand what the new media newspapers needed to embrace in order to survive. But eventually they realized that they needed someone like Marilyn to . . . well, run the news. So they hired her back and promoted her to managing editor. Go figure. As editors go, she was all right. Of course, the bar isn't set very high when it comes to newspaper editors.

"What are you doing, Gil?" she asked.

"Being introspective."

"You look hungover."

"Yeah, well there's that too."

"Rough night?"

"I had the date from hell."

"You're getting too old for this."

"But I still have my boyish charm, right?"

I sipped on some more of the black coffee. It helped.

"Any idea what Stacy wants to talk to me about?"

"Bob Wylie."

"Ah, yes. Our nationally renowned crime fighter and potential future mayor."

"I think he wants to drop a big trial balloon about his candidacy for mayor through the *News*. Do it with you on the air as part of *Live from New York*. Stacy thinks that would be a terrific opportunity to promote us as a new media/print crossover. We put it on the air, we live tweet it, we post podcasts on the website, and eventually, of course, we put it in the paper."

Life used to be so much simpler for me.

I was a newspaper reporter, which is all I'd ever wanted to be. I rose from cub reporter to star writer to columnist at the *Daily News* like a skyrocket. I thought it would always be like that for me. But then things went horribly wrong—some of which were my fault and some that weren't. I almost got fired from the paper, then did get fired at another point—but wound up breaking a couple of front page stories that got the *Daily News* national attention. Now I was a star again. Just not in the same way as before.

Somewhere along the line the paper decided to take advantage of all the notoriety I'd gotten by using me as a publicity vehicle. I wound up doing a lot of webcasts, social media live chats with the readers, and making appearances on TV and radio and everywhere on the Internet to promote the paper's biggest stories.

Then, a few months ago, Stacy came up with the idea to partner with a local TV news station to promote our big stories on air. It is called *Live From New York*. We talk about the news the paper is covering and give viewers an inside look at the *Daily News* people who are covering it. At the same time, the telecast is livestreamed on both of our websites. Guess who Stacy picked to be a big part of it? That's right: yours truly.

Now I was on TV regularly talking about the big news stories—even more than I was actually reporting them. It was heady stuff, I must admit. People recognized me on the street, there was more money, it was kinda neat being a broadcast celebrity. But I missed being a real reporter.

Marilyn Staley sat down now in front of my desk.

I asked her if she wanted to hear all the details about my date the night before.

She said she'd just as soon not.

"Hey, is that a touch of gray you're getting there?" she said to me.

"What are you talking about?"

"Your hair. I see a speckle or two of gray."

"Probably just the light in here makes it look like that."

"Sure, I guess that's it," Marilyn agreed.

I looked out the window next to my desk. Spring had finally come to New York City. We'd had a helluva winter—four months of relentless snow, ice, and cold that seemed like it would go on forever. Now I could see the sun shining brightly, people walking on the sidewalk outside in their shirtsleeves. It was as if Mother Nature had finally said, "Enough already."

I loved spring. My favorite season of the year. A time for new beginnings, a fresh start, another chance to make right all the things in your life that had gone wrong in the year before. Spring always cheered me up and made me feel young again and optimistic about the future.

"Damn, that's going to bum me out all day," I said.

"What?"

"Your comment about me getting gray hairs."

"Getting gray hair isn't the worst thing in the world, Gil."

"Not the best either."

"How old are you?"

"I just turned thirty-eight."

"Well, people do start turning gray at that age. And somehow they still manage to go on with their lives."

"You mean like George Clooney?"

"Interesting comparison."

"An apt one too."

"You're telling me you think you look like George Clooney?"

"On his good days."

Marilyn sighed and stood up. She had a higher threshold for

my personality than most people did at the *News*, but I think I'd just about reached it with her. She started to walk away toward her office, then stopped and turned around.

"By the way, there's a woman waiting outside to see you," she said.

"So I heard."

"She apparently wants to talk to you about a story."

"Yeah, people keep telling me that."

"Do you know what the story is?"

"No, Zeena didn't feel compelled to ask her that question."

"The woman's name is Victoria Issacs."

I stared at Marilyn.

"Do you know her?" she asked.

Yeah, I knew her, all right.

Not really as Victoria Issacs though.

I remembered her by another name.

Houston.

CHAPTER 2

'D only met Victoria Issacs once before. But she'd played such a big part in my life that I felt as if I'd known her forever. Not as Victoria Issacs, the person she was now. But as Houston, the person she used to be.

Houston was a famous New York City prostitute. She got her name from Houston Street in downtown Manhattan, where she'd first worked before moving up to expensively priced escort services with high rollers all around town. She'd become a legend in the world of hookers.

Which is why I made her the focus of a series I did for the *Daily News* about prostitution in New York City. I quoted her at length in the articles, talking about her life on the streets and in hotel rooms and the kinky stuff men paid her to do.

The only problem was I never actually talked to Houston. Instead, I'd strung the quotes together secondhand from people who said they knew her, and then made it sound like they came directly to me from Houston. Which is a journalistic no-no. The truth eventually came out, and I almost lost my job. A lot of people even questioned whether Houston ever existed. I believed she did, but I had no proof. To this day, what I did on that story is my biggest mistake in journalism. It will haunt me until the day I die.

Much later, I was finally able to track down Houston. She

was living as Mrs. Victoria Issacs now. Her husband, Walter, was a prominent corporate attorney; she had two beautiful children and a townhouse on Sutton Place. She'd discovered art and spent much of her time painting. No one—not her husband, her family, her friends—knew about her past life. I could have written a story about it all, which, by proving Houston really did exist, might have helped clear up the stain on my reputation from the controversial series. But I didn't. Instead, I walked away and let Victoria Issacs keep living her new life.

I figured that was the last time I would ever see her.

But now here she was sitting in front of me again.

"How are you, Mr. Malloy?" she said to me.

"I'm just fine, Mrs. Issacs. And you can call me Gil."

"Please call me Vicki."

"Well, Vicki," I said, "now that we're both on a first name basis . . ."

"You're wondering why I'm here?"

"The thought had crossed my mind."

"I guess I'm probably just about the last person in the world you'd expect to walk into your newsroom."

"You'd sure be on my short list."

She looked good. Damn good. She had to be well into her thirties now, but she was still drop-dead gorgeous. Long blonde hair, wearing a fashionably short skirt, a silver chain-link belt, a low-cut pale blue sweater, and expensive-looking boots. She crossed her legs while she talked, and I couldn't help but notice they were mighty fine-looking too. I could see why men had paid her hundreds of dollars—sometimes thousands—for an hour or two of her companionship.

We were sitting in an empty office at the *Daily News*. There were plenty of empty offices at the paper these days due to all the layoffs in recent months. All newspapers were struggling to stay alive, and belt-tightening was a big part of that. I'd suggested we move out of the newsroom because I didn't want anyone there overhearing our conversation. I figured she felt that way too.

Except she hadn't really said anything yet. Oh, she'd talked about her kids, community work, and paintings that she was doing, even about watching me on TV—but nothing about why she was there.

I listened quietly to all of it, sneaking a peek once or twice at her legs as she crossed and uncrossed them. I deduced that she was wearing old-fashioned silk stockings, that her calf muscles were in terrific condition, and that the skirt she was wearing might even have been shorter than I had first suspected. Hey, I'm an investigative reporter. You can never accumulate too much information.

"Mr. Malloy, there's something I have to tell you," she said.

"Gil," I reminded her.

"Gil, this is very difficult for me to talk about. But I didn't know where else to turn. The last time we met—the only time—you agreed to keep my past a secret. I was impressed with your honesty, your kindness, your sensitivity to how devastating it would be if the people in my life now ever found out about Houston. I . . . well, I need someone with that kind of sensitivity now."

"I can do sensitive," I said.

"I just have to be absolutely certain before I tell you what I'm about to say that you'll handle all of this very discreetly."

"I can do discreet."

She sighed.

"I'm still not sure how to even begin. . . ."

Victoria Issacs suddenly burst into tears.

"My husband is gone," she said.

"Gone how?"

"He hasn't come home in two days."

"Have you reported this to the police?"

"No."

"Maybe you should."

"I can't involve the police."

She'd stopped crying now. She took a tissue out of her purse and dabbed at her eyes with it.

"I think Walter has been cheating on me," she said.

"Okay."

"I've suspected it for a while."

"With one woman or more than one?"

"I'm not sure."

"Did your husband admit to you that he was seeing someone else?"

"No."

"Do you have anything beyond your own suspicions to indicate that he is cheating on you?"

"No."

"Then how do you know for sure?"

"A woman senses something like that. Especially a woman like me. Husbands would cheat on their wives with me all the time. I know the signs from being on the other side of that equation. I don't know if it's one woman or more than one or even prostitutes that he's paying. But he's more interested in them than in me."

Looking at her again, I couldn't imagine why Walter Issacs would want to cheat on this woman. No matter how beautiful some new girlfriend was.

"Listen," I said, "you're not the first woman whose husband has cheated on her. A majority of marriages in America wind up with some kind of infidelity. The rest of them . . . hell, they're thinking about fooling around too, but they haven't gotten up the courage to actually live out the fantasy. The whole idea of the happy marriage is pretty much a mirage these days, as far as I can tell."

"You sound very cynical about marriage."

"I guess I am."

"Have you ever been married?"

"Once."

"It didn't work out?"

"She's married to someone else now. So no, we did not live happily ever after. The only difference here is I can't understand why your husband would want to cheat on you. You're the kind of woman men sneak out on their wives to cheat with. Like you said, you know how that works better than anyone from all the men who paid you all that money back in the day to be with you. So why would your husband need to go to anyone else when he had you waiting at home for him?"

She smiled slightly now. "I learned a lot about men as Houston," she said. "Men are always attracted to what they don't have. Even if what they have is pretty darn good. I was far more appealing to men as a flirty and promiscuous call girl than I am as a wife and a mother, I guess. The grass is always greener, or something like that. Anyway, that's how most men screw up their marriages. By not realizing how good a woman they've already got and going looking for more excitement."

I nodded. She could have been talking about me and how I messed up my marriage to Susan, but I didn't tell her that.

"So you think that your husband's disappearance is somehow related to his playing around with other women?" I asked.

"I think so. I'm not sure, but . . . yes."

"Okay, your husband is shacked up with someone else. I'm sorry, but it happens."

"I just hope that's all it is."

"What else could it be?"

She reached into her purse. At first, I thought she was going to take out more tissues for her eyes. But instead she had a piece of paper in her hand.

"Did you ever tell anyone that I used to be Houston after that day you found me?" she asked.

"No."

"You're sure about that?"

"Of course, I'm sure."

"Not even your editor? Maybe to make sure you got your job back? Or a close friend? Or some woman you were sleeping with, in a moment of passionate outburst? Have you ever told anyone, anywhere, anything about how I really was the Houston in your story? I have to know the truth."

"I've never told anyone," I said. "Why would I? I have as much to lose as you by doing that at this point. Hell, knowing the truth about Houston and keeping it from my editors—it would have been a great follow-up story—that's as almost as bad a journalistic sin as pretending I found and talked to you in the first place."

"I have to know that I can trust you."

"We share a secret, Vicki," I said. "You and I both. We need to be able to trust each other."

She hesitated for a moment, looking down at the piece of paper in her hand that she'd taken from her purse.

"I found this note under my front door," she said. "While I was worrying about why my husband hadn't come back. I didn't know what to do. I didn't want to tell the police. Or any of my friends. All I could think of was you. You were the only person I could talk to about this. I kept hoping you'd have some answers. I almost wished you had told someone about Houston. At least it would make some sense then."

"I've never told anyone," I repeated.

"Then how do you explain this?"

She handed me the piece of paper.

I read the note.

It consisted only of a few words. Someone had written them on the paper in large letters with a red Magic Marker. The note said:

"I know where your husband is, Houston."

CHAPTER 3

I WAS living on East 36th Street, just off Lexington, in the Murray Hill section. I'd moved there from Chelsea after breaking up with the last woman I'd been seeing. Before that, I'd been on the Upper East Side, where I'd moved from Gramercy Park after my marriage broke up. I had a problem staying in an apartment by myself where I'd spent a lot of time with a woman I loved. Too many memories, I guess. It was easier just to move on. At the moment, I was considering the possibility of moving to Brooklyn or Staten Island to get away from Peggy Kerwin.

I let myself into the empty apartment, grabbed a beer from the refrigerator, plopped down on my couch, and turned on the TV set. TV was the perfect solution for loneliness. TV was my true friend.

I clicked around through the channels—watching snatches of news, sports, cable reruns—and thought about Houston and her missing husband.

Before I left work, I'd talked to a police detective I knew named Frank Wohlers. I trusted him and I figured he could check into it quietly for me. I told him how Walter Issacs was a prominent attorney, and that his wife—who was a friend of mine—had become concerned because he had not come home. I did not tell him about his wife's suspicions that he was cheating on her with other women. Or how I knew the wife. Or about the note she'd gotten, addressed to Houston. Those details might have to come out later, but I was hoping Wohlers would find out some answers without them. He said he'd make some discreet inquiries and get back to me as soon as he came up with anything.

There were still several problems I had with all this.

First, what would make Walter Issacs disappear? He'd never done that before, so why now? Even if he was running off with another woman, there were more logical ways to leave your wife. There was also the possibility of foul play, of course. But then wouldn't he have shown up in a hospital or—worst case scenario—the morgue by now? I suppose he could have been kidnapped, but why target him? He was a successful lawyer, but he wasn't famous or particularly high-profile or controversial. Kidnapping didn't make any more sense than any of the other possibilities.

My second concern was over my own involvement in this. If whoever wrote that note knew about Victoria Issacs's past life as Houston, then maybe they knew about my knowledge of it too. How I'd tracked her down and never told anyone—most notably my editors at the paper—that she really did exist. I didn't like the idea of anyone else knowing that secret besides her and me.

Finally, and perhaps most troubling of all, Houston, I had thought, was finally in the past. The most traumatic thing I'd ever gone through, it dramatically affected my career, my marriage, my whole psyche, for years. I wound up having anxiety attacks from it. Attacks so bad that I needed to see a doctor and a psychiatrist and take medicine to battle the stress. It left me a different person. But now I had thought it was finally over. That illusion was shattered when Victoria Issacs—aka Houston—walked into my newsroom that morning.

I finished off my beer, grabbed another one from the refrigerator, and switched around the channels looking for something to take my mind off all of this and my empty apartment and the many other problems in my life.

One of the cable channels was showing reruns of *Mister Ed*. Perfect. Wilbur was in trouble with his neighbors because Mister Ed had been making annoying phone calls to them. Everyone thought it was Wilbur making the calls, and he wasn't able to convince them it wasn't because he couldn't tell them that . . . uh, his horse talked. With TV fare like this, who needed a woman around?

It had been more than six months now since Sherry DeConde left. We'd met while I was working on a big story that involved her and wound up in a pretty passionate romance for a while. She was a theatrical agent in Greenwich Village, and we split our time between her townhouse there and my apartment in Chelsea. In the end, it didn't last though. She was much older than me, twenty-five years or so, although she still looked damn good and damn sexy. We might have survived the age difference, but we both also carried a lot of messy baggage from our pasts that in the end couldn't be forgotten. Sherry had been married four times. She wanted to marry me too. She thought that would solve everything. I kept holding her off on the marriage stuff, and then one day she was just gone. The next time I heard from her she was in Europe. She traveled around there, finally settling down in Italy, where she met a count or something and married him. When I asked her why, she said: "I get married, Gil. It's what I do."

My ex-wife, Susan, had married again too. To an estate lawyer, or something like that. Susan was a prominent assistant district attorney in Manhattan, and the two of them together were a definite power couple. For a long time after our divorce I'd held out hope that she'd come back to me. Endured the other men in her life, even an engagement to another guy. But there wasn't much I could do after she got married. That was pretty much the end of it for me.

And then there was the other woman in my life. Houston. I gotta say again that I couldn't stop thinking about how good she looked when she came to see me at the *News*. The first time I saw her she looked more like a housewife and a mother. This time I could see the "Houston" sexiness that drove so many men mad for her. Maybe she'd glammed herself up to try to win her husband back. Whatever, it was all academic. She came to me because she was worried that her husband might be badly injured or dead or something. I decided it would be extremely tacky for me to ask her out on a date while she was waiting to find out.

I needed someone else.

There had to be another woman out there for me.

I mean what I was looking for in a woman really shouldn't be all that difficult to find.

All I wanted was someone who was attractive, intelligent, interesting to talk with, a nice person and . . . well, not married.

———

I'd DVR'd a previous appearance I'd done recently on *Live from New York* with Bob Wylie, who was the deputy mayor for New York. I figured it might be useful to re-watch now since Stacy wanted me to interview him again. It used to make me uncomfortable to watch myself on TV. But now I sort of liked it.

At the moment, Wylie was the leading contender to be the next mayor. He had quite an impressive résumé—in politics, law enforcement, and private business. He'd been police commissioner in a few cities, most notably St. Louis, and then moved to New York, where he set up a lucrative private security business. After the current mayor of New York was elected, he recruited Wylie to be his top deputy mayor—creating a new role for Wylie in which he oversaw all aspects of law enforcement. This included the police, city anti-terror agencies, school safety, and coordinating with transit, fire, and federal agencies as well as community officials. The mayor and Wylie hailed this establishment of an overall law enforcement czar as an innovative approach for fighting crime in the twenty-first century.

It was a good idea. Maybe too good, at least for the mayor. Wylie racked up an impressive record in the job, dramatically cutting back crime and strengthening police ties with the community at the same time. But it was Wylie, not the mayor, who got most of the credit for it. He was a good-looking, charismatic guy who exuded energy and self-confidence. He'd become a media darling and his popularity soared. Now he was expected to run against the mayor in the upcoming election and—from what I'd found out at the *News* this morning—it appeared he wanted to drop a big hint about that to me.

The appearance I'd DVR'd was of Wylie at the Police Academy. He was there to talk to the graduating recruits about the rewards and responsibilities of a life on the force. One of the graduates was Vincent D'Nolfo—who I'd met when he worked as a bodyguard for a TV star named Abbie Kincaid. D'Nolfo and I hadn't gotten along very well at first, but—after Abbie was murdered—we kind of bonded and kept in touch. He'd been an Army Ranger in Iraq and Afghanistan when he was younger, but then bounced around between private security jobs. I suggested—and even put him in touch with someone in the department I knew—he take the NYPD entrance exam. He did it just before reaching the maximum age of thirty-five, and now was one of the oldest police recruits on record. I set up an on-air meeting between him and Wylie which turned out to be pure media gold. D'Nolfo told Wylie a moving story of how his best buddy in Iraq had died saving his and other soldiers' lives during an ambush. He said he always carried a picture of his dead friend with him in his pocket now and knew that the friend would somehow watch out for him on the streets of New York too. Wylie spoke eloquently as he praised D'Nolfo's service to both his country and his city.

Afterward, Wylie took me aside and talked to me privately for a while.

"That was great," he said. "Hell, you just did more to make me look good than my goddamned PR director has done since he started."

"That doesn't surprise me," I told him.

"What do you mean?"

"Most PR people are useless," I said. "Like that old joke about them: How many PR people does it take to change a lightbulb? I don't know, I'll have to get back to you on that one."

Wylie smiled at me.

"Can you and I speak frankly, Malloy?"

"Sure. Speak frankly."

"I've asked around about you. People say you're a helluva reporter. Smart, talented, relentless, fair . . ."

"All qualities of mine. And don't forget modest."

"They also say you're a total pain in the ass to work with."

"That might be a little too frank," I told him.

He said he had a lot of people working for him. Some good, some not so good. His top aide was a guy named Tim Hammacher who was tough, not afraid to upset people—a real ball-buster, as Wylie put it. He wanted someone else like that to join his team. Someone like me, he said.

"Do you mean in the deputy mayor's office?" I asked.

"I'm talking about in the mayor's office when I get to city hall."

I figured the whole thing was a win-win situation for me. If I did wind up taking a job with him, it would mean a lot of money and power and prestige. I doubted that I would make the move because my only real ambition is to be the best reporter in the world. But it didn't hurt to have an ally in the potential future mayor. I'd told him that day at the Police Academy I'd think about the job offer. I figured I could string him along that way for a while. In the meantime, I could get some inside stuff from him and this guy Hammacher on his campaign.

———

My part of the *Live from New York* telecast was over now. I clicked off the DVR and went back to channel surfing. Just in time too. The *Mister Ed* episode was wrapping up. Wilbur was in the barn with Mister Ed when his wife, Carol, brought him his lunch there. Then she kissed him and left. God, I envied Wilbur. A pretty wife. She brings you your lunch and kisses you. Plus you have a talking horse too.

Now that was a perfect marriage.

Not like my marriage.

Or Walter and Victoria Issacs's.

I wondered what had happened to Walter. I could call Wohlers and ask him if he'd found out anything yet. But Wohlers worked the day shift, and he probably had gone home by now. Besides, he had promised to get back to me with any information.

One way or another, I'd soon find out something.

The best-case scenario was that Issacs had indeed run off with some other woman and not told his wife.

The worst-case scenario . . . well, I wasn't sure about that.

But I had a bad feeling—a reporter's instinct, I guess—that there wasn't going to be a happy ending to this story.

"So where the hell is Walter Issacs?" I said out loud to myself.

CHAPTER 4

HEY found him the next day. Stabbed to death in a posh midtown hotel room.

"It's bad," Wohlers said when he called me at the office with the news.

"What happened?"

"Maid found the body when she went in to clean the room this morning. He'd been stabbed multiple times. I mean we're talking about a lot of stab wounds. There's blood all over the place. It looks like he's been dead for a couple of days. I'm here now. Hotel Madison, just off of 47th Street."

"Any idea what Issacs was doing at the Hotel Madison?"

"I think he was having some kind of sexual assignation."

"What makes you think that?"

"There was semen found on the sheets of the bed."

"Always a clue."

"So you want to tell me again how you're involved in this, Malloy. And exactly what you know or don't know about Walter Issacs. And his wife. This is a murder case now. No more bullshit."

"I'm on my way to the hotel now," I said. "I'll tell you what I can when I get there."

I grabbed a cab outside the *Daily News* building. On the way uptown, I dialed Victoria Issacs's number. I was sort of hoping she wouldn't pick up. I really didn't want to be the one to break this news to her. But it turned out I didn't have to worry about that. She already knew her husband was dead, and the gory details of how it happened. The cops had managed to notify her before I made the call.

"Why would someone do this to Walter?" she sobbed to me over the phone. "I just don't understand. Why would anyone kill him? Why would anyone want him dead? Can you tell me who would want to do something like that?"

I said I couldn't.

She clearly didn't know either.

Maybe Wohlers would have some answers.

When I got to the hotel, I was the only reporter there. Wohlers had cut me a break by not alerting the rest of the press yet. So I got as many basic details as I could and called the story into the *Daily News* desk. There wasn't much to say. But the headline PROMINENT LAWYER SLASHED TO DEATH IN POSH MIDTOWN HOTEL was sure to generate hits on the website as soon as it posted. Especially since it was a clear beat on every other news organization in town. I'd write a complete story for the paper too, of course, but that would come later. I just wanted to get something out there quick. Then hopefully I'd have more exclusive material for the print edition in the morning.

"So stabbing was the cause of Issacs's death?" I asked Wohlers.

"Take your pick—stabbing, strangulation, or beaten to death."

"What is this—a multiple choice quiz?"

"No, it looks like Issacs had all those things done to him. There were ligature marks on his wrists and ankles too that indicated he'd been tied up or restrained for some period of time. But it looks like the stab wounds were what finally killed him."

Wohlers told me that the hotel clerk at the front desk remembered Issacs checking in three nights earlier.

That matched the timetable of when his wife said he disappeared.

"He was with a woman. Blonde. Maybe about thirty. Very, very attractive. A stone-cold fox was the way the clerk put it. They booked the room for three nights. She called down later and specifically said they didn't want any maid service. They wanted to be left alone for the entire stay. That's why the body wasn't discovered until this morning."

Blonde. About thirty. Very, very attractive. I thought about how that fit the description of Victoria Issacs. Could she have done it?

No, I didn't believe that.

She had sounded in pretty bad shape over the phone. Crying. Sobbing. Screaming. Sure, the thought had occurred to me at first that she could have been the one who killed him. In a jealous rage after tracking him down to the hotel room where he was having an affair with another woman. But, after hearing her reaction on the phone, I discarded that possibility. No one could be that good an actress. Not even Houston.

"Any identification on the woman?" I asked.

"Issacs just signed in under his own name."

"Did you ask the hotel people if there was a security camera at the desk?"

"Gee, now why didn't I think of that? I guess I've just been flailing around here aimlessly until you showed up to give me some crimefighter tips, Malloy."

I ignored the sarcasm.

"Yes and no on the security camera," Wohlers said. "Yes, there is a security camera. No, it wasn't working. They had some kind of malfunction with the system and the hotel hadn't bothered to fix it yet."

"Terrific."

"There are cameras in the elevators. We're trying to get some of that video now."

"So it sounds like he checked in with this woman, they had sex, and she killed him for some reason. Probably that first night. Then she slipped away, and no one discovered the body until the maid went into the room today. That makes sense, right?"

"Except for one thing. The woman ordered room service the next morning. She called down from the room and asked for eggs over easy, bacon, toast, and a big pot of coffee. The order was for just one person, not two. Probably because Walter Issacs was already . . ."

"Dead," I said.

"She kills him, then eats breakfast while the body is still in the room. Weird, huh?"

"Any of the help see her?"

"The waiter who brought the order up to her room. He said she came out when he knocked, took the meal, and then went back inside. He doesn't remember much about her except that she was, well . . ."

"A stone-cold blonde fox," I said.

"That's right."

———

Wohlers wanted some answers from me. About Victoria Issacs. I had thought about how much I would tell him. In the end, I told him everything. I didn't think I really had too much choice.

"She was a prostitute," I said.

"And you were one of her customers?"

"Not exactly."

"What exactly then?"

"I wrote about her for the paper. A long time ago. A series of articles I did on prostitution in New York. She was a high-priced hooker back then. She had a different name. It was Houston. She gave up the life, married this lawyer, had some kids—and it seemed like she'd turned her life around."

"Houston? Wait a minute, wasn't that the one you got in all the trouble with? The woman who supposedly never existed?"

"She turned out to be real."

"Did you ever write about that?"

"No."

"Why not?"

"I had my reasons."

I told him about how she'd come to see me after all this time to ask for my help in tracking down her husband.

"Why didn't she just come directly to the police?"

"She didn't want to involve the police."

"Because she suspected her husband was having an affair . . ."

"Well, that was one reason."

"And the other?"

"She got a note at her house. An anonymous note. It said: 'I know where your husband is, Houston.' That's why she came to see me. No one else knows that she once was Houston except for me and her—and now whoever it was that wrote that note. Which could be—very probably is—the same person who murdered her husband."

"Aw, jeez, Malloy," Wohlers groaned. "What a nightmare. Do you have any idea how messy this case could get?"

"Yeah, I do," I said.

———

The security cameras on an elevator at the Hotel Madison had caught the blonde who checked in with Walter Issacs.

In the hotel's security center Wohlers and I watched the video of Issacs and the woman getting into one of the elevators. It had taken a bit of convincing to get Wohlers to allow me to be there with him, but he finally relented after I pointed out that I was the one who first tipped him off that Issacs was missing. I breathed a sigh of relief when I saw the woman on the screen. It wasn't Victoria Issacs. You couldn't see her face, but I could tell enough from what I could see that it had to be someone else.

"That's not his wife," I said to Wohlers.

"So who is she?"

The video was in black-and-white, but you could still tell she was definitely a blonde and definitely very hot. A sexy body in tight jeans and a sleeveless top, tottering on high heels. She had a tattoo—it looked to be in the shape of a heart—on her left arm. On the elevator she stayed standing with her back to the camera.

"Turn around, honey," Wohlers muttered. "Smile nice and pretty into the camera for me."

But she didn't. As the elevator went up to their floor, she kept her back to the camera as she plastered herself all over Issacs. Kissing him—running her hands through his hair and all over his body. Watching it, I couldn't help but think about how turned on with sexual excitement Issacs must have been at that moment. No way he could have suspected what was about to happen.

But why did it happen?

Did this woman do all this stuff spontaneously in the elevator and then kill him because something went horribly wrong when they got to the room and had sex?

Or was the whole thing planned? Did she deliberately lure him there and put on this whole act with the idea of murdering him from the very start?

Or was there some other scenario that we or I hadn't even considered?

When the elevator doors opened, Issacs and the blonde woman

got out and headed toward the room. She seemed to make a slight gesture, and then they were gone. There was no security camera in the hall. The screen went blank.

"She never turned to face the camera," Wohlers said. "You can't see her face."

"Yeah, bad luck, isn't it?" said the head of security for the hotel.

"Bad luck," Wohlers grunted.

I could tell he'd seen something on the screen that bothered him.

"Run it again," he told the security chief.

"Sure."

We watched it one more time and saw the same things. The elevator ride, with her all over him as they headed to the room. The blonde hair, the tight jeans, the sexy top, the tattoo on her arm. The woman and Issacs walking off arm in arm together after the doors opened. And the gesture she made at the end.

"Can you freeze that at the end?" Wohlers asked. "Run it slow motion? Whatever you can do . . ."

"No problem."

We watched it over a few times. I realized what Wohlers was looking at now. The gesture at the end. No question about it. As they got off the elevator, the woman took her right hand off of Issacs and seemed to make a movement with it behind her back. It looked deliberate.

"Give me a close-up on that."

"On what?"

"Her hand behind her back."

"Why?"

"I don't know. That's why I want to see it closer."

At first, it was still hard to make out. But zoomed-in, with the video stopped, I finally understood what the gesture was.

Wohlers did too.

"It's her finger," I said with amazement.

"Right."

"Behind her back."

The security guy looked at the screen.

"What are you guys talking about?"

"Her middle finger," Wohlers told him. "She's got it extended."

"Why?" the security guy asked.

"This woman knew exactly where the camera was," Wohlers said. "That's why she made sure not to turn her face toward it. But she wanted to let us know she did it deliberately. And so . . ."

"She's giving the finger to the camera," I said.

Wohlers nodded. "Basically, she just told us to fuck off."

CHAPTER 5

WROTE the story for the Web and next day's paper. Adding new information along the way as I learned it from Wohlers. I was still way ahead of any other media outlet in town. They were just breaking the basic facts while the *Daily News* had the whole story.

Well, not all of it. I included details about how horrific the crime scene was; how Walter Issacs was found with stab wounds and bruises all over his body; how he had apparently had sex with his killer before he died; and all about the taunting blonde on the elevator that could be seen with him on the security camera. That was all great stuff, and pretty much all of it was exclusive.

I left out what I knew about the note addressed to "Houston." And my own personal connection to the widow. For the sake of the investigation Wohlers wanted to keep quiet about the note, so I was okay on that front for now. But I knew I would have to deal with my bosses at the *Daily News* about it eventually. And that wasn't going to be pleasant.

No question about it, I had a big ethics problem. I'd told the paper years ago that I couldn't find Houston, which was true at the time. They didn't fire me; they took a great deal of criticism for that and my Houston story—yet still they gave me another chance. That I found Houston should have been a big story too, and a redemption of sorts for the paper and for me. But I kept the news to myself. I didn't want to ruin her new life. I thought it was the right thing—the ethical thing—to do. But it was the wrong thing for me to have done as a reporter. A reporter is supposed to report the facts, not parcel them out as he sees fit. So I had somehow managed to do a good ethical thing and a bad ethical thing at the same time. This ethics business sure got tricky.

I needed to make a preemptive strike. Go to Marilyn Staley, Stacy Albright, and the rest of my editors and tell them everything. It was going to come out sooner or later—probably sooner—so I could at least get ahead of it by making a clean breast of everything. There was no way to know what would happen afterward. Sure, I was riding pretty high at the paper these days. But a newspaper reporter can go from the penthouse (i.e., the front page) to the outhouse very quickly. I knew that better than anyone.

For the moment, I fell back into the best security blanket I knew. Just being a reporter. I threw myself into the story and tried to put everything else—all the difficult decisions I had ahead of me—out of my mind.

For now.

————

The next day I was at work still trying to figure out the best way to handle all of this when my desk phone rang. I recognized the number. It was someone I hadn't heard from in a while.

"Hi, Gil." It was my ex-wife, Susan. "Congratulations, you seem to be doing great. A big star on TV. And back on Page One again. I'm really happy for you."

"Thanks," I said, wondering what the call was all about. "What's going on with you?"

"Oh, the usual. Work, work, work—you know the drill."

"How's your husband, the escargot lawyer?"

"Estate lawyer."

"Whatever."

She laughed.

"Wow, you must really want something from me, Susan."

"What do you mean?"

"You used to always get aggravated with me when I made a remark like that."

"I'd just like to talk with you, Gil."

"Talk how?"

"Lunch. Drinks. Something like that."

"The last time we had lunch together you announced to me that you'd gotten married."

"I always felt badly about the way that happened."

"So what's your ulterior motive this time?"

"I have no ulterior motive."

"Everyone has an ulterior motive."

"Not me. I'd just like to see you again. It's been too long."

That's when I knew she had some kind of agenda. We made plans for drinks later in the week. What the hell else was I going to do? Besides, I was interested to see her too after all this time. Always good to be reminded of exactly what you missed out on in your life.

Later that day, I got a postcard from Sherry DeConde in Rome. It was addressed to me at the *Daily News*, probably because I'd never given her my new address after I moved out of Chelsea. There was a picture of the Colosseum on the postcard. On the back she had written: "Sometimes these days I feel as old as this. You always made me feel young, Gil. I still think about you, hope you don't ever forget me. Love, Sherry."

Jeez, what the hell was going on here? All the women from my past were suddenly coming back into my life. Susan. Sherry. And, of course, Houston. When the phone rang again, I kinda half expected to hear from Rosemarie Langford next, the girl I took to my high school senior prom, telling me how much she'd loved the corsage I gave her.

Instead it was Wohlers. He said he was heading over later to do a full interview with Victoria Issacs about her husband's murder. He said she had asked if I could be there too. It was highly irregular, he pointed out, but she insisted.

"What's the deal between the two of you anyway?" Wohlers asked.

"I told you. We shared this secret about her being Houston. I guess it's given us some kind of bond together."

"Are you schtupping her?"

I sighed. "Lieutenant, I don't think people say 'schtupping' anymore."

"Okay, but you still didn't answer my question."

"No, I am not schtupping Victoria Issacs."

"Because she could be a suspect, you know."

"C'mon, even you don't believe that. We saw the woman on the video and it's not her."

"No, we saw the woman on the video who went up to the room with him. They might have had sex up there. But then maybe it was Victoria Issacs who came by later to murder him in a jealous rage for cheating on her."

"Victoria Issacs did not kill her husband."

"Yeah, you're probably right," Wohlers said.

CHAPTER 6

T HE news meeting that morning turned out to be quite a scene. Lots of arguments. Yelling. Screaming. Name-calling. And I gotta say the whole brouhaha was pretty much all because of me.

"We need to put all the resources we can—starting with Gil, of course—on this murder story," Marilyn Staley said.

"Malloy can't do that," Stacy Albright said. "He's the point man on our big *Live from New York* TV interview with Deputy Mayor Bob Wylie when he drops his first big hint that he's running for mayor. Wylie specifically asked to do this with Malloy. This interview is all set. It can't be changed."

"Stacy, we're talking about a sexy front page murder story here," Marilyn said impatiently.

"And I'm talking about a helluva big exclusive on the mayoral race," Stacy snapped back at her.

"Sexy murder trumps mayoral race," Marilyn told her.

Tension between the two of them had been building for some time, ever since Marilyn got rehired as managing editor. Until now, they had managed to coexist in a temporary peace, with Marilyn concentrating on the day-to-day news coverage for the paper and Stacy spending her time building up the Web and social media presence for the paper.

Now the two top female editors at the *Daily News* were battling it out. Over me.

Not that I was a stranger to having two women fight over me. I mean that had happened plenty of times. Okay, maybe not in real life. But I sure had fantasized about it a lot. I decided to take the high road on this one though and act as peacemaker.

"I have an idea," I said. "What if . . ."

"Shut up and stay out of this," Marilyn snapped at me.

"Yeah, what does this have to do with you?" Stacy said.

"I'm the guy you're fighting over," I pointed out.

That stopped them both temporarily.

"Look," I said, "interviewing Wylie is a onetime thing. I can do that in an hour. So I go ahead with that as planned. That's all I have to do on the mayoral race for now to give us the Wylie exclusive. Then the rest of the time I'll work on the Issacs murder story. Make sense?"

Marilyn and Stacy looked at each other warily, each to see what the other one's response would be. I didn't really have a side in this fight, but I was kinda rooting for Marilyn. Even though she had once fired me from the *News* and demoted me during all of the original Houston controversy a few years back. On the other hand, Stacy had given me the opportunity to become a TV star. Although I respected and even sort of liked Marilyn, at least as much as it is possible to like and respect an editor, I didn't feel that way about Stacy. I have a unique set of values when it comes to judging people.

"Do you really think that you can work on both these stories at once?" Marilyn asked me now.

"C'mon, this is Gil Malloy you're talking to. I can leap tall buildings in a single bound. Disguised as a mild-mannered reporter for a great metropolitan newspaper—fighting for truth, justice . . ."

"Cut the crap, Malloy," she said.

"... and the American way." I shrugged. "I figured you'd want to hear the ending."

"Can you do both stories at once? Yes or no?"

"Uh, yes."

Marilyn looked back at Stacy again.

"I guess I can live with that arrangement," she said.

"Me too," Stacy agreed.

Ah, Malloy, you talented son of a gun. Ace reporter. TV star. And now add peacemaker to the résumé too. Maybe when I was done with these stories, I could hire out to the UN and go try to straighten out that whole mess in the Middle East.

———

"What do you think about Bob Wylie?" I asked Zeena as I passed by the receptionist desk.

"Why?"

"I'm supposed to interview him about the mayoral election on *Live from New York*."

"I'd vote for him."

"Really?"

"Sure."

"Why?"

"He's hot."

"Excuse me?"

"You know, like . . . ," she put her finger in her mouth, licked it, and held it up to make a sizzling sound, ". . . hot. Handsome. Nice body. Terrific buns. Now, that's what I call a law enforcement figure. I mean this guy could put a pair of handcuffs on me anytime he wanted."

I sighed. As Winston Churchill once said, the best argument against democracy is a five-minute conversation with the average voter.

On my way out of the newsroom to meet Wohlers for the Victoria Issacs interview, I ran into Marilyn Staley.

"Thanks for stepping up for me in the news meeting the way you did, Gil," she said. "I don't know how this thing with Stacy and me is going to play out. But it's good to know you're on my side."

"Don't worry, I got your back, Marilyn," I said.

Then—when I got to the elevator bank, there was Stacy holding a cup of coffee.

"Gil, I know you have to go along with the crime story thing for a while," she said. "But you and I both know how big the mayoral connection with Wylie could be leading up to the election. The man is on his way to Gracie Mansion. I don't see any of the other contenders stopping him. And—with you on the inside of his campaign—we'll be there with him every step of the way. I really appreciate your support in the meeting. It really makes me feel better knowing I have you on my team."

"Right back at you, Stacy," I smiled.

Malloy's the name, diplomacy's my game.

CHAPTER 7

VER the years I'd interviewed a lot of families of crime victims—and it never got any easier.

Sometimes they fell apart completely, screaming and crying and pleading to God for answers. Other times they were angry and demanded revenge against the criminal who took their loved one away. And then there were those who reacted with no emotion at all, acting almost as if they didn't understand what had happened.

But interviewing Victoria Issacs about the murder of her husband was going to be different.

Because I knew her.

Because I liked her.

And because—for better or for worse—her life and mine had somehow become inexorably intertwined ever since I wrote that memorable Houston story for the *News*.

"What are you going to say to her when we get there?" I asked Wohlers as we drove up to the townhouse on Sutton Place where she lived.

"I'm going to ask her if she knows who killed her husband."

"She doesn't."

"Yeah, well . . . I'd still like to hear her answer."

Wohlers was driving with one hand and eating a meatball sandwich with the other. He was a big man—maybe six-foot-five,

240 pounds—and the most prodigious eater I'd ever seen. He told me he'd just had time to grab the sandwich at the deli before he picked me up near the station house. Eating a meatball sandwich can be a messy business under any circumstances. But doing it while driving a car is almost impossible. I looked at his shirt and saw a big stain of meatball sauce. There was also something yellow—maybe mustard—from a previous meal. At one point, he dropped one of the meatballs on the floor of the car as he made a turn. He reached down and picked it up when we stopped at the next red light, then popped it into his mouth. I was hungry too when I got into the car, but watching him eat had pretty much made me lose my appetite.

"Do you really think Victoria Issacs knows something?" I asked.

"She knew her husband was fooling around. You told me that. Jealousy over a cheating spouse is a pretty good motive for murder."

"I thought we went through all that on the phone."

"You say Victoria Issacs is not the blonde on that hotel security camera video. But I haven't seen her yet. Maybe she wore a disguise."

"Walters Issacs took that woman on the video to the hotel to have sex."

"So you never heard of a man taking his wife to a hotel for sex?"

"Victoria Issacs is not a killer. She's a good person. A good mother. A good wife."

"Who just happened to be the most notorious hooker in New York City at one time."

"Turning tricks is not the same thing as murder."

Wohlers grunted, finished the meatball sandwich, and wiped off the last of the sauce with his sleeve. "They're both against the law."

Victoria Issacs greeted us wearing a pair of blue jeans, a green sleeveless top, and open-toed sandals. Subdued enough attire, but she still looked sexy. I did my best not to leer. But I did wonder idly what the mourning period was for a widow whose husband had cheated on her, before she could have sex again. Three months? Six months? That was a long time to wait. Of course, if I ever did have any kind of personal relationship with Victoria Issacs, it would only complicate the whole Houston mess even more. Then again, I was already deep into the Houston thing again anyway, so I might as well go for it all.

We sat in the living room—the same living room where she and I had sat when I tracked her down as Houston a few years earlier. There were pictures of her two young daughters on a table next to me. She said they were staying with her husband's relatives until the funeral was over. I did not see any pictures of Walter Issacs. I wondered if maybe they had been there, but she took them down when she found out about the tawdry circumstances of his death.

"Wow!" Wohlers said to me under his breath, when she was out of earshot.

"Yeah, wow," I muttered.

I thought maybe he would get right to the picture of the woman in the elevator. She hadn't seen it yet. No one had, the photo hadn't been made public. If she could somehow identify the woman, that would help answer a lot of questions.

But he started out slowly instead, quietly asking her questions about her husband and herself.

"Did you know your husband was spending the night at the hotel?" Wohlers asked her.

"No, not specifically. I didn't know where he was. That's why I went to see Malloy. I was scared."

"But had he ever spent the night in a hotel before?"

She got a tight expression around her mouth.

"Yes, he sometimes did that when he was working late."

"Working in the city?"

"Yes."

"So why would he stay at a hotel in the city when he had this townhouse?"

She didn't answer.

"Mrs. Issacs, he was there with another woman. We believe he had sex with the woman before he was killed."

She stared at him blankly.

"Do you think that maybe this woman's jealous husband or boyfriend killed Walter?" she asked.

"No, we think the woman did it."

"But why would she do something like that?"

"Well, that's what we're trying to find out. Mrs. Issacs, I need to ask you about the letter you received just prior to us finding your husband. The one that talks about your past as a prostitute named Houston."

She whirled around and glared at me.

"You promised you wouldn't tell anyone!"

"I kept my promise. Until now. Now it's become a murder investigation, and all bets are off. I'm sorry. I had no choice."

"You promised . . . ," she said again angrily.

Well, so much for my plan to woo and seduce the Widow Issacs. I'd gone from a good guy to a bad guy in her eyes in those few seconds it took for Wohlers to tell her that he knew about her being Houston.

"Will this have to be made public?" she asked Wohlers.

"That depends on whether or not it becomes relevant to the investigation into your husband's murder."

"What does one thing have to do with the other?" she asked pleadingly.

"You got a note from someone who knew you were Houston and seemed to know what had happened to your husband before anyone else," I said. "We gotta figure that's going to be relevant to the murder investigation."

I think she already knew that. She was just hoping she could delay the world finding out as long as she possibly could. I knew the feeling too. Because I was going to have a lot to answer for at the paper myself when this became public.

I could see the conversation between Marilyn and Stacy going something like this:

Marilyn: "I think we should suspend Malloy."

Stacy: "I think we should fire Malloy."

Marilyn: "I think we should suspend him and fire him."

Stacy: "Is tar and feathering still legal in this state?"

Marilyn: "I'll provide the tar if you get the feathers."

Well, on the bright side, at least the two of them would be able to finally agree on something.

Wohlers took out the picture from the video showing the blonde on the elevator with Walter Issacs.

"I want you to look at this photo, Mrs. Issacs, and tell me if you recognize the woman with your husband at all. You can't see her face. But there might be something . . ."

"How would I know her?"

"Maybe she's someone in your social circle."

"My husband wouldn't fool around with any of my friends," she snapped.

She said it as if it was a conversation she'd had before, like with her husband. Maybe she was willing to look the other way and ignore his fooling around as long as he didn't do it with anyone they knew.

"Please look at the picture, Mrs. Issacs," Wohlers said.

"All right, I will. But it's a waste of time. I'm telling you, I don't know anything at all about who this woman is . . ."

There was a stunned look on her face as she saw the woman on the video.

Even without the face, she recognized something.

"Oh, my God," she said. "It's Melissa!"

CHAPTER 8

T HE woman with my husband is Melissa Ross," Victoria Issacs told us. "But why would she want to hurt Walter?"

"How did you recognize her so quickly when her face wasn't visible in the picture?" Wohlers asked.

"The tattoo on her arm. It's a heart. Split in two pieces. Melissa talked about it with me the first time we met. She said it symbolized how men always broke your heart. She was very proud of that tattoo. She kept saying I should get one too. She said it would make me feel better about . . . well, about what my husband was doing to me. About his cheating."

"So tell us what you know about Melissa Ross."

She looked down at the photo.

"Melissa is a private investigator. I hired her to spy on Walter. I've never done anything like that before. But I just didn't know what else to do."

Now it was my turn to be angry. She hadn't told me any of this when she asked me to go looking for him.

"Why didn't you tell me that in the beginning?" I said to her.

"I didn't think it was important."

"You didn't think it was important to inform the guy you asked to search for your missing husband that you'd put a private investigator on his tail to catch him in the sack with another woman?"

"Okay, I was embarrassed. I'm still embarrassed by it, Gil."

She talked about how she'd suspected her husband of cheating on her for a long time. How he'd been staying out late at night. Every time she confronted him, he denied it though. She began hoping against hope that maybe she was wrong. Even though she knew in her heart she wasn't. So she hired the private investigator, Melissa Ross, to find out the truth once and for all about his infidelities. She said Melissa Ross specialized in that kind of work—catching cheating husbands in the act.

"How did you find out about her?" Wohlers asked.

"She bought one of my paintings," she said, looking up at her artwork on the walls of the living room. "I've been painting for a number of years now, and I finally did my own show at a gallery in SoHo. It was my first exhibit and I was very excited, and I was also nervous that no one would buy my work. But Melissa did. She bought two of my paintings and told me how much she liked my style. We talked about art, and then we talked about other stuff. I liked her. Eventually she told me she was a private investigator and what she did. So I hired her to follow Walter for me."

"When is the last time you heard from her?"

"A few days ago. She said she had some information for me. But she wasn't ready to tell me just yet. She said she'd be in touch, and that I'd finally get some answers about Walter."

"Can you describe her at all for us?" Wohlers asked.

"She's very beautiful."

"So everyone says."

"Well, she is."

She looked down at the photo of her husband with Melissa Ross on the hotel elevator one more time. She began to cry again.

"Did you tell Melissa Ross about your past as Houston?" I asked her.

"No."

"Then why did that note you got know you were Houston?"

"I have no idea."

———

I had a hot story here, no question about it. I had the identity of the blonde killer. Melissa Ross, a private investigator who hired her services out to women with cheating husbands.

Of course, there were still a lot of things I didn't know.

Like why she had killed Walter Issacs.

And exactly how she managed to do it.

And why she stayed around in the hotel room all night.

And where she was now.

And then, of course, there was the most pressing question of all. If she sent the note to Victoria Issacs, how did she know about her really being Houston?

Now I just needed to focus on getting the story out. I grabbed a cab back downtown to the *Daily News* offices. When I got there, I filled in Marilyn and Stacy on what I had, pounded out a quick first story on my computer, and we put it up on the website. The headline said: EXCLUSIVE: BLONDE BEAUTY ID'D IN KILLING OF TOP LAWYER.

After that, I kept working to gather more details from the cops and everyone else I could think of before the rest of the media in town caught up to the story.

There was no sign of Melissa Ross anywhere.

Police descended on her office, which was in Queens. Inside, they found a cluttered but otherwise typical office. It had a desk, a computer, file cabinets, a couple of chairs, and a sofa for clients to sit on. The cops found a half-drunk cup of coffee, an empty pizza box, and an unfinished crossword puzzle. But no Melissa Ross.

It was the same thing at Melissa Ross's apartment building a few blocks away when the cops burst in there with guns drawn. Nothing seemed to be missing. The closets were filled with clothes.

Everything looked completely normal, except Melissa Ross was nowhere to be found.

Neighbors said they didn't really know her that well, only saw her coming and going from the building. Often at night.

"The last time I saw her she was all dressed up," the building super told me when I got him on the phone. "Tight pants, low-cut sweater or blouse, really high-heeled boots. She looked very, well . . ."

"Hot?"

"Yes."

"Did she say where she was going?"

"She said she was on her way to work."

"Dressed like that?"

"I think it was part of her job."

Through the night I kept adding to the story, until it was more than thirty inches in length—and with sidebars on what we knew about Melissa Ross and a profile of Walter Issacs.

The one thing I still didn't include though was the note Victoria Issacs had gotten—just before her husband was found murdered—calling her Houston. Wohlers hadn't released anything official on that. He and I—and Victoria Issacs, of course—were the only people who knew about that note. Well, there might be more—Wohlers probably would have given the information to other people in the police department. Or, if he hadn't done that yet, he would have to include it in the case file. And sooner or later, it would become public.

Which would leave me with a lot of explaining to do with my bosses at the *News* about why I knew the identity of Houston and had never told anyone or done a story about it.

The way I saw it I had three choices: (1) walk in to Marilyn and Stacy right now and confess everything, (2) just go home tonight, savor all the acclaim over my big scoop, and then worry about the rest of it in the morning, or (3) keep hoping that no one ever found out about Houston, the note mentioning her name, or my involvement in any of it.

I was too tired to do (1), and—even in my most delusional state—I realized that (3) was just wishful thinking. So I opted for (2). Procrastination is a specialty of mine. Whatever the problem, I'm very good at putting it off for as long as possible.

I decided I'd deal with it tomorrow.

Tomorrow would be time enough to come clean.

Tomorrow would be fine.

Tomorrow would be . . . well, interesting.

CHAPTER 9

ERE'S what we know about Melissa Ross so far," I said to Marilyn and Stacy the next morning. "She's thirty-one years old. Divorced. Lives in Kew Gardens, Queens. Has a small private investigations office on Queens Boulevard. Ex-actress, ex-model, ex-cop too. She was on the police force for a while."

"How long was she a cop?" Marilyn asked.

"Only lasted a couple of years before she got fired. She kicked her commanding officer in the balls. Sent him to the hospital. Poor guy had to go on disability and retire from the force."

"Why did she do it?"

"She said he came on to her. Tried to grope her."

"Did he?"

"Apparently."

"So maybe the creep had it coming," Marilyn smiled.

"Still seems like a bit of an overreaction," I pointed out.

We were sitting in Marilyn's office, which gave her a bit of an advantage at the moment in the power game she was playing with Stacy at the paper. It was a big, nicely furnished office filled with memorabilia from her long years at the paper—awards, pictures, trophies. The subtle message to Stacy was: "I'm still the managing editor and you're the city editor, which means you work for me." On the other hand, the *Daily News* website—Stacy's pride and joy—had set a single-night record for traffic the previous evening with my story about the hunt for blonde killer Melissa Ross.

"There was other stuff too with Melissa Ross," I told them. "A bunch of civil complaints, even though she was only on the force a few years. Suspects claiming that she used physical force on them. A couple of them went to the hospital. One guy sued. But most of the others dropped the charges. It was too embarrassing for them to admit that they'd been beaten up by a woman."

"Sounds like she's got something against men," Marilyn said.

"Hard to believe, huh? But I guess not all men are as sensitive, politically correct in the workplace, and all-around adorable as me."

Marilyn rolled her eyes.

"Her husband was a cop too. The marriage didn't last long," I said.

"What happened there?" Stacy asked.

"She caught him cheating on her."

"Did she kick him in the balls too?"

"What she did was waited until he was asleep one night, then handcuffed him to the bed. Hands and feet both, spread-eagled there when he woke up. She gagged him, kept him like that for days. Beat the crap out of him. Kept threatening to castrate him with a butcher knife. Finally, when she was out of the apartment, he managed to get the gag free and call for help. A neighbor heard and called the cops. They found him like that."

"Did he press charges against her?" Stacy asked.

"No, he started to—but then changed his story to say it was just some kind of sex game that got out of hand. I mean what cop would want to testify publicly in court about how his wife did that to him? He'd be a laughingstock. So they never prosecuted her. He divorced her right afterward. Hell, I imagine he was happy just to be rid of her."

"Beat him up? Threatened to stab him?" Marilyn muttered,

looking down at a picture of Melissa Ross on the front page of the paper. "Sounds like what she did to Issacs. This is a scary woman."

"Anyway, before becoming a cop, she got some modeling and acting gigs because of her great looks. She did a few commercials and fashion magazine photo layouts, even appeared in a recurring role on a TV soap opera for a while. But she never hit it big. Then she joined the force, and stayed until she had that blowup with her commanding officer.

"After that, she set herself up in this private investigation business. Specifically in helping women find out if their husbands were cheating. Some of it involves typical PI stuff—following a cheating husband, getting pictures of him with a lover, tracking down receipts from hotels, etc.

"But she has another ploy too. The 'honey trap.' That's what they call it. She meets a guy somewhere, comes on to him—and sees if he goes for it. Pretty hard for any man to turn down a come-on from a woman who looks like her. If he bites, she goes back to the wife and tells her that her husband was willing to be unfaithful. But she never actually sleeps with the guy. Just sets up a bedroom date to show the wife she can't trust him."

"So why did she sleep with Issacs this time?"

"Maybe she fell in love with him."

"Then why kill him?"

I shrugged.

"Christ, I don't know . . . maybe she's fickle."

"Any other family besides the ex-husband?" someone asked.

"She has a mother on Long Island," I said. "I got her on the phone. But the mother told me she hasn't been in contact with Melissa for years. They had some kind of falling out."

"Okay, Melissa Ross hates men, hates the way men treat her and other women—and sets up this business to get back at them," Marilyn said. "Only this time she gets more than just simple re-

venge by revealing his infidelities to the woman. She gets the ultimate revenge. She has sex with him, then she kills him. So now we
just wait until the police find and arrest her to get all the answers
on why she did it."

"That should be easy," Stacy said. "I mean we know who she
is, where she lives and works. And a woman who looks like that
should be easy to find."

———

"I have something else I wanted to discuss about the Melissa Ross
story," I said when that was finished. "There's a Houston angle."

"Houston?" Marilyn said. "Your Houston?"

I nodded.

"What does Houston have to do with Melissa Ross and the
Walter Issacs murder?"

"Mrs. Issacs is really Houston," I said.

I told her the story about how the legendary New York City
hooker named Houston had found what she thought was true
love, gotten married, became the mother of two daughters—and
thought she had put the life of Houston behind her for good. I also
told her how someone—presumably Melissa Ross—had sent her
a letter addressed to Houston about her missing husband. Ergo,
Melissa Ross—the person who killed Walter Issacs—knew that she
was also killing Houston's husband. Maybe that's even why he was
killed. Because of her past as Houston, not anything happening
now.

"My God, that's unbelievable stuff!" Stacy said.

"How long have you known about this?" Marilyn asked, zero-
ing right in on the question I hadn't answered yet.

I had thought long and hard about how to handle this. I figured I could either tell her nothing, everything, or something in
between. I opted for the last choice.

"I didn't know until now," I said. "Victoria Issacs knew who I was, of course. That's why she came to me when she was looking for someone to help find her missing husband. I guess I was the only reporter she could think of in her desperation. When I talked to her later—after her husband's death—she told me about getting the note from someone who knew about her husband and about her own past as Houston. I don't understand what the connection is, but I wanted you two to know about this first."

I looked at both of them. Stacy was buying everything. Marilyn seemed a bit more skeptical. But all she said was: "Can we print all this Houston stuff?"

"Why not?" I said.

CHAPTER 10

MET my ex-wife, Susan, for drinks at a posh bar on East 21st Street.

The bar was in the same Gramercy Park neighborhood where we'd lived together when we were married. We hung out in that bar a lot in those days. Back then it was a funky, kind of down-and-dirty New York City place. The drinks were cheap, the noise was loud, and the bar was jammed with everyone from construction workers to struggling writers and out-of-work actors.

Now it had been renovated into one of those chic, trendy spots you read about in *New York* magazine. Soft jazz playing, expensive paintings on the walls, tasseled velvet chairs instead of bar stools. I hadn't been there in a long time. But Susan picked the place to meet, not me—so I just went with the flow.

Susan was already there when I showed up. She looked good. Not that it was a surprise. Susan always looked good. But this night she looked especially good. She was wearing a sleeveless black dress and gray suede boots, and her hair was longer than I remembered it being the last time I saw her, hanging down over her bare shoulders. I wondered if she looked like that when she was in court. Might cause a few mistrials.

"Well, you certainly made it back onto the front page in a big way," she said.

54

"I do have a nose for news. But you'll be happy to know I'm still the same modest, unassuming, humble journalistic superstar I always was—and I'll even give you an autograph before we leave."

"Seriously, how do you find all these big stories?"

"Sometimes they find me, Susan."

We were sitting in velvet chairs at one of the small tables. A bartender wearing a white shirt and pleated vest gave us a menu with a dazzling selection of specialty drinks to choose from. Susan ordered a sweet vermouth martini. I ordered a beer. The bartender looked at me disapprovingly.

"I like beer," I said to him. "Is that a problem?"

"No problem at all," he replied, but not like he really meant it.

Susan was particularly curious when I told her about the Houston story I was going to do. She had gone through the Houston scandal with me—watched it destroy my career back then and seen our marriage disintegrate along with it. I repeated the stuff I'd said to Marilyn and Stacy about Houston being Mrs. Victoria Issacs. I didn't tell her the rest about Houston though. Just the public version I was hoping to stick with as long as I could.

"How—and why—does Houston fit into all of this?" she asked when I was done.

"I don't know."

"Jeez, it's almost like this Houston business somehow keeps following you—and now has come full circle for you."

The waiter came with our drinks. He placed the vermouth martini in front of Susan and smiled broadly at her. Then he plopped down a beer along with a glass. No smile for me. I thought about drinking the beer straight out of the bottle to annoy him even more. But I decided that might seem petty and poured some into the glass.

"So how are things with you?" I asked Susan.

"Good."

"Your job at the DA's office?"

"Good."

"Your new apartment?"

"Good."

"And your marriage to Dave or Dan or Dale or whatever his name is—the amazing estate lawyer?"

She started to answer, then paused and took a big sip of her martini.

"Not so good," Susan said.

———

Now suddenly it all made sense. The invitation for drinks. How good she looked. Even the decision to meet here at one of our old favorite spots. After all the times I'd needed her in the past, she finally had come to me for help.

"I think I made a big mistake by marrying him," she said.

"Why?"

"I don't know if I can talk about it with you."

"You can't invite me out for drinks, announce to me that you think your marriage was a mistake, and then not give me any details."

My beer was almost gone. But I didn't want to go through the big deal it would take with the waiter to get another one right now. I just wanted her to keep talking. As it turned out though, she summoned the waiter over and ordered another round.

"Does he hit you or physically abuse you in any way?" I asked, starting off with the obvious.

"No."

"Does he have a drinking problem, a drug problem, or any kind of substance abuse issues?"

"Absolutely not."

"Does he have kinky sex hang-ups that make you uncomfortable and . . . ?"

She smiled and shook her head no. "Actually, I'm probably kinkier than he is. No, the bedroom stuff is okay. Not great, but okay. That's not the issue. None of that is. The problem is . . . well, this is going to sound stupid . . . I miss the laughs."

"Laughs?"

"You always could make me laugh. Even when you and I were going through hard times—and there were a lot of them back then when we were married—there were moments when we still laughed together. There are no laughs in my life right now."

She took a big gulp of her new martini.

"I really miss the laughs, Gil."

———

We sat and talked and drank for a long time. The bartender brought us several more rounds of drinks. By the end, I think I'd started to win him over. He still plopped the beers down on the table in front of me, but he wasn't scowling anymore. I even got him to bring me a bowl of peanuts.

Susan basically laid out the story of a marriage in trouble. She hadn't known him that well when she got married and probably rushed into it too fast, she said. I mean she and I had gotten married before we knew each other that long too, but our troubles were for different reasons. Most of them my fault. This time though she had just suddenly realized he wasn't the man she wanted to spend the rest of her life with.

By the time we left, she was pretty drunk. I walked her out onto Lexington Avenue in front of the bar to get a cab. She pressed against me and put her head on my chest as we waited.

"I could go home with you tonight," she said, looking up at me.

"For the night? You and me?"

"Yes, that would be the sleeping arrangement."

I wasn't sure what to do. For a long time after our marriage ended, I'd hoped for, fantasized about—and pleaded with her—to let me have sex with her again. But she always wanted to move on with her life. And now here she was offering herself up to me, no questions asked.

"I can't tonight—I have someone there," I lied.

"A girlfriend?"

"A woman."

"Is it serious?"

"Not at all. She was just there last night and stayed around today. She'll be gone in the morning. We could talk about this some other time."

"So I'll take a rain check," she said.

Then she kissed me. This wasn't a peck on the cheek. Or even a goodbye kiss on the lips. This was a passionate, openmouthed assault that left me breathing heavily and seriously reconsidering the wisdom of my phony story about the imaginary woman who was staying in my apartment.

"By the way," Susan said as she got into the cab I hailed for her, "I know you were lying about having another woman there tonight."

"How do you know that?"

"I'm a lawyer. I can read people."

"I just didn't think it was a good idea right now."

"Don't forget the rain check," she said and got into the cab.

On my own way back home, I thought about everything that had happened between us that night. About the way she opened up to me about her unhappiness and marriage. About how damn great she looked. And—most of all—about my impulsive decision to turn down her advances.

It really made no sense when you thought about it. I'd spent most of my time over the past few years figuring out ways to get her into bed with me again. And now—when the big moment happens—I say no. I didn't feel guilty or worried about her husband's feelings or anything noble like that. To be honest, I don't have a lot of lofty rules or principles when it comes to having sex. I've always operated on a pretty simple principle, which is:

If it feels good, do it.

Sleeping with Susan sure would have felt damn good.

So why didn't I do it?

CHAPTER 11

BOB Wylie came to the *Daily News* office to make his *Live from New York* appearance the next day. He brought Tim Hammacher with him, the top aide he'd mentioned before. Wylie introduced us. I told Hammacher I'd heard a lot of good things about him. He did not say he'd heard good things about me. He made it clear instead that he didn't think Wylie's appearance was a good idea.

"I don't want you taking any cheap shots against us," he said.

"Why would I take cheap shots?"

"Because you're a tabloid reporter."

"Guilty as charged."

"And tabloid reporters take cheap shots at people."

"I promise to abstain just for today."

"Good. Then you and I will get along just fine."

Hammacher was about my age, with short reddish hair and wearing a three-piece suit. He kept checking his phone for text messages while he was talking to me. And this guy was the best on Wylie's team? Jeez, no wonder he needed me.

The original idea had been to focus the interview on Wylie exploring a run for mayor in the upcoming election. Not that it was a big secret or anything; there'd been lots of speculation and hints from his camp about a mayoral candidacy. But this would be the first time he addressed it directly, and that was big news.

Now though the sensational murder of Walter Issacs at the Hotel Madison was something I needed to ask him about too.

I told Wylie and Hammacher that before we went on the air.

"Let's do the murder stuff first," Wylie said. "You ask me about that, and I'll do my best to give you the status of the investigation. I'll segue from there into a big picture view of crime in New York City—and the great strides we've made in combatting and controlling it in the past few years. After that, we go right into the politics of the mayoral race."

I nodded. That seemed to work.

"Have you given any more thought to coming to work for me in the campaign and then at city hall after I win?" Wylie asked.

"I have."

"And?"

"I'm still thinking about it."

Hammacher snorted in disgust. "Well, I wouldn't wait too long," he said. "There's a lot of people trying to get on our bandwagon right now. You don't want to be left behind."

"Or, to use another analogy," I said, "the train is about to leave the station and I need to get aboard in a hurry?"

"Something like that. So where are you on this right now, Malloy?"

This guy was really starting to get on my nerves.

"I'm still standing in the station," I told him.

———

Everything went well at the beginning.

On the Issacs murder, Wylie went through what he knew about the hunt for Melissa Ross in an efficient, no-nonsense style that made you feel confident he was completely on top of the case—and that Melissa Ross would soon be in custody.

He then talked about all the successes during his term as deputy mayor. Plunging crime rates. More convictions. Safer streets. Better community relations. Innovative law enforcement techniques using modern technology to fight crime. Finally came the money quote about his political plans: "I think I can do even more for this city as mayor. And so I am seriously considering a run for city hall." It all sounded very impressive. Bob Wylie sure seemed like a winner. Maybe I should get aboard his campaign train. I wanted to be a winner too. I could use some winning in my life.

After that, we opened it up to questions from the viewers and people watching it on Livestream from their computers. Sort of like a town hall meeting, only twenty-first-century style. Some people called in their questions. Others would email, tweet, or text them in—and we'd post them online along with Wylie's answers. It was awfully complicated for a traditional newspaper guy like me, but fortunately we had a lot of young kids who'd grown up with social media to take care of that stuff.

We had someone screen the calls and online stuff for us, asking viewers what they wanted to talk to Wylie about, etc. Toward the end of his interview, a woman called who said she wanted to ask a question about the Walter Issacs murder. The screen on my computer alerted me to the topic, and I said sure. The more we got Wylie to talk about the murder case, the better. It was definitely the big story at the moment, even bigger than the mayoral race.

But when the woman came on the line, she addressed her first question to me—not Wylie.

"Did you ever see the movie *Basic Instinct*, Gil? The one where Sharon Stone stabs to death the man she's having sex with. I love that movie. It always gives me ideas. Exciting ideas. Sex and death. An unbeatable combination."

"Who is this?" I said.

"Oh, you must know who it is. Didn't you watch my performance on that security video from the Hotel Madison? Me and the late Walter Issacs? You were the one who broke that story. Your paper has been way ahead of everyone else in writing about me. I've very impressed. I'm becoming a big fan of yours."

"Melissa Ross?"

"You can just call me Melissa. I'm famous now because of you. The whole city knows my name. You can make me even more famous too. We'll both be famous, Gil, you and me together. I need someone to work with in the media. You're the choice. I didn't plan it that way—you just turned up on my radar by accident. But now I've decided you're the right person for the job."

I looked over at Wylie. He was stunned, but quickly pulled himself together.

"The best thing you can do right now is surrender," Wylie told her. "Let's set up a place to meet. You have my personal assurances that no one will harm you if you give yourself up peacefully."

"Not yet. I still have more work to do. You know what they say: 'A woman's work is never done.' "

"What are you talking about?" I asked. "What work?"

"There will be an email arriving in your inbox momentarily explaining it. I just sent it to gmalloy@nydailynews.com."

Then Melissa Ross hung up.

Sure enough, a few seconds later, I heard a ping telling me I had a new email. I called it up on my screen. The subject line was: "TO THE MEN OF NEW YORK CITY."

I read it with growing amazement and horror:

So this guy walks into a bar and announces he wants to tell a dumb blonde joke:

"I'm a blonde and I have a black belt in karate," the woman bartender says to him. "The woman sitting next to you is a blonde with a black belt in karate too. And the woman on the other side of you is also a blonde with a black belt in karate. Now, do you still want to tell us your dumb blonde joke?"

"Nah," the guy says. "Not if I have to explain it three times afterward."

You know, a lot of people really do think blondes are dumb. Walter Issacs, the not-so-alive guy the police found at the Hotel Madison, did. He won't make that mistake again. (Ha, ha!)

Bottom line here, folks: We all go through our lives with blinders on. Getting up every morning, going to work—each day the same as the next. Pretending that what we do really matters somehow or actually makes a difference in this big cosmic universe of ours.

And then one day everything changes.

I don't want to get all melodramatic here and bore you with endless Dr. Phil-like psychobabble about self-discovery and self-empowerment and all that crap.

Not my style. Me, I'm about action. Action speaks louder than words. And sometimes you just have to act to make people sit up and take notice.

Another dumb blonde joke:

Q. Why did the blonde cross the road?

A. I don't know, but neither did she.

Here's one thing I do know. There's going to be a lot more blood spilled here before this is over.

If you don't believe me, go to the Yorkville Apartments on 84th and Second.

You'll find him there.

Victim #2.

Part II

BASIC INSTINCTS

CHAPTER 12

T HE new victim's name was Rick Faris.

Faris was an advertising executive with a big Manhattan agency. He had a wife named Karen and three young children, who lived in Mountain Lakes, New Jersey. Like Victoria Issacs, Faris's wife had recently hired Melissa Ross as a private investigator to find out if he was cheating on her.

Faris was found in an apartment at the Upper East Side address in the email. He had told his wife he was staying in Manhattan for a late meeting with a client. But there was no client and there was no late meeting. It turned out the apartment was a secret love nest he kept in the city to bring back women he picked up in bars.

Witnesses said they'd seen him leaving a singles bar in the neighborhood with a very attractive blonde woman on the evening he died. The woman fit the description of Melissa Ross.

The details of his murder were similar to Walter Issacs's death. He'd been stabbed, beaten, and strangled. Rope marks on his arms and legs indicated he had been restrained prior to his death. There was also evidence of semen. It appeared that Faris had had sex with the woman before she killed him, the same as Issacs.

The crime lab teams went over everything in the apartment, of course. But there was nothing there. No unknown fingerprints. No strands of blonde hair. No evidence of any kind. No actual witnesses either. No one in the building or neighborhood had seen or heard anything unusual after Faris left the bar with the woman.

Everyone covered the new murder in a big way. BLONDE BEAUTY KILLS AGAIN was the *Daily News* headline. This was now more than just another sensational murder story. It was a sensational serial killer story. A sexy blonde woman who had cold-bloodedly murdered two prominent men—and now threatened to claim more men as victims. Plus, she was talking about it—taunting us—in the media, just like Son of Sam once did. There'd been other serial killers over the years, but most of them targeted women. This was a woman killing men. And having sex with them before they died. The story dominated the news cycle for every newspaper, TV station, and media website in town.

I managed to stay ahead of the pack with some big exclusives. First, of course, I was the one who had broken the story of the killer's call and email to *Live from New York*. We broadcast it live, then got it up on the Web. Plus, I scored an interview with Rick Faris's grieving wife. I'm not sure exactly how that happened. I suppose it had something to do with the fact that my name had become so linked with the story of the murders. I also knew the lawyer who was acting as a spokesman for the Faris family—he'd worked with Susan when she and I were married, and we'd gotten together socially with him a few times. I guess luck played a part in it too. I probably just made my request for an interview at the moment they decided it would be a good idea for Mrs. Faris to give one.

I never worry about why I get an exclusive though.

Only about the ones I miss.

——

I sat in the living room of Karen Faris's house and talked to her about her dead husband. Or tried to talk to her anyway. For a while, I could barely get a coherent sentence out of her. She just kept crying every time I mentioned her husband's name.

Finally, Karen Faris calmed down enough so that I could ask her a few questions.

"Tell me about Melissa Ross," I said.

"She's a private investigator. I was worried that my husband was being unfaithful. But I was afraid to know the truth. I was pretty confused. She told me it was better to know the truth than to live a lie. She told me she could help me. She told me she'd helped lots of other women when men had done them wrong."

"And so you hired her to spy on your husband?"

She nodded and looked down at a picture of her husband that sat on an end table next to her in the living room. Rick Faris was a decent-looking guy, about forty, with gray-tinged hair and a big smile on his face in the picture. He looked like the kind of guy who smiled a lot. He had his arm around his wife in the picture and she was smiling too.

Karen Faris began to cry again.

"I understand how difficult this is for you, Mrs. Faris," I said softly. "But I would like to ask you some more questions about your husband and about Melissa Ross. Is that all right with you?"

"Yes, of course," she said.

She tried to wipe away some of her tears. I took out a Kleenex and handed it to her. I smiled at her as I did it. She smiled back. Ah, Malloy, the women just melt when you flash them that smile. Well, at least it seemed to work on the grieving widows. She dabbed at her eyes with the Kleenex and then blew her nose.

"How did you find out about Melissa Ross and what she did at her agency?" I asked.

"At my women's group."

She said she had started going to a women's empowerment class for emotional support. They encouraged her to deal with her husband's lies and find out once and for all the truth about his infidelities.

"So I hired Melissa. She began following Rick. From the moment he left the house until he came home again. Lunch hour, after work drinks, and . . . well, whatever else he was doing. She said that was the only way she could find out what my husband was really up to when he was away from me. The only way I'd know whether or not he was cheating."

"And what did she find out?"

"She found out the truth."

"That your husband was cheating?"

She started to answer, then stopped. Her eyes welled up with tears again.

I moved over and sat down next to her now. I put my arm around her to comfort her. She smiled at me again. I started to take my arm away, but she clung to it for support. Almost desperately hung on to me. I was starting to feel uncomfortable and just a little bit guilty at being that intimate with her.

"Was he cheating on you with another woman?" I asked gently.

"Other women," she said. "There was more than one. He was seeing several different women."

"What did you do after Melissa told you this?"

She looked down again at the picture of her husband on the table next to her.

"What did you do when you found out your husband was cheating?" I asked again. "Did you confront him with the evidence? Did you fight over his extracurricular activities? Did you threaten to divorce him?"

Karen Faris shook her head no. "She gave me pictures," she said. "Pictures of him with other women. Pictures of them kissing. Pictures of them holding hands. Pictures of them doing things . . . things that left no doubt what Rick was doing when he wasn't here at home with me. But I never showed the pictures to him, like Melissa said I should. I threw them away. The pictures. The wiretaps Melissa did. The tape recordings she made. I threw everything into the trash and burned it."

I was confused.

"But you wanted the private investigator to find out all this for you. . . ."

"That was a mistake."

She looked at the picture of her husband again.

"It was my fault, you know."

"I don't understand, Mrs. Faris."

"I hadn't been good enough for Rick. That's why he started spending time with other women. They were giving him something I wasn't. I was the problem, you see, not Rick. No, it wasn't your fault, Rick—it was mine. I just wasn't being a good enough wife to a wonderful man like you."

She wasn't really talking to me anymore, she was talking to her dead husband.

Apologizing to him for making him run around with other women to have sex with instead of her.

Unbelievable.

"I made up my mind to change," she told me now. "Made up my mind to become the type of woman worthy of Rick again. I started working out every day at the gym to get my body back to where it was when Rick and I first met. On that last day—the day he died—I had worked out for nearly three hours at the health club. When the workout was over, I was so delighted to find out I weighed almost my old weight again. The weight I used to be when we got married. The weight I used to be when Rick found me attractive and didn't need to look for sex somewhere else. I even bought some sexy lingerie. God, I hadn't done that in years for him. I wanted to please my husband so much. I wanted to please him so much that he'd never be tempted to be with other women anymore. I wanted . . . I just want my husband back."

She said she had even started making sure she cooked his favorite foods again. That's what she was doing when she got the news he was dead.

"I was making him a beef stroganoff casserole. It was his favorite dinner. I spent all day working on it, making sure it was just right for Rick. I stirred up the filet mignon, seasoned it with Rick's favorite spices and then put it into a frying pan so it could simmer on a low flame for a long time. It made the meat more tender that way. Then I started working on the pasta and—most important of all—the sauce, which I made by hand. I wanted everything to be perfect for Rick. It had been a long time since things had been perfect between us. But this was going to be a new start for us. I was going to make our marriage the way it used to be—full of love and affection and passion."

The tears began to flow again. Karen Faris sobbed uncontrollably. She picked up the picture of her and her husband. Held it to her chest. Then kept calling out his name over and over again.

That was the way I left Karen Faris.

Crying in the living room of her now empty house.

I felt a bit sorry she was in such bad emotional shape over her husband's murder, I suppose.

But mostly I was excited because it was a great interview.

The headline on my story said: ANGUISHED WIDOW SOBS: "I JUST WANT MY HUSBAND BACK." I included all the details she had told me, including the sexy negligee she bought and the lovingly prepared beef stroganoff dinner that he never got the opportunity to eat.

I also talked about her hiring Melissa Ross to spy on her husband's philandering, quoted her on the things Ross had said—and pointed out that this was all the same pattern that Ross had followed with Walter Issacs and his wife. There was no question now that Melissa Ross was the killer. Now all the police had to do was catch her.

Until then, I was going to ride this story for everything I could.

Did I feel bad for poor Karen Faris?

Sure I did.

Just like I felt bad for Victoria Issacs.

But mostly I felt good over getting the exclusive interview.

Welcome to the murky moral world of a tabloid reporter.

CHAPTER 13

THERE was no one waiting for me when I got home to my apartment. Just like the night before. And the night before that. That was okay with me right now though. Hey, even Superman needed some downtime alone after a long day of crime fighting. This was like my own personal Fortress of Solitude.

I grabbed a beer out of the refrigerator and then checked the latest messages on my phone.

One was from Peggy Kerwin. She wanted to know when we could get together again. I hadn't gotten up the courage to tell her I really didn't want to see her anymore. So instead I just kept making up excuses about being busy. I was hoping she'd get the hint. She didn't. Peggy was so sweet, so nice, so trusting—and unfortunately so boring. Damn. How in the hell was I going to get out of that one?

Another was from Victoria Issacs. She wondered if I knew yet when the Houston article was going to run. In preparation for it she'd already told her children and a few close friends about her past as the legendary prostitute, but she wanted to know when everyone else would find out. I understood. Her entire life was going to change when the article came out. I felt a little bit guilty about that, even though it wasn't really my fault. Both of us—Houston and me—just seemed to be caught up in a conflux of life-changing events that were somehow beyond our ability to control.

Tim Hammacher called too. He said Wylie wanted to know if I was ready to make a decision about coming to work for him. Hammacher said Wylie had been deluged by job applicants for his campaign team—and he would have to make some decisions very soon. He mentioned the train leaving the station analogy again and at the end of the message even made a sound like a train whistle blowing. Cute.

And then there was a message from Susan. Ah, Susan. The love of my life. Except when she said she wanted to love me, I said no thanks. I still wasn't sure exactly why I had done that. She sounded kind of apologetic about it in the voicemail she left, without really apologizing for anything. Just thanked me for listening to her problems, admitted she'd had a bit too much to drink, and said we should probably talk again soon. I wondered idly if she was still living with Dale the estate lawyer or if he had moved out or they were sleeping in separate beds or whatever.

I drank some more beer and thought about who to call back first.

I didn't really want to talk to Peggy Kerwin or Tim Hammacher. I didn't mind talking to Victoria Issacs, but I really had no answers for her—the paper hadn't made a final determination on when to go with the Houston disclosure. I wanted very much to talk to Susan, but I had no idea what to say to her at this point.

In the end, I shut off my phone and decided to deal with all of it later.

———

I walked back into the kitchen and thought about what to make for dinner.

I had a cookbook that Sherry DeConde had given me for my

birthday before she left that had some great recipes in it. There was a chicken marsala that sounded good. A ham and eggs dish. Even a rack of lamb that was supposed to be easy to make.

The problem was that making any of these things would require me to go out to the store to buy the food. I would have to turn on several parts of the oven, including either the broiler or the oven. And then there were the dirty dishes to deal with when I was done. It all seemed like a lot of trouble for a meal.

I finished off the beer I had and grabbed another.

Beer, the dinner of champions.

Then I picked up my phone and called a nearby coffee shop for delivery—which comes complete with paper plates.

I watched TV while I ate. There was a *Superman* episode on one of the cable channels that I hadn't seen in a while. It was about an eccentric scientist who builds a robot that gets kidnapped by bad guys to help them rob places. Superman, of course, saves the day—and saves the robot from a life of crime. I wanted to stand up and cheer.

I thought some more about all the decisions I had to make.

I decided that I would just let the Peggy Kerwin thing play out to its eventual conclusion. At some point, she would get tired of calling me and give up. She'd find someone else as boring as her, they'd have boring kids, and all of them would live boringly happy lives ever after without me.

Tomorrow I would find out from Marilyn and Stacy exactly when the stuff about me and Houston was going to run in the *News* and on air with *Live from New York*. Then I would tell Victoria Issacs I would offer to do anything I could to help support her through what I knew would be a difficult time for her. I figured I owed her at least that much.

I had a plan on how to deal with Wylie too. It was a pretty good plan, if I do say so myself. I'd come up with it somewhere between my second and third beers. I would tell Wylie that I really was seriously considering working for him. But I couldn't make any decision or announcement until I finished with the Melissa Ross story, whatever way it came out in the end. That would give me some more time to play along and stay on the inside of the police investigation. Hell, there was no way I was ever going to be happy in any job in my life other than being a real reporter, but he didn't have to know that. At least not yet.

The only thing I had no answer for was the Susan situation.

I thought about it while I watched Perry White, Clark Kent, Lois Lane, and Jimmy Olsen putting out the *Daily Planet* and keeping Metropolis safe.

I loved Perry White. He was everything I always wanted in a newspaper editor. Angry, irascible, impatient—but the kind of guy who was always in charge and who you knew would make the right decisions in the end. I wished I had a Perry White making editorial decisions for me at the *Daily News* right now. Or even helping me out with my personal life too.

"Great Caesar's Ghost!" Perry White screamed at one point on the screen. "You call yourself a reporter? What in the hell is the matter with you anyway? What exactly is your problem?"

"My problem is," I yelled back at the TV, "that I'm in love with my ex-wife. She's married to another guy. But she doesn't love him anymore. I think she still loves me. But I'm really not sure what to do next."

Perry didn't answer, of course.

He was talking to Clark, Lois, and Jimmy—not me.

It also dawned on me that talking about my problems to characters on a TV show made nearly sixty years ago was probably not the most productive—or sane—way for me to deal with them.

John Hamilton, the actor who played Perry White, had died a few years after the show was on in the 1950s. George Reeves, the TV Superman and Clark Kent, died back then too, of either a suicide or a deadly love-triangle or gangland murder—depending on which Hollywood legend you believed. Hell, even Christopher Reeve, who played Superman in the later movies, was dead now.

I needed to talk about Susan and my other problems with someone who was a real person—not a TV character.

Someone who could ask me questions, respond to my answers, and give me some good advice on where to go with my life.

And, ideally, someone who was alive.

CHAPTER 14

S O where is Melissa Ross?" was the first question from Marilyn Staley at the morning news meeting.

"The police don't know," I said.

"Why is she killing these men she has no apparent connection with—and having sex with them first?" she asked.

"They don't know that either."

"And how does she do it? Issacs and Faris were both good-sized men. How did a woman like Melissa Ross overpower them so easily?"

"I guess we'll have to wait until the police can ask Melissa Ross those questions to find out," I said.

"Except the police can't find Melissa Ross."

I was a bit baffled by this too. It had all seemed so easy at the beginning. The cops knew who the killer was, they knew where she lived, and they knew where she worked. Plus, she was a stunning blonde woman—which made it hard for her to remain unnoticed. Since both victims' wives had hired her to spy on their husbands, the cops had put out a public appeal for other Melissa Ross clients to come forward. They were also going through the files and videos and other evidence found in her office, to reach out to anyone who had been in contact with her recently. It seemed like only a matter of time until they tracked her down and arrested her.

But she had already killed once again. And was threatening to carry out the murders of more men as part of some sort of bizarre vendetta she seemed to have against men because of the way they had treated her.

"Maybe she uses a gun," someone suggested. "That would explain how she controls her male victims."

"Except she didn't shoot them."

"Ross might be a black belt in karate or something," an editor suggested.

"Or maybe she waited until they were asleep," someone else said, "then handcuffed them to the bed, like she did with her ex-husband."

I had another thought. I pointed out the references in her phone call to the movie *Basic Instinct*.

"Do you remember that opening scene in *Basic Instinct*?" I said. "The one where Sharon Stone killed the guy in bed with an ice pick, stabbing him over and over again? She tied the man up to the bed in some kind of kinky sex play before she killed him. He was completely helpless. Had to take whatever she wanted to do with him. Sexually. Or, in that case, being stabbed by an ice pick. And he let her tie him up. He wanted her to do that. He was turned on by it."

"Do you think maybe Issacs and Faris wanted to be tied up?" Marilyn asked.

"Why not? Melissa Ross says she wants to play some kinky games. She takes out handcuffs or rope. Says she'll do all sorts of stuff to the guy while he's tied up. He's excited, he'll do pretty much anything at this point to get into her pants. It wouldn't have been hard for her to convince him how much fun they would have."

"So she ties him up and has sex with him?"

"Yes."

"Why not just kill him as soon as she's gotten him tied up?"

"Maybe Ross wanted the sex too. Only on her terms. On top of him. With him powerless and her totally in control of everything. Maybe that excited her."

"And when the sex was over?"

"The guy asked her to untie him. She refused. That's when she started to go to work on him. He's not so excited anymore. He's just scared. Maybe at first he thought it was some kind of a joke she was pulling on him. Just more sexual teasing and game-playing. But this was no game. She was determined to kill these men after having sex with them."

"Boy, talk about a guy's dick getting him into trouble," someone muttered.

———

Stacy wanted to talk about the mayoral race next.

"Wylie seems to like you for some reason, Malloy," Stacy said.

"Why wouldn't anyone like me?" I said.

"I have a list of reasons in my office . . . ," Marilyn started to say.

"The point I think Stacy is trying to make," I said, "is that I am in the perfect position to get us exclusive stuff from Wylie. About the mayoral race and about the murder investigation too."

"Exactly," Stacy said. "Now we need to leverage that unique relationship between you and the deputy mayor to maximize both readership and traffic results emanating from the window of opportunity. I propose you engage in another interactive session which combines an on-air presence with innovative social media techniques to further promote our brand in cyberspace."

Honest to God, she really talked like that.

"Translation anyone?" I said, looking around the room.

"I think she wants you to do another interview with Wylie," an editor said.

"So why didn't you just say that?" I asked Stacy.

She didn't seem offended by any of the banter though. I'm not even sure if Stacy knew people were making fun of her. Or if she cared. She just thought she was smarter than anyone else, and she didn't need our approval, because she had all the answers. I made a mental note again to root for Marilyn Staley in the battle for power the two of them were waging at the *Daily News.*

Marilyn weighed in on Stacy's plan.

"I need Gil to write a story for tomorrow's paper on the latest in the murder investigation," she said. "And I need him to keep on that story until it's over and Melissa Ross is in police custody."

"He can do that and the political stuff for me too," Stacy said.

We also talked about when we'd go public about Victoria Issacs being Houston. I had mixed feelings about doing this watered-down version of the Houston story, but it was better than the alternative of telling the whole truth about the story.

"Is it too much to ask you to do all of this, Gil?" Marilyn wanted to know.

"Nah, I'm good," I said. "And then I could get a paper route and deliver the *News* door to door with any free time I have left."

———

At the end of the meeting, Marilyn brought up another thing about the murders of Walter Issacs and Rick Faris.

"We need a name for the killer," she said.

"Her name is Melissa Ross," Stacy said, not quite understanding what Marilyn was saying.

"No, I mean we need a nickname. All of the serial killers that have made big news always had a great nickname. That's what we need for this woman. A nickname that sticks. A nickname that terrifies people. A nickname that works in headlines and on-air teases so that everyone will know who we're talking about. You understand what I'm saying? Son of Sam. Zodiac. The Hillside Strangler.

Only this one is a woman. A woman who's killing men that she picks up and goes out with. So what's her nickname?"

Everyone in the room thought about it for a minute.

"Femme Fatale?" I said.

"Too obvious."

"The Lady Killer?" Stacy suggested.

"Confusing. It sounds like the lady is the one being killed, it's not clear that she's the killer."

The other editors threw out a series of other possibilities, all quickly shot down by Marilyn.

She looked down at a picture of Melissa Ross on her desk. The one of her in the Hotel Madison elevator. Marilyn stared at it for a long time. Looking at everything about Melissa Ross. The blonde hair. The tattoo on her arm. The sexy body, the revealing clothes, the way she was all over Walter Issacs in the elevator. The same man she would cold-bloodedly murder shortly after this picture was taken.

"Blonde Ice," Marilyn said suddenly.

"Huh?" someone said.

"Blonde Ice. It captures the whole blonde thing, the whole sexy woman thing—and the heartless way she eliminates people, in this case the men who fall for her charms and come on to her."

I liked it. So did all the other editors in the room. Even Stacy nodded her grudging approval.

Marilyn was right. It was what this killer—what this story—needed. The perfect nickname. And now they had it.

Blonde Ice.

As all the other people in the room began filing out after the news meeting, I looked over at Marilyn and said:

"So where'd you come up with that name?"

"Actually, they used to call me that at one of the places where I worked before I came back to the *News*."

I looked at Marilyn now. She did have blonde hair. And she could give off an icy, cold demeanor if she didn't like you. No question about it, Marilyn Staley definitely could be a hard woman, a tough woman, a woman without mercy when she needed to be. Just like Melissa Ross.

"Yeah, I can see that," I said.

I smiled at her.

"Except you never killed anybody," I pointed out.

Marilyn looked over at Stacy Albright, who was going out the door, then back at me.

"Not yet," she said.

CHAPTER 15

HAD a feeling—call it a crazy hunch—that Tim Hammacher, Bob Wylie's top man, didn't like me as much as Wylie did. I sensed it from his body language, the inflection in his voice, the subtle hints that a skilled reporter like me picks up on. And then there was something he said to me too.

"I don't like you, Malloy," he told me as we sat in his office.

That was the thing that pretty much clinched it for me.

"I think this is a bad idea for Bob to bring you aboard our campaign team," Hammacher said. "I've told him that, and I'll tell him again. You have a smart mouth, you don't work well with people, you have a spotty résumé filled with all sorts of red flags about your trustworthiness, and you pretty much act like a jerk all the time. Have I left anything out?"

"I don't take criticism well."

I didn't like Hammacher very much either. He was one of those guys who seemed to live a charmed life and could do no wrong. There were diplomas in his office from Princeton and Harvard Law School. Awards from the bar association, civic groups, and school associations for his outstanding work. Pictures of him with his wife, family, and everything else indicative of the perfect life. He golfed, he played tennis, he sailed. Tim Hammacher was just a damn swell kind of guy. I'd met a lot of people like Hammacher in my life. And I never liked any of them.

"The bottom line," Hammacher said to me now, "is I expect anything you write about the deputy mayor to be a positive affirmation of the contributions he's made to the city over the past few years. And what he can do in the future as mayor. I don't want to see any negativity or snarky comments in what you do. Not if you have any hope at all of convincing him—and me—that you're worthy of being a part of our team. Do we understand each other?"

He gave me a hard stare across his desk.

"Yikes!" I said.

"Excuse me?"

"That stare of yours has me quaking in fear."

"Malloy . . ."

"Do you practice that in the mirror every morning before you come to work?"

"Now, listen . . ."

"No, you listen to me. First, I'm not looking for a job on your team. I'm on a team, the *Daily News* team. Wylie broached a possible offer to me for the future, and I was flattered. But I'm not going to be angling for a job with you at the same time I'm covering your campaign. That's a no-no for a reporter. So we're only talking in very general terms about this topic at the moment.

"Second, my job is not to write puff pieces about you or your boss. I'm a reporter, not a public relations agent. I will accumulate the facts, do my best to interpret them in a fair and impartial manner, and then write my stories about your campaign the way I think they should be written.

"Third, and probably most importantly, I don't give a damn whether you like me or not. Let's just say that winning your approval is very far down on my list of priorities."

I gave him my own hard stare back. We both sat there staring at each other. It was childish, I know. But it made me feel better.

"You just screwed yourself, Malloy," he said finally.

"Wouldn't be the first time."

———

I'd gone there in hopes of getting another one-on-one meeting with Wylie. I wanted to get exclusive news about the Melissa Ross investigation, of course. But I was also ready to talk to him candidly—although not as candidly as I did with Hammacher—about my feelings on his job offer.

Instead Wylie called a press conference. I trooped into the press conference room with a herd of other reporters and listened to him answer questions about the murders of Walter Issacs and Rick Faris, his thoughts on the mayoral race, and pretty much everything else the press wanted to bring up.

The political stuff was pretty easy for him.

"The latest polls show you ahead of the mayor by a wide margin," a reporter said. "What's your reaction to that?"

"I haven't had a lot of time to follow the polls. I'm pretty busy with the job I have now. But—to answer your question—the people of New York will decide the next mayor, not some political polls. I'm confident in their judgment."

"Do you think you'd make a good mayor?" another reporter asked.

"I think you should look at my record as deputy mayor overseeing law enforcement—the drop in street crime, the rise in arrests and convictions, the safety people now feel when they walk the streets of New York City—and make your own decision about what kind of mayor I would be."

"Is that a yes or no to my question?" the reporter laughed.

"My record speaks for itself."

"What about the mayor's record?"

"The mayor should answer that question. It's his record, not mine."

"Do you and the mayor get along these days?"

"He's my boss."

"Maybe he won't be your boss after the next election," the reporter said.

"Well, that decision is going to be up to the people of New York, isn't it?" Wylie smiled.

The reporter from the *Post* sitting next to me leaned over and whispered: "He's really good, isn't he?"

"Damn good," I muttered.

"How can anyone ever compete against someone with all of that charisma and charm?"

He was right. The current mayor was deadly dull, a sixty-five-year-old man who looked and acted like he was eighty. No, there was no way for him to compete against Wylie—no chance for him to win reelection—unless something happened to change the current political situation. Something to stop the Wylie steamroller that now seemed certain to put him in the mayor's office.

But the wild card was still the Blonde Ice murders. If the police captured Melissa Ross and closed the case quickly, Wylie would be an even bigger hero to the people of New York. But if not . . . well, the tone of the questions changed dramatically when the press switched topics.

"Where is Melissa Ross?" a reporter asked.

"We don't know," Wylie said.

"Why is she killing these men she has no apparent connection with?"

"We don't know that either."

"Well, what do you know?"

For a second, it looked like the press conference might get out of control. But Wylie was too good to let that happen.

"I know this—we will catch Melissa Ross, and we'll do it very soon," Wylie said, pounding on the podium in front of him. It was a real nice dramatic flourish. "The people of New York City have my personal guarantee on that. I assure you we will apprehend this woman and make sure our city is safe."

Wow, I thought to myself. He was really putting himself and his reputation on the line here. I kind of admired that. Wylie was all in now on the Blonde Ice case, whether he liked it or not.

On his way out of the room, I managed to intercept him briefly.

"How's it going, Scoop?" he smiled.

"Well, we've got a helluva story here," I smiled back. "A serial killer running wild. Plus, it's a female serial killer. Even better. And you just making this dramatic guarantee to stop her before she kills again. I couldn't ask for a better storyline than that. So—once you catch her—you'll be a big hero in the media all over again."

"Lucky for both of us, huh?" Wylie grinned.

He seemed to suddenly realize that might sound insensitive since people were dying, but I knew what he meant.

"That last remark is off the record, of course," he said quickly.

"Of course."

He relaxed again.

"I heard you had an interesting discussion with Tim Hammacher earlier," Wylie said to me.

"Let's just describe it as a full and frank exchange of views."

"Tim is really a pretty good guy when you get to know him. I know he can be a bit overbearing at times. But he's intelligent, hardworking, resolute, loyal—he's a real model for other members of my office and my campaign team."

"Yeah, he sure sounds swell. . . . When I grow up I want to be just like him."

"I'd like for the two of you to get along," Wylie said.

CHAPTER 16

So why didn't you take your ex-wife up on her offer to come back to your apartment and spend the night with you?" Dr. Barbara Landis asked me.

"Beats me."

"You must have some idea."

I shook my head no.

"That's why I came to see you, Doc. So you can help me understand my subliminal feelings. Delve deep into my subconscious thoughts. Bare my soul and all that stuff. Isn't that what you do for a living?"

Barbara Landis was a psychiatrist. I'd been seeing her off and on for a few years now. Mostly off. The *Daily News* sent me to her when I started having serious anxiety attacks after the Houston scandal first broke and nearly destroyed my career. The worst attack happened in the middle of the newsroom, when I lost consciousness and scared the hell out of everyone. Including me. Landis had helped me through that and a few other crises. I liked her. I trusted her—to a point anyway—and I don't easily trust people. Plus, I couldn't think of anyone else to turn to for help. So there was that too.

"Is it because Susan is still married?" she asked me now.

"Maybe."

"And that offended your moral principles on some level?"

"Sure. Why not?"

"Well, we're living in a different age now. Moral principles and standards have changed dramatically from what they used to be. The marriage vows are not always sacrosanct; many people stray from their marriage vows and many men—in your situation—would not have been concerned about the right or wrong of such a sexual encounter. They would have simply chosen the sexual thrill."

"I don't want to be one of those guys," I told her.

"Actually," Landis said, "you are one of those guys."

"What do you mean?"

"You told me in the past about how you cheated on your wife when you were married. That you'd slept around with some other women under less than virtuous circumstances. So why take the moral high ground now?"

"Maybe I don't want to be one of those guys anymore," I smiled.

Landis wrote that down in her notebook. She always wrote everything down in a notebook during our sessions. I was starting to get uncomfortable. I wondered if maybe it wasn't such a good idea to come here and bare my soul to this woman, after all. Maybe I should just go home and talk to imaginary TV characters some more. The good thing about them is they never ask you a lot of tough questions.

"I've got a new joke," I told Landis. "A guy walks into a psychiatrist's office and tells the doctor he's been having this bizarre fantasy that he's a dog. The psychiatrist tells him to lie down on the couch so they can talk about it. 'I can't,' the guy tells the psychiatrist. 'I'm not allowed on the furniture.'"

Landis sighed.

"Mr. Malloy, we've talked in the past about your penchant for making jokes when you don't want to discuss some of your issues.

How you use humor to hide your true feelings and avoid confronting problems. This creates a serious obstacle in our patient-doctor relationship and negatively impacts the likelihood of a positive outcome to the treatment that I am providing you."

"I'm not sure I understand exactly what you're saying, Doc."

"What I'm saying is that if you keep acting like a jerk, I can't help you."

"That is clearer," I said.

She looked down at her notebook. I imagined she was reviewing some earlier notes she'd written about me. No iPads or modern technology for this woman. Just a spiral notebook and a big fountain pen. Old school all the way.

"Let me ask you the question again then," she said. "Why do you think you rejected the sexual advances of your ex-wife?"

I looked around the office. There were lots of diplomas and degrees and awards from medical associations. Pretty impressive. This woman must really know what she's doing. I mean they don't just hand those diplomas and degrees out like candy, right? I took a deep breath and plunged ahead.

"Okay," I said, "I know I wasn't the greatest husband in the world. Not by a long shot. And yes, I did cheat on Susan at the end when we were going through a really crazy period with the Houston scandal and a lot of other stuff that happened. And then later, after we were divorced, I sometimes felt like she was cheating on me when she was with other men. Because I was convinced we would eventually get back together. But this time I'm not the cheater and I'm not the cheatee. I'm the third person in the mix. The one she'd be cheating on her current husband with. This is uncharted territory for me, Dr. Landis. I guess I'm just not sure how to handle the situation."

Landis smiled. "Okay, that's some progress. Now that wasn't really so difficult to do, was it?"

"There's more. I've been thinking a lot about the story I'm working on now. About the way Victoria Issacs's seemingly perfect marriage fell apart because her husband was cheating on her with the same kind of woman that she used to be. About Karen Faris all alone in that empty house and blaming herself for her husband's cheating ways. I guess maybe that's why I decided I didn't want to be that kind of guy—someone like Walter Issacs or Rick Faris—ever again. I suppose I'm just a romantic at heart. I want to believe that the perfect love, the perfect marriage—the whole live happily ever after thing—is really possible."

Landis wrote that down too.

"And then there's the Houston connection to all this, which also freaks me out. I mean that original Houston story I did—and screwed up on—changed my life in so many ways. That's why I came here to see you in the first place, during all of the fallout from the Houston scandal. Now she's somehow back in my life, and she appears to be a catalyst for all the new things that have happened. I don't understand why. And truthfully, it scares me. I just feel that there is some kind of unseen force behind all this—some kind of fate or predestination or whatever—that is pushing Houston and me together again for a reason. And all the rest of it—the murders, the new revelations coming out about my past, even Susan's marriage crisis—is a part of this. I know that sounds crazy. But I feel that somehow Houston is the reason for everything that's going on in my life at the moment. Just like she was before."

Dr. Landis closed her notebook. She looked at me with a concerned expression.

"Did I say something wrong?" I asked.

"No, you actually made a great deal of sense."

"What's wrong then?" I asked.

She stood up and paced around the room. Arms folded, lost in thought, without answering right away. As she walked, I couldn't help noticing that she was actually a very nice-looking woman. Not that I was going to ever act on that impulse. She was in her midfifties, married with a family. She even told me once that she was a grandmother now. Plus, there was the pesky ethical issue that she was my psychiatrist. I was pretty sure there were rules that prevented psychiatrists from jumping onto the couch with their patients. I didn't want to get into trouble with the American Medical Association or anything.

"Why exactly did you come to see me?" Dr. Landis asked.

"Uh, because I'm a patient and you're a doctor and you're supposed to cure me."

"You haven't been here in months, Mr. Malloy. And then suddenly today you show up at my door."

"I guess I didn't have any problems bad enough to bring me here until now."

"Did you attempt to discuss these problems with any of your friends?"

"No."

"Why not?"

I shrugged.

"Do you have friends, Mr. Malloy?"

"Sure, I have lots of friends."

"Then why didn't you go to one of them to talk about these things that are bothering you?"

"I don't talk to my friends about stuff like that."

"Doesn't sound like they're very good friends then."

She sat down again.

"You're a very likeable guy. Funny. Personable. Entertaining. I'm sure you do have a lot of friends. But mostly people you work with or know from business dealings, right? Other reporters. Some cops. A few government sources maybe. But they're all about your job. I'm not sure they're real friends beyond that. Anyone to talk to when you really have problems like you're having now. So you don't have to hold imaginary conversations with characters on TV shows."

I had told her about that at one point, I guess. I sort of wished I hadn't now.

"In many ways, you act very . . . well, I guess the word I'm looking for is 'immature.' You need to establish a more mature lifestyle for yourself."

"Mature," I said.

"Mature, Mr. Malloy. You need to confront the real problems in your life. You need to talk to someone that you're not afraid to reveal some of your secrets to—in the same way you've done with me. Do you have anyone in your life like that, Mr. Malloy? Anyone besides me that you feel you can totally trust?"

I thought about it.

"Just one person," I said.

"Who?" she asked, even though she already knew the answer.

"Susan."

"But now you can't go to her with your problem because she is the problem. You're not able to deal with that. Hence, you return to my office for this session."

"That's a pretty good assessment of my situation at the moment, Doc," I had to admit.

"So what are you going to do about Susan?"

"I don't know."

"Then maybe you should talk about it with her."

CHAPTER 17

Do you think I'm mature?" I said to Zeena when I got back to the office.

"Who?"

"Me."

"Is this the beginning of a joke or something?"

"Not a joke, Zeena. Do you think I'm mature? Yes or no?"

"No."

"Now, why would you say something like that?"

"Well, let's see . . . you're always getting into trouble around here, you screwed up your marriage and pretty much every other relationship in your life, and you move like every five minutes from one apartment to another. Not the acts of a particularly mature person."

"Anything else?"

"Yeah, you always have this childish compulsion to get the final word in with everyone."

"Hey, you're not exactly a bastion of maturity yourself, Zeena."

"See what I mean."

I sighed.

"Nope, you're definitely not a mature person, Malloy."

"Am too," I said.

Then I stuck my tongue out at her.

———

The Houston revelation was definitely going to be tricky. Talking about it with Dr. Landis had really made me realize that.

On the one hand, it was vindication for my journalistic reputation—proof that the legendary hooker I'd written about really did exist. On the other hand, I was fudging—okay, I was lying—about some of the facts on how I'd finally found her. A lesser man might have had some moral qualms about all this. I was just hoping I could pull it off without getting caught.

The plan was to break the story over a multimedia platform—as Stacy put it—to maximize the saturation of our target audience. Or something like that. I'd announce it on an episode of *Live from New York*, taking everyone through the Houston connection with the Blonde Ice story and my own background with her. Then I'd open it up to questions, tweets, emails, or whatever else from the audience, which I'd address as candidly and fully as possible. Meanwhile, I'd also write an article about all of it that would first go up on the website and then appear in the print edition of the next day's *Daily News*.

On the night before this was to happen, I sat in my apartment and went through all the stories and articles I'd kept about me and the Houston scandal years earlier. No matter how many times I read them, I still couldn't believe I'd screwed up so badly. It was almost as if all the stuff was about someone else. Another reporter named Gil Malloy, not me.

First, there was the adulation I got for my series about prostitution in New York and my "compelling, heartbreaking, and eloquently written" profile of the legendary hooker named Houston. That was what the *Daily News* said when they submitted it for a Pulitzer. I was riding pretty high when that happened.

Then came the questions about Houston. Did I really talk to her? Did she even exist? I finally confessed that my "interview" with her was really a series of secondhand quotes I'd put together from other sources who claimed they knew Houston. But I had never found her.

The dominoes fell pretty quickly after that.

The *Daily News* withdrew my story from Pulitzer consideration. I almost lost my job. My marriage to Susan fell apart—partly, but not wholly, because of the Houston mess. And I wound up being so stressed I started having anxiety attacks and had to get medical help.

Yep, Houston had really screwed up my life.

And now here she was again.

There must be some kind of message or lesson somewhere in all this.

But damned if I could figure out what it was.

———

Stacy wanted me to get Houston to appear on camera with me. I pointed out that the woman was the grieving widow of a murder victim. That her entire life would unravel once her past was revealed. That she had two young daughters she would have to protect from all the scandal about to swirl around her. Stacy said to ask her anyway. I did. She said no.

The show itself and all the rest of it went pretty smoothly. There were lots of questions about what I did or didn't do all those years ago. How I felt about it now, did I have regrets, etc.? I answered the questions as candidly as I could. People also asked about my current connection to Houston. I answered these more carefully, sticking to the story that I didn't know who she was until she came to my office that day recently looking for her missing husband.

The only uncomfortable moment—for me anyway—came when

someone pointed out that my proving Houston really did exist didn't excuse my journalistic sin in claiming quotes from her.

This person asked me how I could justify that.

It was a good question.

I said that I couldn't justify it in any way.

"As a journalist, I have an obligation to always tell the truth and be entirely forthcoming with the reader," I said. "In this case, I did not. I could give you all sorts of excuses about how I believed the sources who gave me the quotes or I was practicing some new kind of journalism or whatever. But the fact is I failed in my duties as a journalist then. I'm sorry about that. I never did anything like that before in my life, and I'll never do it again. Yet I know this will always be a blot on my record as a journalist that I can never erase."

And that really was the truth.

No matter what I did, no matter how many stories I broke, no matter that Houston really did exist—I'd constantly have to prove myself all over again. It always reminded me of the story of Sisyphus, which I really related to. Sisyphus was a character in mythology sentenced by the gods to forever push a heavy rock up a hill, only to see it roll back down to the bottom each time. He was destined never to change his fate. Maybe that was the same fate Houston and I would have to endure for our entire lives. The rock was at the bottom of the hill for both of us, and all we could do was try to keep pushing it back to the top.

———

When the show was over and the story had posted online, I called Victoria Issacs to ask her how she was coping with all of this.

"There's an army of reporters and TV cameras and all sorts of other media camped outside my front door right now," she said. "My husband is dead, my reputation is ruined, and my life will never be the same again. Other than that though, I'm doing just peachy."

I wanted to tell her I was sorry, but I knew that was pointless.

She knew as well as I did that the story of Houston had to eventually come out, and we'd worked together to break the news to the people in her life with as much preparation as possible.

But, in the end, she was caught in the same Houston paradox that I was.

Houston had been the best thing in her life at the beginning. Houston made her rich and famous and successful. And then Houston had taken all that success away. Just like it did with me once—and might do again before this was all over.

I thought about a line from Raymond Chandler in *The Long Goodbye* that I always remembered—and it somehow seemed to fit both of us.

"There is no trap so deadly as the one you set for yourself."

CHAPTER 18

WATCHING the videos police had found on Melissa Ross's computer made me feel kind of dirty.

I'd been pestering Wohlers for another exclusive, so he agreed to let me see them. A consolation of sorts for all the help I'd been to him on the case.

There was some steamy stuff that the cops found in those files. But not all of them were sex videos, per se. There were pictures and videos of cheating husbands and boyfriends out to dinner with other women, walking with them down the street, kissing or making out with them on park benches or cars, and lots of other surveillance material she'd collected.

Some of it was definitely hardcore.

Ross had apparently been able to get inside houses and hotel rooms to plant video devices. I wasn't exactly sure how legal that was. There was a good chance the video evidence of infidelity would never stand up in a divorce proceeding. But then it probably didn't matter to her clients. The revelations to the wife would be damaging enough.

It wasn't hard to figure out her next move once the video or pictures were captured. Her clients—the aggrieved parties, the women being cheated on, the wives and girlfriends who had hired

Melissa Ross to do the spying—were shown the escapades of their husbands' or boyfriends' unfaithfulness.

Then they could confront the man with this evidence. Or not confront him, as in Karen Faris's case. But at least they knew the truth.

I wondered what these wives were thinking once they'd been convinced of their husbands' infidelities. Was it better to know or not to know? Was it better to continue on in a loveless marriage with your head buried in the sand and believing your husband's lies that he wasn't seeing any other woman? Or did the truth somehow either make it more bearable to go on in the relationship or easier to summon up the courage to end it once and for all?

I supposed that each case was different. For every Karen Faris who was willing to look the other way after seeing proof of her cheating husband, there were other wives on the phone with a divorce lawyer vowing to take their husbands for everything they owned.

———

On the screen now, a balding, slightly potbellied man was getting a blow job in what appeared to be a hotel room, from a brunette woman who looked like she knew exactly what she was doing. He sat on the bed in the room while she kneeled down in front of him. Several times she looked up, and her face was visible on the video we watched.

"That's not Melissa Ross," I said to Wohlers.

"Nope."

"A hooker, you think?"

"Probably," he said.

"She sure looks like she has a lot of expertise."

We watched for a few more minutes, until the man exploded onto the woman's face in the video.

Across the bottom of the screen a time stamp gave the location where the video had been shot, a hotel called the Trafalgar that was in Times Square, and the exact date and time of the incident—which had been a few months earlier. There was a name too, Robert Johnson.

"Robert Johnson is the cheating guy," I said to Wohlers as I wrote down the name off of the screen.

"Yep, so we've got to find this Robert Johnson—and go talk to him."

"You think he knows anything?"

"That's what we need to find out. We need to talk to as many of these people on her videos and in her files as we can. Maybe we can get a lead that will help us find her that way. But there's no other information about this guy Johnson on the video. So we have to cross-check everything against the material in her files. Plus, there's plenty of other men in those files and pictures and videos that we took out of Melissa Ross's office. We need to go through all of that too."

"Sounds like a big job," I said.

"Tell me about it."

I wrote down as many names as I could from the other videos he played for me—hoping that I could track down and talk to some of these men myself.

———

Meanwhile, I did track down Melissa Ross's ex-husband, Joe Delvecchio. The former NYPD cop was working as a security guard/bouncer at a club in midtown.

But he made it clear to me he did not want to talk about his former wife—or the circumstances of what she did to him.

"I had to quit the force because of her," Delvecchio told me. "After what happened . . . well, you can imagine what it was like for me. All the jokes, all the derogatory remarks about my manhood, all the questions about how I could let a woman do something like that to me. I was the victim. But I wound up suffering the most. Not just the job, I lost my reputation."

Delvecchio was a big man, well over six feet. He was good-looking, muscular, a real macho guy. He glanced around now at the club-goers on the dance floor, looking for any signs of violence or trouble.

He talked about why he had never brought charges against his ex-wife and why he refused to ever discuss it with anyone.

"The people here, they don't know anything about me. I'm just the guy that keeps everyone in line. They need to be a little bit scared of me. What do you think would happen if they read in your paper that I was the guy who got handcuffed to a bed and beaten up by some crazy woman?"

"Maybe they'd understand. Like you said, you were the victim."

"So was the guy who got his dick cut off by Lorena Bobbitt. How did that work out for him? They made jokes about him on late night TV even though he was the victim too. Me, I don't like being a joke."

I pointed out to him that my paper—even without his cooperation—could still shoot pictures and video of him as he left the club, on the street, or outside his home. We could still tell the whole story of what happened to him at the hands of Melissa Ross. Then all the people at the club where he worked would know exactly who he was and know the humiliation he'd suffered. He would still be a laughingstock, whether he cooperated or not. Or, I suggested, we could work out a compromise. I'd interview him—but I wouldn't use his name; I wouldn't use his picture; and I wouldn't specify where he was living or working now. Delvecchio wasn't wild about the idea. But, in the end, he agreed to go along with the compromise.

"How long were you and Melissa married?" I asked Delvecchio once we sat down to begin the interview.

"Six months. Actually, a year technically. But the last six months of that were in divorce court. We both wanted it done. But, even when a divorce is mutual, it's not that simple. I found that out."

"How was the first six months of the marriage? Was it passionate? Scary? Weird?"

"All of the above. Melissa was always volatile. She'd fly off the handle at me over every little thing. Screaming. Yelling. Sometimes she got really violent. Hitting me, punching me, and even worse. That scene at the end . . . that wasn't the first time she'd threatened to kill me."

"If she was so volatile, why'd you marry her?"

"C'mon, Melissa is hot! I mean hot in looks, hot in bed. I knew that she was high-maintenance, but I figured all that craziness was worth it to be with a hot chick like Melissa. I was wrong about that."

"What did she get so mad at you about?"

"Jealousy about other women mostly. She accused me of flirting with them, fooling around with them behind her back. Not coming straight home after work. She claimed I was cheating on her."

"Were you?"

Delvecchio shrugged. "A couple of times."

"Even though you had this hot chick at home?"

"She wasn't always so hot when it came to me. There were nights she refused to have sex because she was mad about something. Other times she was all over me, mostly when she wanted something from me. It was almost like Melissa used sex as a . . ."

"Weapon?"

"Yeah, that's right."

"Did she ever tell you why she was so angry at men?"

"Men always hurt her, she used to say, men always broke her

heart. That's why she got the tattoo on her arm, the one with the two pieces of a heart split apart. I hated that tattoo. She already had it when I met her. I tried to get her to have it removed. But she said she was keeping it. Whenever I brought it up, she just told me that someday I'd break her heart too."

Eventually we got around to talking about that final scene between him and Melissa Ross. I asked him what had set it off.

"There was this waitress who worked at a bar near my precinct," Delvecchio sighed. "I'd been flirting with her for a while, and she kept flirting back. Well, this one night I went there and drank a lot. One thing led to another, and the waitress and I made it in my car. I was so drunk I didn't realize I still had a pair of her damn panties in my jacket pocket when I got home. Melissa found them. We had this big fight and then I finally collapsed dead drunk on the bed. When I woke up, I was handcuffed to the bed. I started screaming stuff at her to let me go and that's when she first threatened me with the gun. Put the barrel in my mouth and talked about blowing my head off. Then she moved the gun down and did the same thing on my crotch. Said she'd blow my balls off first."

Delvecchio shook his head.

"She kept me like that for days, I guess. Gagged me so no one could hear me. And kept talking about castrating and killing me. I think she might have eventually if I hadn't managed to get the gag out of my mouth and scream loud enough for help that someone in the building finally heard it and called police. That's the way they found me. Cops from my own precinct saw me like that and what that woman had done to me. I was glad to see them at that point, of course, and I told them what she had done. But later . . . later was when all the embarrassment and humiliation set in. So I changed my story, said it was some kind of consensual sex game and didn't press any charges. But everyone knew the truth. So eventually I had to leave the force. I just couldn't face anyone there anymore."

He looked onto the dance floor, where couples moved effortlessly to the music. The incident with Melissa Ross had happened years earlier. But I could see that telling the story again had made it seem very real for Delvecchio.

"What did you think when you heard about her and the murder at the Hotel Madison and the apartment of the other guy?"

"It scared me," Delvecchio said. "It made me realize all over again how crazy she really was. And how . . . how I could have wound up dead too back then just like those two poor bastards."

———

After I left Delvecchio, I went back to the office and read over all the notes I'd made that day.

One thing was obviously clear. Melissa Ross had a lot of anger in her toward men. She felt she'd been used and abused by men all of her life. Then she married a husband who cheated on her and confirmed everything she'd always experienced in the past from the men in her life. She hated men. So she took out her anger in a series of escalating incidents—kicking her commanding officer in the crotch; handcuffing and torturing her husband; even starting up her own private investigator's business that specialized in catching cheating men for other women.

But then one day she suddenly crossed the line between these man-hating actions and the actual killing of men.

Why?

What had turned Melissa Ross into a cold-blooded murderer?

Then I remembered something she had written in the email she sent: "We all go through our lives with blinders on. Getting up every morning, going to work—each day the same as the next. Pretending that what we do really matters somehow or actually makes a difference in this big cosmic universe of ours. And then one day everything changes."

So what changed for Melissa Ross?

Why now?

If I could figure that out, then maybe it could help me and the police stop her before she killed again.

CHAPTER 19

'M getting a divorce," Susan told me.

"That's great!" I said.

"Excuse me?"

"Uh, I mean that's terrible."

"No, I think you meant what you said the first time."

"Okay, I did."

"You could at least make a token effort to hide your jubilation over my life falling apart."

"I just never thought Dave was the right person for you."

"Dale."

"Him either."

She shook her head.

"You're really loving this, aren't you?"

"Yes, I am."

We were eating lunch outside on a bench near her office in Foley Square. My choice of venue. There was a street cart vendor who was one of my favorites. He sold incredible chili hot dogs. Topped with cheese, onions, and sauerkraut. I ordered two for myself. My upper limit for consuming these chili hot dogs was three, which I had done on a few memorable occasions.

"So what happened?" I asked her between bites after we sat down.

"He came home from work, and I told him we needed to talk. I said some of the same things I told you the other night. That he was a great guy, but the marriage wasn't working. There was no magic in it, and I wanted more. He understood completely. He's a smart guy and I think he must have realized the same thing as me. Maybe even before I did. We agreed on a timetable for the divorce, the logistical decisions on who would live where and how to tell our friends and family. It was all very civilized."

"Wow, that's a lot different than when you told me you wanted a divorce."

"The circumstances were different then."

"As I recall, you dumped a pile of dishes, silverware, pots and pans on my head while I was asleep—and then threw a whole bunch of my clothes out of the window."

"After you came home dead drunk during one of your 'lost weekends' of feeling sorry for yourself about the Houston scandal."

"Oh, I definitely had it coming."

I took another bite of my chili dog and contemplated how to proceed next. This was a very crucial moment in my relationship with Susan, after what happened between us last time at the bar. A delicate moment. I didn't want to move too quickly. I needed to be cool and rational and measured about my next move. Yep, slow and easy was the way to go. Subtlety was the key.

"So do you want to have sex again with me?" I blurted out.

She was eating a salad she'd gotten from another food cart. She took a mouthful now, chewed it slowly, and looked out at the street as if she was contemplating what to say next. A young couple walked past us pushing a baby carriage and with a small girl alongside them. They looked like a happy family. I sometimes wondered if Susan and I might have wound up like that if I hadn't made a mess of our marriage. Now all I could do was try to put the pieces of that marriage back together again.

"Well, you did proposition me the last time I saw you," I pointed out.

"I was drunk."

"And now?"

"I'm sober."

"So you don't want to sleep with me?"

"Not at the moment, no."

"Or marry me?"

"Same answer. Sorry, Gil, I hope you understand."

"Sure," I said. "A lot of women say no to me after they've sobered up."

She smiled sadly.

"I think I need to take a hard look at myself before getting into any other kind of relationship," she said. "I think this has to be about me too, not just Dale. I mean he seemed like the perfect guy. And, in some ways, he was. Decent, hardworking, smart, he took good care of himself by working out at the gym and eating healthy . . ."

I looked down at the second chili dog in front of me. I'd already finished off the first one. Maybe I should pass on this one to impress her with my own healthy eating habits. Except I was still hungry. Of course, I could always get a salad instead. But it was only a fleeting thought, never a serious consideration. In the end, I picked up the second chili dog and devoured a big piece.

We talked at some point about the stories I was working on. She was as baffled as I was about Melissa Ross.

"I don't know if I ever remember a case of a female serial killer like this one," she said. "I mean there have been women who've killed a series of people. But generally those were for a specific reason. Like a black widow who killed her husbands for insurance money. Or a nurse who killed sick people in hospitals out of some kind of 'Angel of Death' obsession. But this is different. She's killed two men—and seems intent on killing more—for no apparent reason other than they cheated on their wives with her. And they only did that when she came on to them, which for most men—as you know—is pretty hard to resist from a woman who looks like that. I just don't get it. There doesn't seem to be any real motive here for Melissa Ross to commit these murders."

"Didn't you always tell me that one of the basics of law enforcement investigation is that there is always a motive for every murder?"

"Maybe I was wrong about that."

"Or maybe we just haven't figured out what it is yet."

"And then there's the question of how she overpowered these men," Susan said. "I think that's crucial here. I mean this whole thing is the most unusual murder case I've ever seen."

She asked me about Houston too.

"That's so weird that she comes back in your life after all this time—and as a part of this story. And you had never heard anything from her until she walked into your office and asked you to find her missing husband?"

I hesitated before answering. Looked down at my chili dog as if maybe it could tell me what to do next.

"Well, that's the official story," I finally said to Susan.

"What do you mean?"

"It didn't exactly happen that way."

"So how did it happen?"

I told her the real story. How I'd tracked Houston down years ago and never told anyone—most notably the editors at the paper. I'd done that at the time for what I believed to be a noble reason. To let her live her new life as she wanted without having to explain her past as Houston. But now this seemingly good deed on my part had come back to haunt me, I said.

"Jeez," Susan said when I was finished.

"Yeah, jeez," I said.

"And no one else knows this?"

"I told my shrink. I'm trusting you not to tell anyone. It could cost me my job at the *News* if they found out I lied—and am still lying to them and our readers—about it."

She nodded.

"Just out of curiosity, why did you just tell me?"

"You're my wife."

"Ex-wife."

"Maybe future wife."

I finished off the last of my chili dog.

"I know we had some bad times at the end of our marriage. But you need to understand what I was going through back then. Basically, I was losing the two great loves of my life. I thought the *News* was going to fire me and not let me be a reporter anymore. And I was losing you too. I went a little crazy. Okay, a lot crazy. But there were a lot of good times between us too. You know that as well as I do. And there can be more in the future. I love you, Susan. I'll always love you. You're really the only woman in the world for me."

"Probably the only woman in the world who could put up with you," she smiled.

She reached over and took my hand. She squeezed it tightly.

"You have to understand my situation, Gil. I need some time to figure things out. I don't want to rush into anything too fast. That's why you have to let me move at my own pace on this. There's a part of me—a big part of me—that can't imagine living my life without you either. But I don't want to do that or commit to anything with you like marriage until I'm sure about my feelings."

"But you might?"

"I might."

"I don't mean to rush you or anything, but do you have any timetable on when you might make this decision?"

"You'll be the first to know."

A little while later, I walked her back to the courthouse in Foley Square where her office was located.

"So that offer you made to me when you were drunk, to have sex with me—it's definitely withdrawn?"

"I told you I wasn't ready for that right now."

"Just confirming."

Before heading back to the *Daily News*, I went back to the food cart guy and bought another chili dog.

It sure seemed like a three-chili-dog kind of day.

CHAPTER 20

I T was two days later—a sunny spring afternoon—and I was sitting with my feet up on my desk in the newsroom, thinking about how I really needed to make it out to one of the Long Island or Jersey Shore beaches this summer—when the new message from Melissa Ross came to me.

I'd just gotten back from an excruciating news meeting with Marilyn and Stacy and the other editors about where to go next with the story. The truth was we had kind of hit a wall. This happened on a lot of big stories. Everyone still wanted to read about it and we sure wanted to write about it, but no one was sure exactly how to do that. We'd done all the angles and sidebars and features to death by this point.

And so all of us at the meeting—including myself, I must confess—had ended it by falling back on the old journalist safety net for an answer: "Maybe something will happen."

It did. I knew somehow from the minute I heard the click on my computer from a new email landing that it was from her. Maybe it was my reporter's instinct or maybe it was just a coincidence that I was sitting there waiting for it at that moment. But sure enough, when I looked at the screen, I saw her name.

I suppose a part of me had been hoping I'd never hear from her again. That she'd get caught, or realize the error of her ways and stop killing, or just disappear and never be heard from again. That had happened before with serial killers. They simply stopped and went away and no one ever knew what happened to them. But not Melissa Ross. No, she was back.

I clicked open the email and read the note:

It said:

TO GIL MALLOY AND THE MEN OF NEW YORK CITY:

Here's another dumb blonde joke for you.

Three prostitutes—a brunette, a redhead, and a blonde—see a guy in an alley shooting up heroin with a syringe. He offers them some of his heroin. Then he hands them the same dirty syringe he was using. "I should warn you though," the guy says. "I have AIDS."

The brunette and the redhead quickly decline.

The blonde takes the syringe from him though.

"Are you crazy?" the brunette and the redhead say to her. "He said he has AIDS. You'll catch it."

"It's okay," the blonde says, "I've got a condom with me."

I love to hear the lies. All of the lies men say about us. Goddamned men! Men are full of bravado and machismo and testosterone-filled bragging. But, in the end, it all disappears quite quickly. And all that's left when that happens is a scared little boy.

Don't get me wrong. I love men. I love to flirt with them. I love to tease them. I love to get them aroused and full of lust and so excited they'd do almost anything to get what they want from me.

And then I take it all away from them. Everything

a man has. The bravado. The machismo. The testosterone-filled ego.

Everything they have is stripped away . . . piece by piece.

And, when it's over, I take away the only thing they have left.

Their life.

And now, instead of another dumb blonde joke, I'll end this with a little rhyme:

Eeenie, meenie, miney, moe

Time to catch another man by the toe

If he hollers . . .

Well, I sure won't let him go.

There was a video attached to the email. Whatever it was, I knew it was going to be bad. But how bad? I clicked on the video and it began to play on my screen.

I saw a car. The trunk was open, and the camera slowly moved closer to it. There was something inside the trunk. At first, it was hard to make out because the video had been shot at night. But finally I saw it was a man in the trunk. Bound and gagged and struggling in vain to get free. It was hard to make out his face in the darkness. Suddenly, the video jumped ahead to what seemed like several minutes later. The man in the trunk wasn't struggling anymore. And I could see blood on his head and the front of his clothes. It looked like he was dead.

She'd displayed him alive and as her captive.

Then she'd cold-bloodedly killed him.

The camera moved closer to the dead man in the trunk now, and his features became more visible.

Finally it was so close that I could see his face clearly.

And that's when I really knew how truly evil and diabolical and brutal Melissa Ross was.

Taking in the images I'd seen of Walter Issacs and Rick Faris like this had been tough enough. But they were just people in a story I was working on—I didn't actually know either of them.

This time it was different.

I knew the dead man in the trunk.

I'd just talked to him a few days earlier.

Tim Hammacher.

Part III

NO ONE IS SAFE

CHAPTER 21

TIM Hammacher's body was found in the trunk of his car the next morning.

The car had been parked on the street outside city hall. A meter maid discovered it when she attempted to put a ticket on the windshield a little after 7 a.m. She noticed that the trunk was partially open, lifted it open, and saw the grisly remains of Hammacher inside.

Just like Walter Isaacs and Rick Faris, he had been beaten and stabbed. He was tied up with heavy rope and there was a gag in his mouth. A stench filled the trunk because he had urinated all over himself—probably in terror. There was semen too, indicating he somehow had sex with his killer before she murdered him.

The big difference between this and the other two murder victims was that police found no evidence Hammacher's wife had hired Melissa Ross to follow or investigate him.

The initial speculation was that he had been targeted because of who he was.

A close confidant of the city's top law enforcement official.

Which scared the hell out of everyone, including me.

"We believe all three killings were carried out by the same woman, Melissa Ross," Wylie said at a hastily called press conference. "The circumstances of all these cases appear to be similar, and we are operating on the assumption that we have a serial killer on the loose. I can assure you that every effort possible is being made to apprehend the Ross woman, and we expect an arrest very soon."

For the first time since I'd seen him in action, Wylie looked rattled and unsure of himself. The loss of someone so close to him had clearly hurt him.

He went through some details about Hammacher and the crime. Tim Hammacher was forty-four years old. He had a wife, Deborah, and three young sons—ranging in age from six to thirteen. He had worked for the city in various capacities for several years, before joining Wylie to work in the new administration four years earlier. Leaving work that night, Hammacher had told people in his office that he was driving home to New Jersey. No one knew exactly why he didn't do that. Or how or why he met Melissa Ross. Or why he wound up dead in the trunk of his car in front of city hall.

"Let me add a personal note here," Wylie said, his voice breaking with emotion. "Tim was very close to me. He was my top aide at city hall. And he was my friend. The murder of any person is difficult to deal with, but it is especially traumatic when you knew the victim as well as I knew Tim. And the murder was so senseless. Tim Hammacher was a good man. I'll miss him."

Reporters began shouting out questions.

"Why did she pick Hammacher as her next victim?"

"Do you think it had anything to do with his connection to you?"

"Was Tim Hammacher having an extramarital affair?"

Wylie just walked away from the podium, without answering any of them.

———

When I got back to the office, Zeena hailed me over to the receptionist's desk. She said I had a ton of people trying to reach me. I told her to hold any further calls while I briefed Marilyn and Stacy on everything. Both of them asked many of the same questions that were asked at the press conference.

"How do the police think that Hammacher wound up in that car trunk?" Marilyn asked.

"The speculation is he picked Melissa Ross up someplace. Probably a club or a bar."

"Wouldn't he recognize her from her picture being plastered all over the media?"

"You would think so."

"Had Hammacher ever done this kind of thing with women before?"

"Well, most people thought he was a devoted family man. But now I'm hearing he really thought of himself as a ladies' man—and chased a lot of them. It just goes to show you that people can have secret lives—dark sides—that we know nothing about."

"How's his wife holding up?"

"About as well as you could expect for someone whose entire world just collapsed around them. Deborah Hammacher lost her husband, her kids lost their father, and everyone knows that he died after having sex with another woman."

"Do you think she had any idea he might be fooling around with other women?" Stacy asked.

"She says no. But I'm not sure I believe her. I just figure a wife usually knows that kind of thing."

"Even if they don't want to admit their suspicions, even to themselves," Marilyn said.

"Exactly. Maybe that's the only way they can endure the pain and keep the marriage alive."

It was the lack of a direct connection to Melissa Ross that was the one big difference between Hammacher and the murders of Walter Issacs and Rick Faris.

"There's no possibility Hammacher's wife might have hired Melissa Ross as a PI to investigate her husband's infidelity?" Marilyn wanted to know.

"No, the cops checked that out right away."

"Did she hire any private investigator?"

"She says no."

"No one that might have told Melissa Ross about Hammacher?"

"Not that the cops have been able to find."

"So Deborah Hammacher doesn't know Melissa Ross. She never heard of Melissa Ross before she hit the news. And she never hired any PI—Melissa Ross or anyone else. That changes the pattern a bit. It really does suggest that the only reason Ross targeted Hammacher as her next victim was . . ."

"He worked for Bob Wylie, the city's top law enforcement official," I said. "She wanted to send a message to us about how powerful and resourceful and downright scary she really is. What better way than to knock off someone as high-profile as this? Wylie threw down the gauntlet to her at his last press conference when he made that dramatic personal vow to catch her before she killed anyone else. She not only killed someone else, she killed the person closest to Wylie. This is all some kind of game for her. A deadly game. And she's making up all the rules."

Zeena opened the door and stuck her head in.

"Malloy, there's a call for you," she said.

"What part of 'no calls whatsoever' didn't you understand?"

"You're going to want to take this one."

"How do you know that?"

"It's your ex-wife. She says it's important."

Zeena was right this time, of course. I did want to take this call. Zeena was always much better about the personal aspects of my life than the professional.

"Hey," Zeena suddenly asked me after I'd followed her outside

Marilyn's office to take the call from Susan, "what's going on with the two of you anyway? Isn't she the hotshot ADA who dumped you, broke your heart, and married some other guy?"

"I prefer to say that we simply grew in different directions."

"So now you're talking to her again?"

"Yes, in my professional capacity," I said.

"Do you want to do the nasty with her again?"

"No, I do not want to do the nasty with her," I sighed. "And I wish you would just stay the hell out of my personal life. I don't see how any of this is relevant to you or your job here, Zeena."

She smiled broadly.

"I figured you did," she said.

———

"I've been trying to reach you since I heard about the Hammacher murder and the new communication with you," Susan said when she came on the line. "How come you didn't call me back?"

I checked my voicemail. Sure enough, there was a series of calls from Susan that I'd missed—along with other people trying to reach me about the story.

"I'm sorry," I said. "I've been so busy I haven't had time to really check all my messages."

"I know you're riding high on this story right now, but you need to stop and think about the fact that you could very well be in danger too. Look what happened to Hammacher. And this Melissa Ross woman has some kind of weird obsession with you. She writes to you about the murders. She calls you about them. Why you?"

I'd thought about that too. I didn't really have an answer. "It could be just a chance thing," I said. "She wanted a reporter and picked me at random."

"I'm worried about you, Gil. She kills men. She's fixated on you for some reason. The most logical extension of that is that at some point she comes after you as a target."

"You're forgetting something," I said. "The only way she can get to a man is by using sex as a lure. That's how she gets to her victims. I know what Melissa Ross looks like. So I'm not going to fall for her sexual lures no matter how pretty she is. Besides, I've already fallen for a pretty woman's sexual lures. Yours."

Susan didn't laugh. I had to admit I was a bit flattered by her concern for my well-being. It showed she really did care. But what she was saying did make me uncomfortable too, because I knew she was right. There was some reason that Melissa Ross began coming to me to get media attention for her murders. I needed to find out what that was. And maybe I should be more worried about it too.

"Tim Hammacher knew all about Melissa Ross," Susan said to me now. "He knew how dangerous she was. And he knew what she looked like. So why would he get in the same car with her? It doesn't make any sense. Sometimes men just can't help themselves though, I suppose. Maybe that's what happened to him. Maybe he still got turned on by her, still wanted to go to bed with her—even though he knew how dangerous she could be. Maybe his sexual urges overcame his common sense."

She was talking about Tim Hammacher, but it kinda felt like she might be talking about me and some of the mistakes I had made in the past too.

CHAPTER 22

THE murder of Tim Hammacher—a top city hall official, a seemingly happily married family man and a pillar of his community—was a shocking development even for hardened New Yorkers who liked to brag about how they'd seen it all and how tough they were and that nothing really ever got to them.

Every man in New York, whether he admitted it or not, now had to wonder if he could somehow wind up being the next victim of the woman the entire media had dubbed "Blonde Ice."

And every woman in New York had to wonder when she kissed her husband goodbye in the morning whether or not she would ever see him alive again.

The search for Melissa Ross was centered on New York City. It made sense that she was still close. She had to have been somewhere near New York City recently, of course, to have carried out the murders of Walter Issacs, Rick Faris, and Tim Hammacher. But she could also be hiding out somewhere else, then returning to New York for the murders—and fleeing again after she had carried them out.

So bulletins were also sent out across the nation. Melissa Ross had no passport, so it didn't seem as if she would be able to flee to another country. Still, special attention was given to the borders of Canada and Mexico in case she tried to cross one or the other.

Tips and leads poured in from the public. There always were plenty of those in a high-profile case like this. Except they all turned out to be dead ends.

Like the guy in Queens who claimed a blonde woman—who he was certain was Melissa Ross—had tried to pick him up in a Kew Gardens bar and lure him back to a motel room. When he said no and told her he knew who she was and what she really wanted to do to him, she ran out of the bar. Cops descended on the bar, talking to everyone who had been there. They finally pieced together the true account of what had happened to the guy. It turned out he had been drinking quite a bit, hitting on women in the bar—and he tried to strike up a conversation with the blonde he mentioned. She fled, all right. But not because she was Melissa Ross and he'd figured that out. She ran away because he was acting so strange and scary when she turned down his advances, claiming she was really out to kill him. When the police finally did find the blonde woman, it was quickly apparent she wasn't Melissa Ross. She wasn't bad-looking, but she was no drop-dead blonde fox either. You'd have had to drink a lot of beers to think she looked like Melissa Ross. Which is apparently what the Queens guy had done that night.

Then there was the West Side woman who saw an attractive blonde woman forcing a handcuffed man into the trunk of a car. The blonde then drove away, but the woman on the street got the license plate number of the car she was driving. The police took the woman's account very seriously. She was a prominent attorney, a partner in a firm on Park Avenue. No drunk in a bar. She saw what she saw, and she was adamant about it to police. It turned out that the incident had happened, just the way the woman described it. An attractive blonde female did indeed force a handcuffed man into the trunk of her car. But it wasn't real. It was all part of an elaborate sex game. When the cops tracked down the license plate number, they found that it belonged to a pretty blonde, all right.

Except it wasn't Melissa Ross. She was a professional dominatrix. She said the man had paid her to stage the kidnapping—and to hold him hostage for a few hours. She said lots of men like that role-play scenario, and that she'd done it many times before. Picking men up off the street, restraining them with handcuffs or rope, then pretending to torture the captive. She got paid as much as several thousand dollars to do this, she said, sometimes for a day-long "kidnapping."

Another time armed cops burst into the Brooklyn home of a woman who a telephone tipster had positively identified as Melissa Ross. It wasn't her though. It was the tipster's ex-wife, and he was tired of sending her alimony payments. If she went to jail for a while until it all got sorted out, he figured, he could slide on a payment or two he owed her. Instead, he wound up going to jail himself for filing a false police report.

There were many more dead ends like this. Everything was checked and re-checked though. No stone was left unturned. In the end, it all led to nothing. They hadn't gotten a sniff of Melissa Ross. She was still out there somewhere. Planning her next move. And, until the police found her, all they could do was wait to see what that might be.

———

Like every other journalist in town, I became consumed by the story and the hunt for Melissa Ross. Waiting for her to be caught. And until that happened, I was desperately trying to come up with angles and story ideas to sate the public hunger for more tidbits about the Blonde Ice killings.

The obvious approach for a newspaper or a TV station or a website was to go to places where singles or cheating husbands might go to meet women—and then interview people there about how worried they were.

The only thing was many of these bars and clubs catering to single men and the pickup crowd were almost empty now. Some of them even closed their doors until the killer was caught. No one was eager to pick up strange women in singles spots right now. Husbands were staying home with their wives. Single guys with their girlfriends. Not all of them, of course. But more and more as the murders occurred.

I talked to one bar owner who said that Melissa Ross had probably done more to save marriages in the past few weeks than all of the marriage counselors in the city put together.

Another night I did a remote for *Live from New York* from the midtown bar where Rick Faris had met Melissa Ross on that fateful night that he was murdered.

There were a few women there, only a handful of men—and no one was really that interested in talking to people they didn't know.

"A few weeks ago, this bar was filled with singles," I said on air. "Hot-looking women, well-dressed men—all of them looking to find the right partners. Or, in other words, looking to find the right person to spend the night with. But now the people who do show up here have a much more important goal. Their goal is to make sure they get through the night alive."

For blonde women, the killings had presented a problem. Blondes used to be a hot commodity. Now men were leery of them, for obvious reasons. There were reports that some blondes were even starting to dye their hair or wear dark-haired wigs to avoid any comparisons with the "Blonde Ice" killer.

"Not a good time to be a blonde," one woman said when I interviewed her in a hair salon as she made sure all the blonde traces were gone. "I used to like being a blonde. Men always looked at me. Well, they look at me now, but in a different way. Yeah, I'll probably go back to being a blonde again when this is all over. But right now . . . hell, it's tough being a blonde in this city."

Old-timers said it was reminiscent of the Summer of Sam, those hot months in 1977 when Son of Sam had hunted young women sitting in parked cars on lovers' lanes across the city.

There had been pure panic back then. Young people afraid to go out at night. Women dying their hair blonde or wearing blonde wigs because Sam had seemed to target dark-haired women in his attacks. An entire city feared that summer that they'd be Sam's next target.

Until now, Son of Sam had been the most famous serial killer in New York history, and that summer would live on in infamy. But it was happening all over again. With a different kind of killer—one maybe even scarier than a crazy postal worker who killed random women for no reason.

The New York tabloids—especially the audacious *New York Post*—had even resurrected one of the most memorable headlines from the Summer of Sam in their coverage of the Blonde Ice murders.

On the day after Tim Hammacher's body was discovered, the *Post*'s Page One headline said simply:

NO ONE IS SAFE!

CHAPTER 23

VICTORIA Issacs called after Hammacher's murder and said she wanted to see me. She gave me a place to meet. The location was a Starbucks on Houston Street in what used to be known as Alphabet City. It was a long way from her Sutton Place townhouse. And not just geographically.

The Starbucks had some outdoor tables, and we sat at one of them. It was early June now and the temperature had hit eighty for the first time this spring, giving us a taste of the New York City summer ahead. She was wearing a beige sundress and open-toed brown sandals, and carrying a straw handbag. I had on a light-weight summer blazer, a T-shirt, and jeans. People walked by us on the street in shorts, tank tops, and—in one case—what looked like a bathing suit.

"I love New York in June, how about you?" I said, humming a few bars of the old Frank Sinatra song.

She smiled and looked around. There was a trendy restaurant on one side of the Starbucks and a big supermarket on the other. Farther down the street, I saw nail salons, cell phone stores, and a CVS.

"This is where I started," she said. "Right here on Houston Street. Everything's so different now. I used to stand on that corner over there all night. Waiting for someone to stop and give me some business. This place was a bodega then. My pimp lived in an apartment on the top floor. There was an adult bookstore, a pawnshop, and a dive bar which was really just a place to buy and sell drugs. Yep, this was where I worked back then."

"Hence the nickname Houston."

"Funny thing about that. You know how everyone in New York City pronounces the name of the street as 'How-sten.' Not 'Houston,' like the city. So I started out pronouncing my nickname like the city street too. But no one else did. They just called me Houston like the one in Texas. Eventually I started using that pronunciation too. Christ, I can't believe I still remember stuff like that."

"So what prompted this trip down memory lane?"

"I just wanted to see it again."

"To see where you'd come from?"

"I guess. And maybe to figure out where I was going next too."

I took a sip of my coffee. She was drinking iced coffee, but I still took mine hot, no matter what the weather. I don't like iced coffee. I like regular hot coffee. I pondered the possible reasons for that while I waited for her to tell me exactly why she wanted to see me. It took a while.

"I spent a year working here on the street, until I managed to move up in the business," she said. "To get away from the pimps and the drug dealers and the psychos who wanted me to do all kinds of sick stuff after I got into their cars. But I did get off the street. And you know the rest. I worked my way up to being Houston, the queen of the call girls. Big apartment on Park Avenue, wined and dined at the best restaurants, and more money than I'd ever dreamed of having in my life. I was—as you put it in that article you wrote about me back then—a legend. Houston, the legend. There's something to be said for being a legend in any field. To being the best at what you do for a living. Even if it's being the best goddamned whore that money can buy."

A family was eating breakfast at a table next to us. There was a young girl of about eight with her mother and father. Victoria Issacs looked at them sadly and then back at me.

"My two little girls are still with Walter's parents," she said. "They say I'm an unfit mother because of my past as Houston and have gone to court to get a temporary restraining order against me that would give them custody. They also claim that the mortgage and deed for the townhouse are in their names because they put up the money for Walter to buy it. They want to evict me from there too. Meanwhile, none of my friends will return my phone calls, I've been suspended from the art museum board that I served on, and our country club on Long Island revoked my membership. None of these people from my new life—the life I worked so hard to build—want anything to do with me anymore. And so here I am back on Houston Street again, where it all started."

"I'm sorry," I told her.

She shrugged.

"I'll be okay. I made it out of here, didn't I? I can do it again. I can build a new life for myself one more time despite all this. I guess that's why I came down here today. To remember what it was like to be Houston. She was a tough lady that Houston. I need to be tough again too. I need to re-channel a bit of that Houston personality."

I drank some more coffee and waited. This was all interesting, but I figured she had something else on her mind.

"I slept with a lot of people when I was Houston. In the beginning, on the street, the majority of them were creeps. But later, when I moved to Park Avenue and raised my rates by a lot, well . . . the quality of the clientele went up too. Some of them were still creeps, no matter how much money they had, but most of them were pretty nice. They just wanted to spend some time outside their real life, to have a fantasy relationship for an hour, or a night with a woman like me. Or at least like the woman I was back then.

"There were bankers and lawyers and Wall Street investors and even some politicians. The public would have been shocked if they'd ever heard about the secret sex lives of some of these high-profile people that paid me money as Houston. But I never betrayed that confidence. Those people came to me knowing I was discreet and would always respect their confidentiality, which I did. Believe it or not, we hookers have rules and standards of integrity that we live by too, or at least I did. Just like a doctor or a lawyer. Or even a journalist like you."

She smiled at me.

"But there were a few times, after I got married and left the business, that I ran into some of my former clients. At charity events, awards banquets, museum openings. Most of them didn't recognize me because I looked and dressed and acted so much differently as Victoria Issacs than I did as Houston. I always avoided any contact with them.

"Except for one time. It was a big concert in Central Park—hosted by the mayor—and one of my ex-clients was there. He was a very powerful, influential man now, and I was pretty important too in my new life. He recognized me right off. And he made a pass at me. I refused. He made another pass and then another. Finally, I said yes. Walter wasn't there with me that night, so we went back to the old client's apartment after the concert and made love.

"I saw him a number of times after that. He always paid me for the meetings, just like he had when I was Houston. That somehow made me feel less guilty about cheating on Walter, I guess. It was just a job to make some money. But, to be perfectly truthful, it made me feel good too that a man still wanted to pay to have sex with me. It was fun being Houston again, even for just a little while.

"But eventually I ended it. I wanted to make my marriage to Walter work, and I couldn't do that if I was still acting like Houston. So I became Mrs. Walter Issacs all the time—a pillar of the community. That's what everyone knew me as. Until you came along."

I still wasn't sure where she was going with all this.

"What are you trying to tell me?" I asked.

"I've been trying to figure out how the Houston stuff fits into all this. Just like you have. What is the connection? I still don't know. But something else has happened now. Another connection I don't understand. But it has to mean something. I didn't have anyone else to talk to about it. That's why I asked to meet with you."

"What kind of connection? To Houston?"

"Yes."

"And to the murders?"

She nodded.

"It involves someone you know."

"Know how?"

"He's been on the front page of your newspaper."

I thought about it.

"Are we talking about Tim Hammacher?" I asked.

She shook her head no.

"His boss."

"Bob Wylie?"

"Yes, Wylie was the man I was telling you about. He used to be a customer of mine."

CHAPTER 24

WENT back to the *News*, drank a lot more coffee at my desk, and tried to figure out what I had here.

Bob Wylie had been a client of—and later had an affair of sorts with—Houston. That meant there was now a Houston connection to the third murder, Tim Hammacher. Not a direct connection, but Hammacher's boss had been a client of Victoria Issacs when she was Houston. That had to mean something. I knew, of course, there was already a Houston connection to the first murder—of her husband, Walter Issacs. I didn't know of any Houston connection to the second victim, Rick Faris. But that didn't mean there wasn't one to find. Yep, no matter how you looked at it, there was a Houston thread running all through this Blonde Ice business.

I had thought that I was the common denominator here. Like Susan had said, Melissa Ross seemed to have some sort of obsession with me—coming to me to announce the murders so far. But what if this wasn't about me? What if it was really about my connection to somebody else?

Houston would be the obvious choice.

I had become famous—or infamous, depending on how you viewed it—for the original Houston story. Victoria Issacs, aka Houston, had hired Melissa Ross to investigate her husband's philandering. I knew now that Houston had once slept—for money—with the boss of Melissa Ross's most recent victim.

But there was one other person who now appeared to have connections of some sort to all three of the murders.

Bob Wylie.

He'd had a relationship with Houston, the wife of the first victim. I also remembered that Melissa Ross had announced the second murder—Rick Faris—when Wylie was on *Live from New York* with me. I didn't give any real significance to that fact then, but now it seemed much more relevant. And later, of course, there was the murder of his man Hammacher. Which seemed to have been done because of Hammacher's relationship with Wylie. Yep, Bob Wylie was linked in some way to the circumstances of all three Blonde Ice murders. This could be the clue I was looking for. The clue I needed to break the case wide open.

Aha! I said to myself.

I wanted to stand up and say it out loud in the newsroom—like a real detective—but I feared my coworkers might find that a tad pretentious. So I just sat there in quiet admiration of myself and my genius for figuring all of this out.

This self-congratulation was tempered a bit by the realization that I still had no idea what the Wylie connection meant or where it was headed or what might come next.

What did I really know about Wylie?

Well, I knew a lot.

But maybe I should find out more.

———

I told Zeena that I needed her to pull together some clips and information on somebody for me.

"Is this professional or personal?" she asked.

"Now, why would it be personal?"

"You know, some woman you're looking to scope out before you take the plunge."

"Zeena, have I ever asked you to do something like that for me?"

"Sure, a few months ago. The woman who turned out to be the triple bigamist."

"Okay, once," I said.

I explained to her that I wanted whatever biographical information she could get me on Bob Wylie. Then I went back to my desk. I figured it would take her a while to do that. But she quickly sent me a detailed file on Wylie's life and career.

"How'd you do this so fast?" I asked.

"Stacy had already asked me to do it for her when she was getting ready to have him as a guest on *Live from New York*. So it was all ready to go."

"Why didn't you tell me that before?"

"You didn't ask."

Fair enough.

I read through all the material about Wylie. Newspaper articles. TV interviews. Some longer pieces, including in-depth magazine interviews and covers. The guy had a Facebook page and a Twitter account too.

With one notable exception, Wylie had led a charmed—almost storybook—life.

A high school football star and honor student in Massillon, Ohio, where he grew up. President of his class. Got scholarships—both athletic and academic—to Cornell, where he was a political science major. Then he went on to get a law degree. But he never practiced law. Instead, he joined the police department. In an interview once, Wylie talked about that decision.

"I cared very much about the law," he said. "But there were so many lawyers out there. Many of them unfortunately devoted their careers to keeping the guilty out of jail because the financial rewards were so considerable as a prominent defense attorney. I could have chosen that route. Or, on the other side of the fence, I might have become a prosecutor who tried to put guilty people in jail. But I decided I could make a greater contribution on the front line of crime. As a police officer. I'm proud of that decision. It's a decision that I've never regretted for a single instant."

Wylie rose quickly through the ranks. Made detective. Then lieutenant and captain. He became the youngest precinct commander in the history of the New York City Police Department.

He was eventually hired as police commissioner by the city of St. Louis. He moved there and put together an impressive record. Crime went down, the streets became safer, corruption was curtailed—and the morale of the St. Louis Police Department was said to be at an all-time high during his tenure as the chief law enforcement official there.

But then he unexpectedly resigned and moved back to New York City. He opened up his own security firm in New York, with high-profile clients who hired him for protection from kidnapping, terrorism, and all sorts of other dangers they faced because of their affluence. Wylie himself became quite wealthy by doing this.

When a new mayor was elected in New York, he wooed Wylie and convinced him to join his administration, overseeing law enforcement as deputy commissioner. Wylie gave up his flourishing business, his wealthy clients, and all the rest of it to take the job.

He quickly became a popular figure in New York. The media loved him. They loved him more than they loved the mayor. And so, in the public eye, he began to eclipse the mayor he worked for. The highlight of the media attention came when his picture wound up on the cover of *Time* magazine with the headline THE MAN WHO HAS MADE NEW YORK CITY A GOOD PLACE TO LIVE AGAIN. Now that it looked like Wylie was going to run in the next mayoral election, most of the political experts had already tabbed him as the clear favorite in the race.

No matter how you looked at it, Bob Wylie was a real feel-good success story.

The only thing that marred it was a tragedy that happened to his wife and children.

When he was in St. Louis, Wylie had met and married Deborah Hawkins, a local real estate broker. They'd had two children—a son, Robert Jr., and a daughter, Samantha. But they all died when a fire swept through their house one night. Wylie normally would have been there too. But, at the last minute, he had been summoned to the scene of a major shooting in which several officers had been wounded. He was at the hospital with the fallen officers when he learned that his entire family had died in the fire.

Many people thought that was the reason he left St. Louis. That the city held too many bad memories for him. By going to New York, he could start fresh again without the constant reminders of everything that he had suddenly lost.

There was nothing startling in any of this. Nothing that jumped out to me as particularly new or interesting or important in the Bob Wylie life story. High school football hero. Academic star in college and law school. Outstanding cop. Successful businessman. A popular, high-profile deputy mayor and now a hot candidate for mayor.

Helluva record.

Helluva career.

Helluva guy.

———

I asked Jeff Aronson to meet me for a drink at a bar near Foley Square. Aronson was the top criminal justice guy on the *News*. He worked out of a courthouse in Foley Square most of the time. But he was plugged into the cop part of stuff too. We'd both started out together at the paper around the same time and we'd both had successful runs—albeit taking different paths. My career was mercurial—full of ups and downs. His was steady all the way.

I didn't want to reveal the real reason I'd asked to see him: to find out more about Bob Wylie. So we just talked in general for a while, about the Blonde Ice investigation and the bizarre phenomenon of a sexy blonde killer murdering men who cheated on their wives.

Aronson was on his second drink before I tried to steer him in the direction of talking about Wylie. He always had exactly two drinks, no more. Then he went home to his wife and four children in New Jersey. He seemed like the perfect husband, the perfect father. But then people had said that about Tim Hammacher too. You never know what demons are inside people.

"Did you ever think about doing something like that?" I asked him when we talked about the three victims.

"You mean cheating on my wife with another woman?"

"Yes."

"Every man thinks about other women, Gil," he said, surprising me a bit with his honesty. "But no, I never have cheated on my wife, and I never would cheat on her."

"How can you be so sure of that?"

"Because my wife and family are too important to me to throw it all away for a brief bout of passion with some woman that I really didn't know. How about you when you were married to Susan?"

"I strayed on occasion for a brief bout of passion."

"So you probably have some sympathy for the three guys that got murdered, huh?"

"All they were doing was trying to get laid. Hard to resist that urge when someone who looks like Melissa Ross seduces you into bed. And they sure didn't deserve to get killed for it."

Aronson was getting close to finishing his second drink now. I asked him about Wylie.

"Well, if Bob Wylie solves the case, he's going to be a big hero in New York City. Should be a shoo-in to be elected mayor then. Of course, if he doesn't catch the Ross woman and there are more men killed, it's going to look bad for him and maybe ruin his chances for mayor. But he's going to catch her soon. She can't run forever. And then he'll make it to Gracie Mansion—the latest in a long line of career successes for him."

"What do you think of Wylie?" I asked.

"Why?"

"Just wondering."

"Bob Wylie's got the whole package. Great résumé, great looks, great charisma. Not a hint of scandal in his many years of public service. The guy's a winner."

"He sounds perfect," I admitted.

"Yeah, almost too perfect."

"What do you mean?"

"This is probably just my old reporter's cynicism talking. Nothing else. But how can a guy that's been in public life for so long not have some kind of secrets—some kind of skeletons in his closet—that we don't know about? It just doesn't make sense. Of course, I have no idea what they might be though."

I did. I knew about him and Houston. But I wasn't ready to talk about that with Aronson—or anybody else at the *News*—yet.

"Word I've heard is that you might go to work for him once he does get elected mayor," Aronson said to me.

"Doubtful."

"Why not?" He finished off the rest of his drink. "The mayor's seat could just be a stepping stone. Maybe governor after that. Senator. Or hell, even a White House run down the line. Wylie's a political rising star and you could go along for the ride. Why not jump at the opportunity to hitch your star to a guy like that?"

"Like you said, Jeff, he seems almost too perfect."

ow did she do it?" Vincent D'Nolfo asked.

"Melissa Ross?"

"Yes, how did she kill them?"

"She stabbed them. Strangled them. Beat them."

"I mean *how* did she do it? How did she overpower all three of these men so easily?"

D'Nolfo and I were at the NYPD shooting range. I'd never fired a gun in my life, but he'd offered to give me a lesson. Said it was the least he could do for helping him onto the police force.

I went through all the potential possibilities about Melissa Ross, like I'd done with my editors at the *News* when this question came up. She could have used a gun, maybe she was a black belt in karate, and—my suggestion—she may have worked a *Basic Instinct* sexual ploy like Sharon Stone in the movie to get them to let her tie them up, and then killed them while they were helpless.

"I don't know," D'Nolfo said. "It's pretty hard to imagine that all these guys would let her restrain them like that. I don't think she could count on that happening every time she tried to kill a man."

"I guess we'll find out how she did it when we finally catch her," I told him.

"Maybe finding out how she did it would help catch her," he said.

I squeezed the trigger on the gun I was holding and began shooting at the target in front of me. I hadn't hit much of anything so far. This was a lot harder to do than it looked on TV or in the movies.

"Damn, you're starting to think like a policeman," I said. "How's it going so far on the job?"

"Pretty good. I got assigned to a precinct in Brooklyn. Everyone treats me really well. Much of it is because of the publicity and praise I got from Wylie on your TV show. Thanks again for doing that."

I squeezed off a series of more shots that went nowhere near the target.

"You're jerking when you pull the trigger," D'Nolfo said.

"The gun jerks."

"No, it's you. Let me show you. . . ."

He took my gun and let loose a volley of shots.

They all hit the target dead center.

"Jeez, that's freaky," I said. "How did you learn to shoot like that?"

"In Afghanistan and Iraq. I had to learn how to shoot to stay alive."

"You must have been a helluva soldier. Big as you are. Tough as you are. And able to shoot like that."

"Just relax," he said. "You're moving around too much when you shoot. You can't hit anything doing that. Always remember three things when you have a gun in your hands: Aim. Steady. Squeeze."

"Aim, steady, squeeze," I said. "That's it?"

"Try it."

I did. I came a bit closer this time, but I was still all over the place with my shots.

I looked again at the precise pattern of shots that D'Nolfo had put up on the target.

"I'm just glad you were on my side."

"Still am," D'Nolfo said.

———

After I got back to the office, I called Lieutenant Wohlers to see if he had come up with anything new on the search for Melissa Ross. He was not friendly.

"I can't investigate this case if I have to stop and give you update briefings all the time," he barked at me.

"I thought we were partners."

"Partners how?"

"I tell you what I find out, you tell me what you find out."

"Yeah, well, when you find something out, let me know—and we'll see how that goes."

"What's got you so grumpy, Lieutenant?"

"This case. This damn case. Every time I think I find something out, it all falls apart on me. And then I'm suddenly going in another direction."

"Where are you anyway?"

"I'm at the coroner's office."

"Well, that would put anybody in a depressed mood, I suppose."

"I gotta get off the phone. I gotta deal with this new stuff right now."

"What new stuff?"

"The next sound you hear will be me ending this conversation."

After he hung up on me, I pondered what had just happened. Wohlers was in a bad mood. Something he just found had upset him. Something new that changed the direction of the investigation, he said. He was in the coroner's office when I called him. Hence, the new information—which is what was upsetting him— must have come from the coroner's office. I sometimes even amaze myself with my steel trap of a mind.

I knew a woman in the coroner's office named Karen Greene. I'd used her as a source in the past. I called to see if she was on duty today. The person who answered said she was. I thought about just talking to her over the phone, but I knew I had to go see her in person at the coroner's office if I had any hope of getting what I needed. Damn. Going to visit a coroner wasn't my favorite way to spend a sunny June afternoon.

When I got there, I looked at the sign on the door that said *Coroner* and hesitated briefly. Then I pushed open the door and went inside. I tried very hard not to think about the gruesome things that went on here. The truth was I hated the sight of dead bodies. I had realized that at the first murder scene I ever went to. Not a good thing for a crime reporter, but being around dead bodies still always gave me the creeps.

Karen Greene was an African-American woman in her forties, who had worked in the coroner's office more than fifteen years. She'd seen it all and done it all. She was working on something—I assume a body—when I walked into a room where she was bent over a table. She looked up with surprise when she saw me.

"I hope I didn't catch you at a bad time," I said.

"Nah, it's really dead around here," she said.

Then she laughed loudly.

"Hilarious," I told her.

"Sorry, just an old ME's office joke."

She took her hand out from beneath a sheet, wiped some blood off on a towel, and then walked over to me.

"What brings you down here, Malloy?"

"I wanted to find out if you'd finished the autopsy on Tim Hammacher," I said, picking the most obvious thing I figured Wohlers would have been here to find out about.

"Gee, the police just asked me that too."

"Lieutenant Frank Wohlers?"

"Ah, yes. Frank Wohlers. The human garbage receptacle."

"I assume you're referring to his propensity for consuming large amounts of healthy and nutritional food."

"And now you're here to ask me the same question."

"Great minds and all—"

"Why would I tell you anything?"

"Angela Bowers," I said.

It had been about a year ago that the body of a little six-month-old girl was found dumped in a garbage can. No one had any idea who she was. Karen Greene took a personal interest in the case and asked me if I'd write an article about the unidentified little girl lying on a slab there. I did, and eventually someone came forward to the police with information. It turned out the child's mother had died of an overdose, and her boyfriend had killed the child and thrown her in the trash can. The *Daily News* then contributed money to pay for a gravestone and a proper funeral for little Angela Bowers. Small solace, but—as Greene put it—at least the little girl had an identity when she was buried. Afterward, she said she owed me a favor for helping. I said I'd collect it sometime in the future. I figured this was as good a time as any.

But Greene shook her head no when I laid that out for her.

"If you write a story before the cops release the information, they'll know it came from me. I could lose my job. I'd like to help you, Malloy, but not enough to put my job at risk."

"I won't publish anything until the police release the information to everyone," I told her. "I'll get the story ready but won't use it before then."

"How can I be sure of that?"

"I promise, Karen."

I can be very convincing when I try to prove to someone how trustworthy I am. Even when I'm not really trustworthy. But this time I was telling the truth.

She nodded and led me into another room with big drawers along the wall. She pulled open one of the big drawers and I looked down at the remains of Tim Hammacher. It took all of my willpower not to run out of the room. Instead, I just averted my gaze as best I could. Looking at Karen Greene as she talked, not at the body lying in front of us. That helped a little.

"There were rope burns around his wrists and ankles, from being restrained before he died," she said. "Ligature marks around his neck too. Not enough to strangle him completely, but consistent with a pattern of cutting off his air for periods of time. Long enough to make him pass out, then regain consciousness a short time later. She probably began the strangulation process all over again then."

"Jesus."

"It gets worse. There were black-and-blue marks and other bruises over nearly every portion of his body. He was apparently beaten repeatedly with a blunt instrument of some kind. We're not sure exactly what that was. Probably something like a baseball bat though. Did a lot of damage to him. He was really torn up inside and out."

"Is that what killed him?"

"No, although it probably would have eventually."

She pointed down to a puncture wound near the heart. I summoned up all my resolve and looked down at where she was pointing.

"That stab wound there was what finally killed him," Greene said. "There were several other stab wounds too. I count more than six of them. Might have been even more. But this one here was done at the very end and was the cause of Tim Hammacher's death."

I thought about what Tim Hammacher had been forced to endure during those nightmarish final hours of his life.

"So these results are similar to what we found out about the first two victims then, I guess," I said to Greene.

"Not exactly."

"What do you mean?"

"The first two autopsies were done by other people. Good people. They carried out the autopsies by the book. Did everything they were supposed to do. But me . . . well, sometimes I like to do a little more. That's what I did this time. I played a hunch. And it paid off."

She reached over to a table and picked up a plastic vial.

"This is male sperm—traces of it anyway—that was found on Hammacher's genitals and on some bedsheets in the trunk of his car where we found his body."

"Sure, Ross had sex with her first two victims before she killed them. So she had sex with Hammacher too. We already knew that the sex came before the killings."

"Did you know this isn't Tim Hammacher's sperm?"

I stared at her in amazement.

"How did you find that out?"

"Because I'm g-o-o-o-d," she laughed.

"Whose sperm is it?"

"Walter Issacs's."

"The first victim."

"Right. After sperm was found on the scene of the first murder, we determined that it was indeed Issacs's sperm. Indicating that he had sex with his killer before he died. When sperm was found at the scenes of Rick Faris and Tim Hammacher, the assumption was it was the same pattern. But it wasn't. Not with either Faris or Hammacher. I ran a DNA check on the Issacs sperm. The killer must have saved some of it, then brought it to the other crime scenes and put it on the bodies before she left. Because it was Issacs's DNA we found in the sperm with Faris and Hammacher."

I tried to make sense out of everything she was telling me here.

"So what you're saying is that Tim Hammacher and Rick Faris didn't have sex with the killer before they died?"

"Yep," Karen Greene said. "Hammacher and Faris got offed without getting off."

CHAPTER 26

EVERYONE has their favorite romantic spots. A candlelit restaurant. A secluded beach hideaway. Maybe even the top of the Empire State Building. My favorite romantic spot is Citi Field. It used to be Shea Stadium. Actually, wherever the New York Mets are playing. I took Susan to a Mets game for our first date. I proposed to her six months later at Shea when Mike Piazza hit a grand-slam home run to win the game for the Mets and the sky lit up with fireworks. I'd taken her to Mets games since then too. But the fireworks hadn't been as spectacular in a while. For the Mets or for Susan and me.

We were sitting in the upper deck behind home plate now, munching on steak sandwiches, clam chowder, and something billed as Belgian-style *frites*. The food at the ballpark is much better now than in the old days at Shea, when the choices were pretty much a hot dog, a bag of peanuts, or a box of Cracker Jack. But on the field, the Mets starter had been shelled for four runs in the first inning, and the relief pitcher had given up three more. Right now, I would have happily traded the new menu for a better Met bullpen.

I'd promised Susan a romantic evening—and so here we were.

"Why did she only have sex with the first guy?" I asked her.

"What?"

"Why just with Walter Issacs?"

"We're talking about Melissa Ross again."

"Yes."

"Well, that's not very romantic."

"It doesn't make sense."

"Maybe she tried it and decided she didn't like it."

"Sex?"

"Whatever."

"She'd had sex before. Plenty of sex. Her husband said she was like a tiger in bed sometimes—when she was in the mood. Other times she didn't want to do it. But we know she got turned on by men."

"So maybe she wasn't in the mood the last two times."

"There's gotta be a better reason than that."

The story about the autopsy results had broken that day. I managed to be in front of everyone else because I knew it was coming—got another Page One exclusive while at the same time keeping my promise to Karen Greene. Win-win.

The news that Melissa Ross had sex with the first victim—and left his semen at the other two crime scenes—had set off shock waves of more fear, paranoia, and speculation about Ross, now known as Blonde Ice.

"Okay, I wonder about the sex angle too," Susan said.

"You know what also bothers me? Hammacher. He willingly went with this woman, willingly let her into his car or whatever. Think about it. This was a public official. A smart, savvy guy. He knew who she was, knew what she looked like, knew what she was capable of. So why did Hammacher let her do that to him? I don't care how sexually aroused he was. He's still not going to make himself vulnerable to a killer. He's going to try to apprehend her. Or try to call for help. He's not just going to let himself become her next victim."

"Maybe she was wearing some kind of disguise," Susan suggested.

"You mean something like a brunette wig to cover up her blonde hair?"

"Could be."

"Or maybe she dyed her blonde hair another color."

"That way it's possible he didn't make the connection to who she was until too late."

"So she could be a brunette or a redhead or even have some kind of crazy punk rocker hair like green for all we know. Christ, the cops couldn't even find her when we thought she was just a blonde."

The Mets had just clawed back into the game with a three-run double.

"They'll find her," Susan said.

"How can you be so sure of that?"

"They always do."

"Always?"

"Well, usually . . ."

"So what if they don't ever find Melissa Ross?"

"Then she gets away with it."

"Always good to get penetrating insights from a law enforcement expert," I said.

Now the Mets scored another run to cut the deficit to three.

"To be honest, I figured you brought me here to talk about something else besides the Melissa Ross case. You and me."

"Oh, that's coming."

"So bring it on."

"Now?"

"Unless you'd rather just go and get another steak sandwich?"

I pondered that for a second.

"Can I do both?" I asked.

A bases-loaded walk forced in another Mets run. Only two down now.

"Look, here's my proposal," I said. "I've made a lot of mistakes. You've made some mistakes too. Like marrying Dale or Dan or Dave or whatever his name was. So we go back to square one. We were happy when we were first married. Let's do that again. You get your divorce, we get remarried, and this time we try to do the marriage thing right. Buy a house. Maybe even start a family . . ."

"And then we live happily ever after?"

"Something like that."

"Wow, you've actually got both of our lives figured out all nice and neat, don't you, Gil?"

"I'm a man with a plan," I admitted.

She picked up one of the Belgian-style *frites*—which I think were really just french fries masquerading under a different name—and nibbled on it thoughtfully.

"Here's my counterproposal," she said. "We keep things the way they've been for the time being. We spend time together. We get to know each other all over again. We become friends. We find out whether you and I can really be together for the long haul—or if this is just some quixotic romantic fantasy on your part. Mine too."

"Friends?" I said.

"Uh-huh."

"Would this friendship at any point involve . . . well, sex?"

"It might."

"When would that be?"

"When I feel I'm ready for it."

"I don't want to pressure you or anything, but do you have any timetable on exactly how long that might be? A day? A week? Five minutes from now somewhere underneath these stands?"

"I'm not ready for sex with you yet," she said.

"Weren't we on opposite sides of this discussion that night at the bar when you wanted to come home and spend the night with me?"

"You said no."

"I've reconsidered."

"Like I said, I was drunk that night."

"Want another beer now?"

She smiled.

"It's just gonna take time before I'm going to be comfortable going to bed with you again, Gil."

"And you'll tell me when you are?"

"You'll be the first to know, I promise," she said.

Then she kissed me.

It was a nice kiss.

While it was happening, a two-run homer tied the game for the Mets.

Things were looking up.

For the Mets.

And for me.

"So where the hell is Melissa Ross?" I said to Susan.

CHAPTER 27

F watching the video files of Melissa Ross's investigative cases had been uncomfortable, meeting the subjects of the videos face-to-face was even more awkward.

I'd already jotted down names and as much contact information as I could from the videos I'd seen with Wohlers and managed to track down several of them. None of them wanted to talk to the press, of course, but I used the same kind of ploy I had with Delvecchio. I pointed out that I had their names and where they lived and worked. Some newspapers and websites had been running "john" lists to embarrass the clients of call girls. I said that I could either do that (not that I really would have) or they could talk to me without being specifically named in my piece. Most of them agreed to do it that way. Malloy, you crafty devil. They can run, but they can't hide.

Well, except for Melissa Ross, of course.

Who seemed to be doing a damn good job of running and hiding.

The first person I saw was Robert Johnson—the guy I'd watched in the hotel on the Melissa Ross video collection. In person, Johnson looked a bit more dignified than the bald, potbellied naked guy I'd seen with the hooker on Ross's surveillance video.

We were sitting in the office of the construction company he owned in Queens. He was wearing a loose-fitting shirt that hid some of the girth around his belly. He also had a toupee on. Not a great toupee, but it covered up the baldness pretty well.

"Yes, she was a hooker," Johnson snapped at me as soon as I began asking questions about how he wound up in that hotel room video. "I pay prostitutes for sex. Is that against the law?"

"Actually, it is," I pointed out.

"My God, the cops are busting johns now? I guess they don't have enough to do, huh? Of course, they could go out and catch that crazy homicidal bitch who took these pictures of me. But that might be too hard. Easier to hassle regular citizens—upstanding businessmen—like myself."

The office was a nice one. Johnson probably did pretty well in the construction business. Well enough anyway to afford to spend money on prostitutes. I wondered about the toupee though. Why did he wear it for work and not for sex in the hotel room? Did it somehow get knocked off during the sexual foreplay with the hooker, assuming there was some sexual foreplay before the final big act where she got him off? Or did he just figure that since he was paying for the sex, he didn't have to look good—the way he did for his clients and employees?

"I'm not here to hassle you, Mr. Johnson," I said. "I'm just hoping you can give me some information that will help catch Melissa Ross before she kills again."

I told him about the collection of other videos—the surveillance of cheating husbands and boyfriends—that had been discovered in Ross's files.

"I guess I got a little careless," Johnson said. "I've been seeing prostitutes for years. I used to try to hide it better. But lately . . . well, I just figured what the hell? Probably would have been better off if I'd simply told my wife what I was doing. She thought I had a girlfriend or a mistress or something on the side. That's why she hired the Ross woman as a PI. All I wanted was the sex. I love my wife. I just don't want to have sex with her. She doesn't want to have sex with me either. So what's the harm?"

"It sounds like she didn't like that arrangement as well as you," I said. "Otherwise, why would she hire Melissa Ross to spy on you?"

"Like I said, she thought I was cheating on her. But I wasn't. It was just sex for money, that's all. We're fine now, my wife and me. We worked it out after she found out from Ross's investigation. Oh, she gave me a lot of grief about bringing potential sexually transmitted diseases home to her and stuff like that. But, damn, we don't have sex anyway. And you know what? I really think she was relieved when she found out it was just a prostitute I was fooling around with. Nothing more going on in my love life than a damn prostitute on the side once in a while."

"How did she find Melissa Ross?" I asked.

"My wife told me she was reading a lot of stuff about unfaithful husbands. Trying to figure out whether or not I was cheating on her. So she went online and googled some information. At some point, she came across an advertisement for Melissa Ross's service. She contacted her, asked her to follow me and report back on what I was doing."

"Does she know anything more about Melissa Ross?"

"Just what she's read in the papers and seen on TV now."

"Does she know anyone else who used Melissa Ross's services?"

"No."

"No idea where Melissa Ross might be."

"Of course not."

I showed him a picture of Melissa Ross now.

"So you don't know her firsthand at all?"

"No."

"Never seen her?"

"Never seen her."

"She never came on to you in a bar, offered to go back to a hotel room with you, promised sex . . ."

"Nope."

"You're absolutely sure about that?"

Johnson looked down again at the picture of Melissa Ross. "Believe me, I'd remember a hot chick like that."

———

I talked to more of the people the cops found out about through Melissa Ross's files. Both women who had hired her and men she had caught on those videos. Some of the wives were still angry at their husbands. Some of them were remorseful for what they had done—hiring a woman that might have murdered their husbands, just like she had murdered the other three victims. And a lot of them, both husbands and wives, were worried that Melissa Ross could still be a danger to them.

By the time I got to Janet Creighton, I'd pretty much given up hope of learning anything from this seemingly endless series of questions for Ross's clients.

Janet Creighton was very much in the Karen Faris mode. She'd worried for a long time that her husband was cheating on her, finally done something about it by hiring Melissa Ross, and now wished desperately she could turn everything back to the way it was.

"My husband left me," she said, as we sat in her living room in Tenafly, New Jersey—a suburb about fifteen miles outside of Manhattan. "He said he couldn't trust me anymore. Because I had him followed. When he found out what I'd done, he just packed his things and left. If only I'd never gone to that Ross woman. Then I'd still have him here with me. But that's not even the worst part. The worst part is that I may have put him in danger from that crazy woman. I lay awake at night worrying about that. Worried that she might come after him next because of what I did."

I went through the same questions with Janet Creighton. Not expecting much. Except this time it turned out a bit differently.

That happened at the end of the conversation, when I asked her how she'd hired Melissa Ross. Had she discovered her on the Internet like some of the others? Or seen the ad for her unique private investigative services somewhere?

"Oh no, I didn't do any of that," Janet Creighton said.

"So how did you find out about Melissa Ross's agency?" I asked.

"In my women's empowerment class."

Her women's empowerment class. Karen Faris had mentioned a women's empowerment class too. When I asked her how she found out about Melissa Ross's private investigator agency and her specialty in catching cheating husbands, she'd said, "At my women's group."

Janet Creighton said her class had been held at a college in Manhattan.

On my way back into the city, I called Karen Faris's number on my cell phone.

"Yes, they were held at that college," she said. "We went in the evening, two nights a week. It was an eight-week course, no credit—just an adult education kind of thing."

"It was officially run by the school?"

"Sort of. They make space available for these types of adult education courses. So they sign off on the curriculum, etc.—but it's not officially a part of the college, I believe."

"Does a college professor lead it?"

"I believe Kate is affiliated with the school in some way."

"Kate?"

"Dr. Kate Lyon. She's a psychotherapist in Manhattan. Specializes in work with women who've been abused in some way. A wonderful woman, she taught me so much. I think she's a visiting professor there. Or maybe it's an adjunct professor. Some sort of title like that."

"Who in the class told you about Melissa Ross and the service she ran?"

"God, I don't remember. It just came up in a conversation there one day. When I heard about what she did for women who suspected that their husbands were being unfaithful, well . . . she seemed like someone who might be able to help me."

"Was Victoria Issacs by any chance in the same class?" I asked.

"Who?"

"Victoria Issacs. The wife of the first victim."

"No, I don't believe so."

"Tim Hammacher's wife, Deborah?"

"I saw her on TV the other day. But I didn't recognize her. No, she wasn't there either."

"Do you remember who any of the other women in your class were?"

"Not really."

"If you could even just recall a few of the names, it would be very helpful."

"We didn't use names in the class. It was all anonymous. Dr. Lyon said it was better that way. It allowed us to express our real feelings even if we didn't feel comfortable letting the others know exactly who we were. That's why everyone only used their first names. There was Janet, Lisa, Carol . . . that's all. And I'm not sure all of the women even used their real first names."

Janet Creighton had told me the same thing.

"So the only person who knows all of the names in the class would be Dr. Lyon?" I asked.

"Yes, I suppose so. Dr. Lyon would know."

———

When I got back to my desk at the office, I clicked on my computer and looked up whatever information there was about Dr. Kate Lyon. I found a medical website that said she had an office on Central Park West. There was a contact telephone number too.

And a picture of Dr. Lyon. She was a dark-haired, middle-aged woman. Pretty ordinary looking. I wondered if she'd had some kind of bad experience that turned her into a man hater too, just like Melissa Ross. On the other hand, maybe she just wanted to help women. I called her number.

"I'm a doctor," Dr. Lyon said after I explained to her what I was looking for. "I can't reveal information about my patients."

"They're not patients. They're in a class. That's not really the same thing."

"Actually, it is. In this case, they were attending the class as a form of treatment or therapy for themselves. I was a teacher, but I was also a doctor—a trained medical professional—talking to a group of women about their problems. So the doctor-patient confidentiality issue is very much in play here."

"The information I'm seeking is very important, Dr. Lyon."

"So are my principles as a professional medical person."

"Can you tell me anything at all about the class?"

"As long as it doesn't refer specifically to any of the women who were in it."

"Okay, let's talk about who wasn't there. If I give you a name, and that woman wasn't in your class, you can tell me that?"

"Of course," she laughed. "The doctor-patient confidentiality only applies to actual patients. I'll be happy to try and help you in any other way I can without violating that oath."

"Was Victoria Issacs in the class?" I asked.

"No, no one by that name."

"Deborah Hammacher?"

"No."

"Melissa Ross."

She laughed again. "I do read newspapers and watch television," she said. "I know who these women are. And no, Melissa Ross was not a part of my class."

"I've been told by two of the women who did attend your class that they heard about Melissa Ross's investigative services—and then hired her to follow their husbands—from others in the class."

"That's very possible. Some of the women were very angry, very desperate about their situation. They might well have been attracted to someone who offered the type of services that this Melissa Ross did."

"But you can't—or, more precisely, you won't—tell me any of these women's names."

"I'm really sorry, Mr. Malloy."

CHAPTER 28

KEPT waiting for the next phone call or email from Melissa Ross. At work, when a message landed in my inbox or when my phone rang, I wondered if it was her. But it didn't happen that way. The phone call, when it finally came, was to me at home.

The ringing woke me up at 2 a.m. I assumed it was the office calling about some big breaking news story.

Until I answered it.

"Hello, Gil," a woman's voice said. I'd only heard it once before, but I knew immediately who she was.

"Hello, Melissa," I said quietly, and still half-asleep.

"I've got another dumb blonde joke for you. There's a blonde and a redhead watching the six o'clock news. It shows a man on the Brooklyn Bridge threatening to jump. The redhead bets the blonde fifty dollars that the man will jump. Which he does. But the redhead tells the blonde she's not going to take the fifty dollars because she cheated on the bet. She'd already watched the bridge drama play out on the five o'clock news. 'So did I,' the blonde tells her, 'but I didn't think he'd jump again.'"

She laughed loudly into the phone. I didn't laugh or say anything.

"You don't sound happy to hear from me, Gil. That's a bit disappointing. After the wonderful relationship we've had . . ."

"We don't have a relationship."

"Sure we do. Tim Hammacher. Houston. You and I seem to travel in the same circle of people. You know what I'm talking about, right?"

"Tim Hammacher was a decent man," I said. "He loved his wife, and he loved his kids. And now they're going to live the rest of their lives without him because of you!"

"Maybe he shouldn't have tried to put his dick into me then, huh?"

"Why are you doing this, Melissa?"

She laughed again.

"How did you get my number?" I asked.

"Oh, please! I'm a private investigator, remember? I just figured the authorities would be listening in on your work phone now to try to catch me. I decided to switch things up a bit."

"So is there another body?" I asked her. "Is that why you called?"

"Do I need a reason to call you?"

"Yes."

"Actually, the reason I called was because I wanted to say goodbye to you."

"Goodbye?"

"Yes, you'll get an email in a few minutes with more."

"What are you talking about?"

"Goodbye, Gil Malloy."

Suddenly the line went dead.

Then I heard a ping on my email. A new message in my inbox. The subject line said: "Yes, Blondes Really Do Have More Fun: I Know I Did!"

I opened it up and read:

It is time for Melissa Ross to disappear. I know that now.
It's been a helluva ride. But I really do need to move on.

Of course, wherever I go, I don't expect the men to be any different. Men are all the same, wherever they are. I stopped at a McDonald's in Pennsylvania today where I caught a young guy at a nearby table sneaking glances at me. He wore a football jersey that said he was a varsity letterman. He was with a pretty young girl wearing a cheerleaders' jacket from the same school. The football hero and his All-American cheerleader girlfriend. Mr. Touchdown and Chrissie Cheerleader, I decided to name them. The perfect young couple.

Except Mr. Touchdown seemed more interested in me. He just couldn't keep his eyes off of me. Like I said, men are all the same. There was a motel next to the McDonald's. I thought about slipping him a note inviting him to meet me there later, after he'd dumped his cheerleader girlfriend somewhere. Then the young football stud and I could have a fun-filled night together. Of course, I'd be the one having the fun, not him.

But I decided not to. I have more important things to do. More important than luring another horny guy into a motel right now. Just for the fun of it though, I stopped by their table as I was leaving.

"Thanks for the invite," I told the football player, "but I don't sleep with guys who try to pick me up in McDonald's. Guess you'll have to make do with your little cheerleader friend here after all. I appreciate the offer though." Then I walked out, laughing to myself about how Mr. Touchdown was going to explain that to Chrissie Cheerleader.

Let me leave you with one more blonde joke:

There's a legend about a bar that had a very special mirror in the ladies' room. If a woman stands in front of the mirror and she tells the truth, she'll be granted a wish. But if she tells a lie the mirror goes POOF—and she disappears forever.

A redhead stands before the mirror and says: "I think I'm the most beautiful woman in the world." POOF—she disappears.

A brunette stands before the mirror and says: "I think I'm the sexiest woman alive." POOF—she disappears.

Then a beautiful blonde stands before the mirror and says: "I think . . . " POOF—she disappears forever.

It's time for me to do that too.

Time for Melissa Ross to just disappear forever.

"So what do we make of all this?" Marilyn Staley asked.

"It sounds like Melissa Ross has stopped killing for some reason," Stacy said.

"We don't know that," I pointed out.

"Well, at least she's left New York City."

"We don't know that either."

"But she said in the email . . ."

"Stacy, this is a woman who has brutally murdered three men for no real reason. She enjoys killing. Not a nice woman at all. So I don't think honesty—as in telling the truth in her communications with us—is really high on her list of priorities."

"Maybe she's going to kill herself," Marilyn suggested.

"She doesn't seem like the kind of woman who would do that," I said.

"But that email did sound a bit like a suicide note," Stacy said.

Marilyn sighed. "I think Gil is right. We can't believe anything she says. She's a woman who likes to play games. And right now you are the person she's chosen to play her game with, Gil. There could be some kind of endgame to all this that hasn't played out yet. You're a man. She kills men. What better way to make a big splash than by killing the male reporter she's been communicating with about the murders?"

"Well, that's comforting," I said.

"C'mon, you must realize that too."

I thought about what Susan had said. I gave Marilyn and Stacy the same answer I had given her.

"I'll be fine. I'm not going to go to a hotel room or get in a car with this woman. I know how to take care of myself. Believe me, you're not going to get rid of Gil Malloy that easy."

The one thing we agreed on was that we had another great story. We went big with it on the Web, on air, and in print.

It was a waiting game after that. Now that we'd received the next message from Melissa Ross, we were going to have to wait some more to see what—if anything—happened next.

Was she talking about leaving New York City and stopping the Blonde Ice killings altogether?

Was she telling us she was planning to murder men somewhere else instead?

Or what if she really was planning to just disappear—like other serial killers had done in the past—leaving us with lots of questions and few answers?

And so everyone waited. I hated waiting. Plus, there was a huge audience for this story, and Marilyn and Stacy were putting a lot of pressure on me to come up with some follow-up ideas and angles in the absence of real news.

Except I had no ideas.

I had no new angles.

Whenever I found myself at a dead end like this on a story, sooner or later I always turned to what I called the "go-back-to-the-beginning" approach. Maybe I could to try to make some headway like that.

"Just put aside everything you've learned so far and go back to the beginning of the investigation," an old newspaperman told me once. "Start all over again. You might think you've covered every possible fact, every possible piece of evidence, every possible lead in the case. But you'll be surprised at how much you missed when you do it all over again."

Well, the beginning of this case was the Hotel Madison. The place where the first murder, the killing of Walter Issacs, Houston's husband, took place.

I went back to the Madison to go through everything one more time. I talked to the employees on duty, went to the room where Issacs's body had been found, walked through the entire timeline of everything I knew about what happened that night.

Issacs had had a drink in the hotel bar, where—according to witnesses—he met a stunning blonde woman. A woman who was later identified as Melissa Ross. Then the elevator security camera caught them passionately making out on the way up to his room. They went into his hotel room, where they apparently had sex—since the semen found on the sheets had definitely been identified as coming from Issacs. Ross murdered Issacs at some point after that, but stayed overnight in the room with the body. She then calmly ordered a room service breakfast, and answered the door when the waiter delivered it. A maid discovered the body when she finally entered two days later to clean the room.

I went through it all, looking for something I might have missed. It took me a while to figure out what that might be. But then it hit me.

The waiter!

The waiter had seen her. He had talked to her.

The police had interviewed the waiter that first day. He had told them his story, then gone home for the day without talking to anyone else at the scene. He didn't seem important at the time, but now he was important to me. Maybe he could tell me something else about Melissa Ross.

The waiter's name was Luis Velez and he was off for a few days, the people at the hotel said. I got someone there to give me Velez's phone number and home address, which was way at the far end of the Bronx. I tried the phone number, but got no answer. I kept trying it, without any success. I thought about going out to Velez's address in the Bronx and knocking on the door, but I dismissed the idea. If Velez wasn't home—and it didn't seem like he was—the trip would just be a waste of time. So I left messages—on Velez's phone and also at the hotel—that I wanted to talk to him.

I had no idea what to do next. I pondered this dilemma for a while and finally came up with a game plan.

When the going gets tough, the tough just give up and go home. So that's what I did.

———

I ordered a pizza from a place on my block and ate in front of the TV. I thought about trying to set a new personal pizza eating record. My high thus far was all eight slices, although admittedly it was a small pie and the pieces were pretty thin. Normally I can eat four to five slices without a problem. Anything more than that and I'm in uncharted gastronomical territory.

I drank some beer with the pizza and clicked around channels with the remote until I found a *Columbo*. I like Columbo, but I always thought he was a bit of a cheat as a detective. I mean he always understood exactly what was going on right from the very beginning. Not like me. If I was as aware as he, maybe I'd have time to come up with clever catchphrases like "just one more thing, sir."

After a while, the beer and all the pizza started to make me sleepy. I knew I wasn't going to make it until the end of *Columbo*. I just wanted to crawl into bed. Yep, I'll crawl into bed with my woman and cuddle with her through the night. Oh, wait a minute . . . I don't have a woman in my life. I have my ex-wife who now wants to be my "friend"; a former lover who is in Italy with her new husband; and a onetime prostitute who's now a grieving widow. Of course, I could always call Peggy Kerwin. She'd come over and cuddle with me. And, as an added bonus, would be so boring that I'd probably have no trouble going right to sleep.

The truth was, I finally admitted to myself, I was letting my thoughts drift to stuff like this because I didn't want to deal with what was really on my mind.

Melissa Ross.

I didn't know where she was.

And I didn't know what she was doing.

That all scared me.

Sure, I'd come on strong with Marilyn and Stacy about how I knew enough to take care of myself and not become another one of her murder victims. I was too damn smart to go to a hotel room with Melissa Ross or get in a car with her or let her into my apartment so she could murder me.

Except—and this was the part that scared me—all of her other victims probably felt the same way, until it was too late.

I checked the locks on the door before I went to bed.

And I walked around my apartment just to make sure no one was hiding anywhere.

I wasn't really scared.

Just being careful.

There's a big difference.

I think.

But the bottom line was I sure hoped the cops caught Melissa Ross pretty soon.

CHAPTER 29

THEY found Melissa Ross the next day.

A teenaged girl in Ohio taking an early morning swim at a place called Munson Lake saw a dark object at the bottom of the water. She dove down to take a look and discovered it was a car. There was a dead woman inside. The girl called police, who dragged the car and the body to the surface.

The driver's license and other identification in the car identified the woman as Melissa Ross. The serial killer the entire nation was looking for.

Everything pointed to suicide. She was still in the driver's seat, with her seatbelt on. There was no sign of a struggle to get out. No evidence of any kind that she tried to save herself. The tire tracks along the side of the lake didn't show any skid marks or anything else to indicate the car had gone out of control. It appeared as if she had simply driven into the water to die.

Also, there was a room key for a local motel in her purse. The room was registered under the name of Melissa Ross. Her real name. Even though she was the object of a massive police manhunt. It was almost as if she didn't care if anyone recognized her anymore. Inside the room, the police found a suicide note.

It read:

To the people and police of New York City: I'm so sorry for all of the pain I have caused. I don't know why I did it. I was just so angry, so filled with hate because of what men had done to me that I wanted to hurt them. But now I can no longer live with myself because of what I have done. I just can't go on. I hope God shows more mercy on me than I did with those men I did all the terrible things to. The world will be a better place once I'm gone.

It didn't take long to confirm for certain that the dead woman was Melissa Ross. Her fingerprints were on file with the police department from when she'd been on the force. The Ohio State Police made copies of her prints from the body and sent them to New York to be checked against the ones on file. The prints turned out to be a perfect match. The dead woman in the lake was definitely Melissa Ross.

"What the hell was she doing in Ohio?" I asked Wohlers.

"She was on the run," he pointed out. "Maybe it just worked out that's where she decided to give up—she was tired of running, knew she'd be caught eventually and have to spend the rest of her life in prison. So she left a note and killed herself."

"It doesn't sound like her. Doesn't sound like the previous notes. The previous notes and phones calls were all arrogant, cocky, taunting—no hint that she had any misgivings of any kind about what she was doing. This one wasn't like that at all."

"She was crazy," Wohlers said. "She probably had up and down moods. Maybe she was on some kind of drugs that made her temperament go through all sorts of volatile mood swings."

"And she used her real name when she registered at the hotel. Jesus, why would she do that? I mean the minute someone recognized the name . . ."

"Who cares?" Wohlers said. "I'm just glad it's over."

———

The *Daily News* newsroom was pure bedlam, of course. We'd already tweeted out the discovery of Melissa Ross's body, sent out alerts for our online subscribers, and flooded the rest of social media with the breaking news. I'd put a rudimentary story on the website, and now I was adding details, polishing it and turning it into a news story with sidebars that would carry us through the rest of the day. Meanwhile, all the editors were trying to figure out the best Page One headline for the morning edition. The favorite at the moment was: BLONDE ICE ICES HERSELF.

There'd be follow-ups and analyses and opinion pieces running for days. But Wohlers was right about one thing. The Blonde Ice story itself was finally over. Even if there were still a lot of unanswered questions.

In the middle of all this, Zeena called me at my desk phone.

"There's someone here at the front desk who wants to see you," she said.

"Okay."

"Are you in?"

"I'm talking to you, aren't I?"

"Sometimes you want me to say you're not in depending on who it is looking for you."

"Who is it?"

"Let me ask him."

"Good idea, Zeena."

She came back on the line a few seconds later.

"He said his name is Luis Velez."

A few minutes later, a Hispanic man of about twenty-five—Luis Velez, the waiter from the Hotel Madison I'd been looking for—approached my desk.

Stacy had walked over to my desk too, to find out what was going on.

"I got a message you wanted to talk to me about the Blonde Ice woman," Velez said.

Stacy laughed. "You're a little late, Velez."

"What do you mean?"

"Melissa Ross was just found dead," I told him. "That's what we wanted to talk to you about."

"So you don't need me now?"

"Sure, you can go," Stacy said. "The Melissa Ross case is over."

Stacy was right, of course. There was no reason to question Velez now. But old habits die hard. And I always liked to wrap up all of the loose ends in any case. So, since Velez was there anyway, I decided to ask him a few questions about Melissa Ross.

He went through everything he remembered from that morning when he delivered breakfast and talked—albeit briefly—to Ross.

"Man, she was hot," Velez said. "I mean what guy wouldn't have wanted to go to bed with her? I was thinking about her after I left. Not because of the murder, I didn't know anything about that yet. Just because she was so hot. I mean smokin' hot."

"I think we've established that Melissa Ross was hot," I smiled.

"Anyway, she ordered two eggs, coffee, and toast. Breakfast for one."

"Did that seem unusual at all?"

"What do you mean?"

"That it was breakfast for only one. There were supposed to be two people in the room."

"Didn't matter any. I don't know who's in the rooms. I just take the food to them. I'm a waiter. That's what I do. She opened the door and took the food. I didn't figure she was a murder suspect or anything."

I smiled.

"And that's it?"

"That's it. I went back to the kitchen. A few days later, cops are all over and I find out I served breakfast to a killer that morning."

Just like Stacy said, there had been no real point in talking to Velez. But at least I'd tried. I thanked Velez for his time and told him we were done now.

Just before he left, Velez looked at a picture of Melissa Ross on my computer screen for the front page of tomorrow's paper.

"Who's that?" he asked, obviously intrigued by the sexy blonde woman in the picture.

"Melissa Ross."

Velez stared at the photo for a long time. He looked confused.

"No, it's not."

"Sure, it is," I told him.

Velez looked at the photo again, and then shook his head vehemently from side to side.

"That wasn't the woman I met in the hotel room," he said.

———

"I don't have time to talk to you," Wohlers said when I called him.

"This is important."

I told him about my conversation with the Hotel Madison waiter.

"Well, he must have been mistaken," Wohlers said.

"He seemed pretty certain now that the woman he saw in the room didn't look like the picture of Melissa Ross."

"So then she was wearing some kind of disguise that morning. Changed her hair color or something so that people didn't recognize her. She probably didn't look exactly like the picture the waiter saw. But so what? She's dead now. We know she's dead. You should be happy. I'm happy. We've solved the case, Malloy."

"Did you get all the autopsy results from Ohio yet?"

"I was just about to do that when you called and interrupted me."

"Let me know what they are."

"Sure. Do you want me to have a squad car stop by the *News* and deliver the coroner's report to you personally so you don't even have to bother picking up a phone or going online to read it?"

"C'mon, Lieutenant, I'm trying to be a good guy. There's something wrong here. Just tell me what else you find out before anyone else in the media gets the information. That's all I'm asking."

"Yeah, whatever," he said.

I sat and waited for what seemed like hours for him to call me back. Finally, he did. His voice was different now. More subdued, almost sheepish. I knew even before he told me the details of the autopsy that I was right.

"I just got off the phone with the people in Ohio. They're not calling it a suicide anymore. The preliminary autopsy showed Ross didn't die of drowning in that lake—she was dead before she went into the water. A long time before. Maybe as long as a week ago. Tim Hammacher died less than a week ago. So, according to this timetable, Melissa Ross would have been dead before Hammacher was murdered. Which makes no sense at all."

"Sure it does," I said. "Think about it, Lieutenant. The waiter insisted the woman he saw in that hotel room that morning after the Issacs murder didn't look like Melissa Ross. The killer only had sex with the victim the first time, not the next two. Tim

Hammacher—who should have recognized Melissa Ross—let her pick him up anyway that night they met in the bar."

"There's more than one killer," Wohlers said.

"Or maybe Melissa Ross didn't kill anybody at all."

"My God . . ."

"We've been looking for the wrong woman all along," I said.

Part IV

THE LADY IN THE LAKE

CHAPTER **30**

THE police held a press conference the next day where they confirmed the news to everyone that Melissa Ross was not the Blonde Ice killer we were looking for after all.

Wylie was not there this time, which was unusual since he always took a high-profile position with the media. Instead, the press conference was conducted by Police Commissioner William Eaton. Eaton had been pretty much overshadowed in his role by the hands-on Wylie in the past. He didn't look particularly happy to be up there in the spotlight now.

"There was a small bruise on her head," Eaton said. "At first, the people in Ohio thought she had hit her head there during the crash, as the car went into the lake. But the abrasion didn't come from a steering wheel or a windshield or anything else inside the car. It was made by a blunt object—a piece of metal or wood, maybe even a club or a baseball bat that had smashed into her head. That's what killed her.

"There's also evidence now that she'd been in the trunk of the car she was found in. We discovered pieces of fabric in her hair and on other parts of her clothing and body that matched up with materials from the interior of the trunk. It looks like she was killed somewhere else, transported in the trunk of the car to the lake, then placed behind the wheel of the car before it was pushed into the lake, to look like she'd committed suicide.

"And, along with these new developments, the medical examiner has now placed the estimated time of death for Melissa Ross at least one week earlier."

I had already broken much of this information in the *News* hours earlier, of course.

"Just to be clear, you're saying that she died before Tim Hammacher's murder?" someone asked.

"That's right."

"So she couldn't have killed him," one reporter said, pointing out the obvious.

"Not unless she figured out a way to come back from the dead," another reporter laughed.

"Maybe she didn't kill the first two either," someone else said.

Eaton had a shell-shocked look on his face and seemed like he just wanted to get out of there. I thought again about how unusual it was that Wylie wasn't here. Sure, it was a tough situation and he was no doubt badly shaken up by the death of his confidant and friend Hammacher. But he had shown up to answer questions even after Hammacher's death. It seemed unlike him to dodge the media, even under these circumstances.

"I thought Melissa Ross was identified by someone going up in the hotel elevator to the room of Walter Issacs, the first victim," a woman reporter asked Eaton. "Doesn't that show she at least killed him?"

"We have a witness now who puts a different woman in Issacs's room the next morning."

"A sexy blonde woman?"

"Yes."

"But different?"

"This woman was definitely not Melissa Ross."

"So you think Melissa Ross took Issacs up to the hotel room, but never killed him—that the second woman did that."

"That is a viable scenario at this point," Eaton said.

"So are we talking about two women murderers—or one?"

"At the moment, we believe there is only one woman killer—and Melissa Ross was a victim of this woman, along with the men that were killed."

"Who is this woman?" a reporter asked him.

"Where is she?" another one wanted to know.

"We don't have any of those answers yet," Eaton said.

The press conference erupted into pandemonium, reporters yelling questions at Eaton in rapid-fire succession.

I shouted out: "Where is Deputy Mayor Wylie and why isn't he here?"

Eaton mumbled something about "no more information at this time" and hurriedly left.

———

When I got back to the *News*, I called Wylie's office. I wanted to talk to him directly about all this. With Hammacher gone, I didn't have a real contact in his office. So I just told the woman who answered that I needed to talk to him about a job offer he'd made to me. I said I was ready to give him a decision. I wasn't, but I figured that was the best way to get him to the phone.

The woman put me on hold for a long time.

"The deputy mayor says he's unable to talk to you now," she said when she returned.

"Did you tell him who I was?"

"Yes."

"Please go back and tell him it's important I discuss the job offer with him now."

She disappeared again, then came back on the line.

"I'm sorry, Mr. Malloy. The deputy mayor says that job offer is no longer available. He has made other plans for our campaign team. But he said he wishes you the best in your career endeavors."

After I hung up, I sat there trying to figure out why Wylie might have pulled the job offer. He had been really hot for me to join his campaign. And now he wasn't. So what changed? Well, Hammacher was dead. But that should have made me an even more desirable commodity to him. What else could it be?

I had one theory.

Houston.

Wylie probably had no idea Houston was still out there until I did my mea culpa broadcast/story about me and her. He wanted me on his staff badly before I revealed that; now he wanted no part of me. Ergo, I was betting Houston had to be the reason. It was a potential scandal for him—top cop patronizing top prostitute. So the last thing he wanted was a guy on his staff who knew Houston and might find out about his secret. No, now he'd want to put as much distance between himself and me as he could. Which is what he was doing.

The more I thought about it, the more that made sense to me.

What didn't make sense was why he hadn't been at the Melissa Ross press conference.

I also was still bothered by why Melissa Ross's body would have turned up in a lake in the middle of Ohio—hundreds of miles from the other murders.

I found a map of Ohio online and studied it. Munson Lake was in the northeast section of the state, about twenty miles south of Cleveland. Melissa Ross had grown up on Long Island and lived in Queens. As far as I could tell, she had never lived in Ohio. There was no evidence she had even been there at any time until the end. So how did her body wind up in a car at the bottom of this lake?

Did Ross drive to Ohio—to elude the police or for some other reason—before being murdered there?

Or, as it seems more likely now, was she killed somewhere else—probably right here in New York City—and then driven to Ohio to be put into her watery grave?

But why? Why Ohio? Why did whoever killed her go to all the trouble of putting her in that lake—and trying to make it look like suicide—instead of just leaving the body wherever the murder took place?

Looking at the map of Ohio on my computer screen, I suddenly remembered something else. I had called up a map of Ohio a few days earlier too. When I was finding out more about Bob Wylie's background. Wylie had grown up in a place called Massillon, Ohio. I found Massillon on the map. It was about twenty-five miles from where Melissa Ross died. Not exactly the same location. Still, close enough that it piqued my curiosity.

But what could Ross's death possibly have to do with Wylie, who grew up in the same general area more than three decades earlier?

———

"I want to go to Ohio," I said to Marilyn Staley.

"What's in Ohio?"

"The follow-up on the Melissa Ross story."

"They've already brought her body back to New York."

"I want to find out what she was doing there. Now it looks like someone set her up. Made it look like she was the killer. Got everyone—the police, the media, the whole country—looking for Melissa Ross as a cold-blooded serial killer. And then, for some reason we don't know yet, this person killed her and dumped her body in this lake in the middle of Ohio. There are a lot of things we don't know here."

"You figure the answers are in Ohio?"

"It's a place to start."

"How long will it take you to get there?"

"The flight to Cleveland is an hour and a half. Then maybe an hour's drive tops from the airport to the area around Munson Lake."

"Okay, book a flight to Cleveland as soon as you can."

"I already have. I told Zeena to do it for me."

"When?"

"Before I came in here to ask you."

She groaned.

"C'mon, Marilyn, I knew the idea would make sense to you too. Flights to Cleveland are cheap, it won't cost too much from your travel budget. And a *Daily News* dateline—with my byline—from the lake where Melissa Ross's body was found is good for the paper. Good for all of us."

"I'm just curious, Gil," she said to me as I was leaving her office. "Do you have some kind of information, some evidence, some lead that you're not telling me about? Something that makes you want to go to Ohio so badly that you set up the trip even before you asked me about it?"

I thought about the potential Wylie connection. Even in my own mind, it sounded crazy.

"No, Marilyn, I'm just playing a wild hunch that this might lead to a good follow-up story," I said.

When I got back to the newsroom, I asked Zeena if she'd made arrangements for the trip to Ohio like I'd asked.

"Almost."

"You did make hotel reservations?"

"You want a hotel?"

"Yes, I want a hotel," I said, with exasperation.

"Okeydokey."

"How about a car?"

"A car."

"You didn't rent a car . . ."

"Why do you want a car?"

"Because I have to drive from the Cleveland airport to this town called Munson Lake."

"Is that a long ways?"

"At least an hour drive. That assumes, of course, that I have a car to drive in. Which I apparently don't. Zeena, why didn't you take care of any of this stuff I talked to you about?"

"Jonathan had surgery for a brain tumor," she said.

"Huh?"

"*General Hospital.*"

Now I understood. Zeena was a daytime soap fan. She had this arrangement with the office that she was allowed to watch her favorite soaps during her lunch hour and breaks. In return . . . well, I wasn't sure what we got in return. I told her to make my travel arrangements as soon as Jonathan was out of medical danger.

———

By the time I got to Cleveland, Stacy had gotten involved with the story. She thought it was a great idea for me to do a live stand-up from the lake—the spot where Melissa Ross's car went into the water—for *Live from New York*.

So there I was standing by Munson Lake doing a remote TV broadcast even before I wrote up my own damn story.

Ah, the exciting new world of journalism.

I ran through the basic facts, pointing to where Melissa Ross's car went into the water. I talked on air with some residents who lived near the lake, including the teenaged girl who had spotted Melissa Ross's car and body on the bottom while she was swimming. Then I did an interview with Munson Lake Police Chief Dan Conigulara.

ME: Chief, how do you think the woman and her car got into the lake?

CONIGULARA: At first, we thought it was an accident. That she lost control of her car on the road and plunged into the water. But that would have been hard to do.

ME: Why?

Conigulara pointed to a fence that was around the lake.

CONIGULARA: There was another fatal accident once here at this lake. A long time ago. After that, they put up the fence so that a car would have a safety barrier to stop it before it got to the water.

ME: So what you're saying is that a driver would have had to deliberately avoid that fence to make it all the way down to the lake.

CONIGULARA: Yes, that's right.

I turned to the camera.

ME: For weeks, police have been hunting for Melissa Ross, believing that she could provide all the answers to this baffling series of murders known as the "Blonde Ice" killings. Now they have found her. But there are no answers. Instead, Melissa Ross's death just raises more disturbing questions about a killer who is still out there, still on the loose, and still apparently looking for more victims.

CHAPTER 31

MASSILLON—the town where Wylie had grown up and went to high school—was about a thirty-minute drive south from Munson Lake. I didn't tell Marilyn or Stacy or anyone else back at the paper where I was going or why. Hell, this didn't even make sense to me, so how could I explain it to someone else? I had no idea what I was looking for, why I was looking for it—or how to go about finding it.

The high school was a lot different now, of course. Most of the teachers and staff who'd been there when Wylie was a student were long gone. Most of them, but not all. I found that out when I introduced myself to the principal, Richard Hanson. Hanson had been a civics teacher—just starting out his teaching career—when Wylie was at the school, and remembered having him in one of his classes.

"Bob certainly has done well for himself, hasn't he?" Hanson said as we sat in his office. "I've heard and read so much about him over the years. He's the most famous person ever to come out of this school. Imagine, one of my students could possibly wind up being mayor of New York City. Isn't that something?"

"I suppose it doesn't come as much of a surprise to you he was so successful, huh?" I said. "You probably saw those qualities in him when he was here."

"Not exactly," Hanson said. "Don't get me wrong, Bob was a

nice kid—but he just wasn't that exceptional in high school. He wasn't a bad student, but no whiz kid. More of a 'B' student than an 'A' one. And, on the football field, he did start some games for the team in his senior year, but . . ."

"Everything I've read about him said he was a standout student and athletic star. Got a scholarship to Cornell and everything."

Hanson smiled. "Bob always sold himself pretty well. Made himself seem a little more important than he really was when he was here. That's one of the reasons he's gotten so far, I suppose. To be honest, many of us were surprised when he got into Cornell on that scholarship. He certainly didn't have the grades you'd expect for it. And it wasn't like he was good enough to get an athletic scholarship. But that's Bob. He's always been in the right place at the right time. Good things just happen to people like that. Like they say, better to be lucky than good, huh? And Bob Wylie . . . well, he's always been lucky."

I talked to a few more people who'd been there when Wylie was a student. They all told me pretty much the same story. Bob Wylie was a charming guy, a popular guy, a nice guy who everyone liked. But he was nothing special as either a student or as an athlete.

I managed to dig up an old yearbook from the year Wylie graduated. There were several pictures of Bob Wylie in it. His graduation photo. One of him on the football field throwing a pass and looking as cool as a young Tom Brady. So how did he do it? How did an average student and not so great athlete wind up getting a scholarship to a top Ivy League school like Cornell? How did he rise to the position of power and influence that he held today in New York City?

Maybe he'd learned a lot—maybe he'd improved himself dramatically—since he was in high school.

Or maybe it was just like Hanson had said: It's better to be lucky than good. And Bob Wylie had always been lucky.

At the back of the yearbook, I found a section called "Favorite

Senior Awards." There was a picture of Wylie with a girl. Holding hands with each other. The headline over the picture said: STEADY SENIOR COUPLE. Underneath, a caption read: "Bob Wylie and Valerie Cartwright. Do we hear wedding bells in their future?"

I looked at the picture of the two of them for a long time. The young, handsome Wylie and the young woman with him. She was actually very average-looking, which seemed a bit out of place next to Wylie. She wasn't bad-looking, but no beauty either. She was gazing at Wylie lovingly in the photo. Wylie? Well, he was looking at the camera.

I remembered from the clips I'd gone through back in the office that Wylie had been married only once.

His wife's name was not Valerie Cartwright.

No real surprise there, of course. Most high school romances fell apart after graduation, when the kids grew up and began to go out into the real world. So Bob Wylie and Valerie Cartwright—the "Steady Senior Couple" back then—broke up and went their separate ways in life. It didn't mean anything at all. In fact, it was no doubt completely unconnected to what I was looking for.

Except I didn't know what it was I was actually looking for.

Maybe Valerie Cartwright could help me figure that out.

———

Valerie Cartwright still lived in Ohio. I tracked her down in a place called Bainbridge Township, less than an hour away from where Wylie had grown up, in Massillon. She'd gotten married to a man named Bill Sidowsky.

It looked like she'd done well for herself. When I pulled my rented car up to her address, the house turned out to be a sprawling, spectacular-looking home on several acres of land. There was a long winding driveway, a swimming pool, a pond out front, and even a guesthouse adjoining the main structure.

A few minutes later, I sat in Valerie Sidowski's living room talking with her.

"Why is a reporter from New York City coming all the way out here to ask me questions about Bob Wylie?" she asked.

"He's being touted as possibly the next mayor of New York. We thought it would be a good idea to do a color piece on him. His life, his background, where he grew up—that sort of thing."

This was the same story I had given to the principal and the others at the high school earlier. It made sense too. Wylie was a big personality in New York now, so it was very logical that a New York newspaper reporter would want to do a profile on his past.

Valerie didn't look that much different from her picture in the high school yearbook. Older, of course. But she was one of those women who never really looked their age. In high school, she'd seemed older than a teenager, and now she looked younger than a woman who was near fifty.

She proudly showed me pictures of her husband and three children on the walls of their living room.

"Bill is chairman of the board of Cartwright International. My father started the company. They're based near here in Cleveland—always have been—but with branch offices now in New York, Los Angeles, D.C, London, Paris, and around the world. That's where Bill is now, on a business trip to Paris. Bill Jr., our oldest son, works for his father. My other son, John, is a financial analyst for a bank in Chicago. And my daughter recently graduated from Cornell. She's on a round-the-world tour right now, figuring out what she wants to do with her life."

I nodded, trying desperately to act like I was interested in all of this. This was how interviews sometimes went. You got the person talking, feeling comfortable. Telling you a lot of information you couldn't care less about. Waiting for the moment to ask the questions you really wanted answers for.

"So how did you and Wylie get picked as 'Steady Senior Couple' in high school?" I finally asked when I thought the time was right, showing her the picture from the yearbook.

"Oh, that was because of Bob, much more than me. Bob was always popular. Everyone liked him. I guess they still do, huh? Me, I was just along for the ride with him when it came to high school popularity. It was really quite exciting being Bob's girlfriend, I have to say. Even after all these years I remember the excitement of being with him."

"How long were you together?"

"We started dating the summer before our senior year. He was so handsome, charismatic, so . . . well, so Bob. We went steady all during our senior year and then he left for college. We stayed together as a couple while he was in college too. Saw each other when he came back to Ohio, and I took trips to New York to be with him at Cornell."

"Who eventually ended the relationship—you or him?"

"Oh, it was him. He sent me a Dear John letter—or whatever you want to call it to a woman—after he graduated from Cornell. I always thought he'd come back to Ohio once he graduated and we'd get married. But Bob had other plans."

"Did it bother you that he went to a college as far away as Cornell?"

"Oh, no," she said. "In fact, the reason Bob went to Cornell was because of me. And my father. You see, my father was on the board of directors at Cornell. He'd graduated magna cum laude there and was a big alumni contributor. He pulled some strings to help Bob get admitted and get his scholarship. The admissions process was very competitive. Bob probably wouldn't have made it there without my father's help."

It started to make sense now. Bob Wylie was a good student, not a great one, Richard Hanson, the principal had said. A good athlete, not a superstar. Hanson was surprised by how he got into a top school like Cornell. Except he met—and started going steady with—the daughter of a prominent alumnus and contributor who could get him into Cornell. Coincidence? Or was Wylie playing politics even back when he was in high school?

"So you and Bob went steady during your entire senior year?"

"Pretty much so. Of course, there are always a few ups and downs in a relationship."

"Tell me about the downs."

"We broke up once. For about two weeks. I found out Bob had been cheating on me. The girl was really pretty, really sexy—much prettier than me, I have to admit. But she was known for sleeping around. To be honest, she kind of had a reputation as the school tramp. I told Bob he had a choice—stop seeing her or stop seeing me. If he didn't make a choice, we were finished."

"And he stopped seeing this other girl?"

"Yes."

She changed the subject quickly. Like she didn't want to re-member that side of him. The cheating side. She talked again about how much she'd been in love with him back then.

"Are you married, Mr. Malloy?" she asked at one point.

"I used to be."

"What happened?"

"We got divorced."

"That's too bad.

"I'm seeing her again now though. We're even talking about getting remarried. Doing it right this time."

"It sounds like you really love this woman."

"Yes, I do."

"More than any other woman you ever met?"

"Susan is definitely the love of my life," I said.

She nodded. "If this person is the one you really love, hold on to her no matter what. Don't ever settle for second best. I believe we all have one special love in our life, one person that we're meant to be with. It's a shame if that turns out not to be the person that you marry. And you lose the one that you really love. A shame, Mr. Malloy." She looked down again at the long ago yearbook picture of her and Wylie. "A terrible shame."

I was pretty sure she wasn't talking about me and Susan anymore.

————

"That girl Bob cheated on you with in high school," I said before I left, "do you by any chance remember her name?"

"Of course, it was Patty Tagliarini." She spelled out the last name. "Like I said, she was pretty in a cheap kind of way. Slit skirts, tight sweaters. That kind of girl can be awfully tempting for a teenage boy. But, with Bob, it was just a temporary thing. He promised me he would never see her again."

"I'd like to talk to her," I said. "Do you have any idea how I might contact her?"

"Oh, you can't. She's dead."

"When did she die?"

"Gosh, that was a long time ago. At the end of our senior year actually."

"How did it happen?"

"She died in a car accident. She got drunk, drove her car off the road, and drowned in a place called Munson Lake."

————

I found some old newspaper clips about it at the Massillon library. The death of Patty Tagliarini had been a pretty big story at the time. There was an article about it on the front page of the Massillon paper: TEEN DIES IN WATERY CAR CRASH. Several follow-ups talked about grief counselors being brought into the school for students and stepped-up efforts to warn young people about the dangers of drunk driving.

There was a picture of Patty Tagliarini. She was pretty, all right. The picture wasn't your standard studio shot. It was from a party. Patty Tagliarini was drinking a beer and posing in a sexy, flirting kind of way for the camera. The story talked about how she'd been known as a "party girl" at school. Another reference said she was "very popular with the boys." Like Valerie Cartwright had said, it was clear that this was a girl who liked to have fun.

According to the article, the accident had occurred at 12:30 a.m. Tagliarini was driving at a high speed—estimated to have been as much as 85 mph—on the narrow road overlooking the lake. She lost control of the car and plunged down a hill into the water. Her body was found outside the car on the bottom of the lake. An autopsy showed that her lungs were filled with water, and drowning was the official—although it seemed pretty obvious—cause of her death. The autopsy also showed she had a blood alcohol level of nearly 2.0—more than double the legal limit for driving. There was evidence of marijuana in her system too. The conclusion was inescapable. She'd gotten drunk, probably gotten high too, and driven the car off the road in an alcohol- and drug-fueled haze.

No one ever figured out exactly what she'd been doing before the fatal accident. Her parents said they'd long ago given up trying to monitor the movements of their wild, party-loving daughter. An empty liquor bottle was found in the backseat of the car, which led authorities to believe she was drinking in the vehicle either just before or even at the time she died.

At the high school graduation ceremony a few weeks later, her seat was left empty in her memory. The valedictorian mentioned her in his speech. And the commencement speaker said a prayer for her—with the students all joining in a moment of silence—before he sent the graduates out into the world with his words of optimism and encouragement.

That was pretty much all there was to the Patty Tagliarini story. The authorities officially closed the book on the case as an accidental drowning.

I remembered something the Munson Lake police chief had told me. About how the fence had been put up after another accident a long time ago. It must have been Patty Tagliarini's accident. The fence was supposed to stop anyone else from going into the water the way she did. But, all these years later, someone had made sure Melissa Ross's car got past the fence and crashed again into that same lake.

I looked down at the piece of paper where I'd been taking notes on what I'd read.

Then I wrote down the following points:

- Bob Wylie went out with Patty Tagliarini in high school.
- Melissa Ross died in the same lake—and in a similar way—as Tagliarini.
- Bob Wylie had been the top law enforcement official chasing Ross.
- What's the connection?

CHAPTER 32

ELISSA Ross had grown up in Rockville Centre, on Long Island—a middle class community about an hour away from New York City. Her mother still lived there, in the same house.

I took the Long Island Rail Road out to Rockville Centre as soon as I got back to New York. Sylvia Ross, Melissa's mother, didn't look much like her daughter. She had unkempt hair, was plain-looking, and wore no makeup. She wasn't that old, probably somewhere in her fifties. But she looked older. She looked worn out by life.

"When is the last time you heard from Melissa?" I asked.

"When she left the police force. After I heard about what happened, I called her. I offered to help her any way that I could."

"What was her reaction?" I asked.

"She told me to go to hell."

"Why would she do that?"

She shrugged. "Melissa had a lot of hostility toward people."

"Especially men?"

"Yes."

"Why was she mad at you?"

On the walls of the living room where we were sitting, there were several pictures of Melissa Ross growing up. One of them was of a little girl in pigtails on a tricycle. Another showed her blowing out the candles on a cake that said it was her tenth birthday. And one was of her in a cheerleader outfit from Rockville Centre High School. Sylvia Ross glanced over at that last picture now, gathering her thoughts before she spoke. I wondered if she was remembering the happy moments between her and her daughter. Or maybe they weren't so happy after all.

"Melissa adored her father when she was growing up," she said. "He took her to the park, showed her how to ride a bicycle, played catch with a baseball in the backyard, even climbed trees with her. I used to kid him about how he was turning her into a tomboy, not a little girl. They were so close."

Her voice trailed off. She looked over at the picture of Melissa as a cute high school cheerleader again.

"When Melissa began to grow up, she . . . well, she began turning into a woman. A very attractive woman. And then I noticed that she and her father didn't seem that close anymore. It almost seemed that Melissa didn't even want to be around him. She'd become nervous, uncomfortable, whenever he came into the room.

"One day Melissa came to me. She said her father would come into her bedroom at night after I was asleep. Or during the day when I was at work. He'd come home from his job in the afternoon, before me, after she'd gotten out of school . . . and . . . do things. Sexual things. At first, Melissa didn't understand why. Not really. She just told me that day, 'Make him stop.' "

She bit her lip and looked like she was holding back tears.

"What did you do?" I asked.

"Nothing."

She couldn't hold back the tears now.

"I did nothing at all," she sobbed. "I didn't believe her. Or maybe I did believe her, but didn't want to admit it. I told her she was making it all up. That her father would never do anything like that. I told her never to say anything like that to me—or anyone else—ever again."

"Did you ask your husband about it?"

"No. I'm not really sure why I didn't. I guess I just didn't want to admit to myself something like that could really be true. It was easier to believe that Melissa was making things up."

"What happened then?"

"Melissa ran away from home. I didn't know where she was or what had happened to her for a very long time. Then I heard she was trying to make it as an actress or model in New York. And, after that, she eventually turned up on the police force. But she and I never really had much communication after she left home. She blamed me for what happened. Why not? I was as guilty as her father. Maybe more guilty. I could have done something to stop it, but I didn't. I just stuck my head in the sand and pretended it wasn't happening. I didn't protect my daughter when she needed my protection. And she never forgave me for that."

"And your husband? Are you sure it was true?"

She nodded.

"After Melissa left, I finally confronted him about what she said had happened. He admitted it. He even bragged about it. He said he didn't see why messing around with her was such a big deal. It wasn't like it was really incest, he said to me. I divorced him after that. So I lost my husband and my daughter. I've been alone ever since."

"Where is your husband now?" I asked.

"He died. Cancer. A really nasty cancer. It hit his bones first, then his brain. They say he lived a long time with the pain before he finally died. I have to tell you, I was glad about that. About how much he suffered at the end. I always thought it was kind of God's punishment for the terrible things he had done."

"Your daughter's body was found in a lake in Ohio," I said.

"Did she have any connection to Ohio? Did she know anyone in Ohio? Can you think of any reason at all that she would wind up in Ohio at the end?"

Sylvia Ross shook her head no.

"I've never been to Ohio in my life," she said. "Neither had Melissa, as far as I know. Of course, I didn't know that much about her life after she left here. But she never mentioned Ohio to me in the few conversations that we did have. I have no idea why her body was found there."

I asked her questions for another half hour. But there wasn't much more I found out until the end.

"You said something before I didn't understand," I said, looking down at the notes I'd made during our conversation. "About the time you confronted your husband over his sexual abuse of Melissa. You said he admitted it, but said it was no big deal because 'it wasn't really incest.' What did he mean by that?"

"Well, I guess because he wasn't Melissa's biological father."

"You mean you had Melissa with another man?"

She shook her head.

"I wanted to have a baby. But I couldn't conceive. I tried everything. Fertility drugs. Egg implants. Nothing worked. The doctor said I couldn't have a child of my own, so I . . ."

"Wasn't Melissa's biological mother?"

"That's right. Melissa was adopted."

———

There was no reason that any of this had any particular significance at this point, of course. Melissa Ross was no longer the killer we were looking for, she was just another victim. So what was I going to learn digging around in her past that could help me crack this case? I mean who really gave a damn about her adoption or her family or anything else about her? Looking at it logically, I was just wasting my time going after more information about Melissa Ross.

Except I'd also learned along the way during my journalistic career that information is the best tool a reporter has. And you never can be sure what's important and what isn't, even if you think you know. You can't just collect the information you think will help you. You need to get all of the information, analyze it, and then see where it takes you. Sometimes that might be in an entirely different direction than where you began. So you follow that trail of information, no matter what. That's why I tracked down the adoption agency that had turned over Melissa as a baby to the Ross family.

I had a bit of a problem obtaining the adoption information at first. The director of the adoption agency talked about the right to privacy of the families involved—and a lot of issues like that. But I had gotten permission from Mrs. Ross, and in the end, the director agreed she had the authority to track down the old files on the adoption.

"The biological mother gave birth on February 26, 1985," she said when she finally found the file. She turned through the pages as she talked. "The child was put up for adoption in June of 1986, when she was one year old. The baby was transferred to our New York facility at that point. Arthur and Sylvia Ross began the adoption process soon after that—and they were given custody of the baby a few months later."

"The baby was a year old?" I asked.

"Yes."

"Is that unusual? I assumed she would have been adopted as a baby. Why would the birth mother wait a year before beginning the adoption process?"

"The birth mother died when the little girl was a year old."

"What about the father?"

"Dead too."

"They died at the same time?"

She read through the file a bit more. "No, the mother died in a car accident. The father had been killed several months earlier. He was in the U.S. Army. Some kind of an explosive incident. The mother lived at home with her family. When she died too, the family decided they couldn't raise a young child on their own—and that's when they put her up for adoption."

"You said earlier that the baby had been transferred here prior to the adoption by the Ross family. From where?"

"Ohio," the adoption director said.

Damn.

"Where in Ohio?" I asked, even though I already knew what her answer was going to be.

"Some place called Munson Lake," she said. "The birth mother drowned there in the car accident. Her name was . . . wait a minute . . . Oh, here it is. . . . Her name was Patty Tagliarini."

CHAPTER 33

WAS still mulling over my options on what to do next when I got
to the office the next morning. I decided to talk to Marilyn about
it. Even though I suspected she might be a tad upset with me. I had
pretty much disappeared after the Munson Lake appearance, to go
to Massillon and then Long Island without telling her or anyone
else at the *News*. That shouldn't be a big problem though, I told
myself. Hell, she'll probably be so glad to see me back that she'll
forget all about me going AWOL.

"Good morning," I said to Zeena when I walked in.

"Don't think so."

"Don't think what?"

"That it's going to be a good morning."

"Why not?"

"Marilyn wants to see you."

"Great, because I want to see her too."

"Don't think so."

"What do you mean?"

"I don't think you're going to want to see Marilyn this morning."

"Why not?"

"She's mad at you."

"How mad?"

"Mad like in 'Where in the hell is that damn Malloy?' "

"I'll stick my head in her office right now, throw a little of my charm at her, and straighten everything out."

"Don't think so."

"Will you stop saying that?"

I headed for Marilyn's office.

"There's nothing to worry about, Zeena. It'll be fine."

"Don't think so," she mumbled again under her breath as I walked away.

———

Marilyn was on the phone when I pushed open her door. I stuck my head in anyway, flashed her a big smile, and announced: "Been away, now I'm back!"

She glared at me, said something to whoever she was talking to on the phone, and then hung up. She did seem pretty mad. Of course, she didn't have to be mad at me. Maybe she'd had a fight with her husband. Or one of her kids came home with a bad grade. Or her eggs were cold for breakfast. Something like that very easily could have been what had her in a bad mood today. It didn't necessarily have to be about me.

"Where in the hell have you been?" she barked.

Nope, it was me.

"Working the Blonde Ice story."

"Without keeping me or anyone else here in the loop?"

"There were some unexpected developments in Ohio."

"So why not share them with the rest of us? Look, I've given you a ton of leeway on this story. I know you've been way out in front on it from the beginning. But there comes a point . . ."

"I found out some pretty blockbuster information, Marilyn."

That stopped her.

"Should I call in Stacy and the other editors too so you can tell us?" she asked.

"No. This is very sensitive information. I'm not sure I can trust Stacy or anyone else with it."

"Which means you think you can trust me?"

I shrugged.

"It's kind of a sliding scale with editors," I said.

"Okay, now you've really whetted my curiosity."

I went through with Marilyn everything I'd found out about Bob Wylie. All about the strange links between him and the area in Ohio where Melissa Ross's body had been discovered. And then how I'd found out about Melissa Ross being the daughter of the woman who died in the same spot thirty years earlier.

"What in the hell does all of this mean?" she asked when I was finished.

"I have no idea. But I'm a reporter. I go with my journalistic instincts. And my journalistic instincts right now tell me there's a connection between what happened in Ohio with Wylie as a teenager in high school—and what's happening now. I just don't know what that connection is."

Marilyn nodded.

"Let me ask you the obvious question. Do you think Wylie was the father of the baby? Melissa Ross's father?"

"No, I checked that out. The father of the baby was a soldier who died in a basic training camp accident. He'd gone to school with the biological mother, Patty Tagliarini, at a different high school. Tagliarini transferred to Massillon after she had the baby. So Wylie didn't even know her until after she gave birth to Melissa."

"Could Bob Wylie have been involved in her death somehow?"

"Not according to the Munson Lake police. They say Tagliarini's death was definitely an accident and she was the only person in that car."

I took a deep breath and plunged ahead with the rest I needed to tell her.

"But there is more."

"From back in Ohio when Wylie was growing up?"

"No, here in New York. Involving Houston. Wylie knew her when she was a prostitute."

"Knew her how?"

"He was a client of hers, and they kept up the relationship for a period of time even after she left the business."

Marilyn stared at me with a look of astonishment on her face.

"How do you know this?"

"Houston told me."

"Do you believe her?"

"She has no reason to lie. She has this whole code about never revealing the identities of former clients. That's why she never told anyone before. But now after Hammacher, the person closest to Wylie, was murdered—she thinks there has to be some sort of link between her relationship with Wylie and everything that's been going on. I think she's right."

Marilyn thought about it all for a few seconds.

"I don't think we have enough to print any of this yet," she said.

"Agreed."

"What we have are a lot of coincidences. A lot of speculation. This stuff could be dynamite politically for Wylie. But we still don't know what any of it has to do with the woman—whoever she really is—that's doing all the killing, including the death of Melissa Ross. We need more information, we need more hard facts."

"More facts would be good."

"So how do we get them?"

"I have a plan."

"Let's hear your plan."

"You're not gonna like it."

"Now, why doesn't that surprise me?"

"Okay, I could ask Bob Wylie about it."

"You're just going to walk into the office of the deputy mayor of New York City—who also happens to be the front-running mayoral candidate—and ask him if he knows why the body of Melissa Ross was dumped into a lake near where he went to high school? And what he thinks it might possibly have to do with a girl he briefly dated who turns out to be Melissa Ross's mother—and died under similar circumstances back then? Then maybe casually throw in another question about him patronizing the most famous prostitute in New York City history who also happens to be the widow of the first Blonde Ice victim?"

"Not a good idea, huh?"

"I'd love to come up with a better one."

"Me too."

Marilyn thought about it for a while.

"When would you do this?" she asked.

"As soon as I can get access to Wylie."

"All right. But be careful. Be discreet. Be diplomatic. Be . . . well, don't be your normal self, Gil."

"Hey, what could possibly go wrong?"

She rolled her eyes.

"I'll just lay it all out there for him," I said. "I'll tell him we need some answers from him. We need the truth about what he knows because this story is going to come out—and it will look better for him if he is cooperating with us. It might get really nasty. But believe me, I'm going to press him as hard as I can."

"Are you sure about this?" Marilyn asked. "I mean it's no secret Wylie has been eying you for a position in his administration. We're all aware of that. If Wylie still gets elected after all this, you might just screw yourself out of that job if you hit him too hard and he survives."

"I already have a job," I said.

CHAPTER 34

HAD another anxiety attack," I told Dr. Barbara Landis.

"Tell me exactly what happened," she said.

"I was home watching TV. *The Andy Griffith Show* was on one of the cable channels. There was a baking contest or something at the county fair, and Andy and Barney were trying to figure out how to tell Aunt Bee her entry wasn't good enough to win. You see, Aunt Bee didn't know how to . . ."

"Mr. Malloy! Stop avoiding the issue and tell me the details of the anxiety attack."

"Yeah, well . . . I suddenly felt uncomfortable. Started gasping for breath. The room looked like it was spinning around. I was afraid I was going to lose consciousness. I really panicked there for a minute. All the same symptoms I've had before. But I haven't had one of those attacks in a long time. So it really sucked to have it happening all over again."

"Did you tell anyone about this or seek some kind of medical assistance?"

"No, you're the first."

"Why are you telling me about it then?"

"You're the hotshot shrink who's supposed to figure out stuff like this."

"There are many secrets you've kept from me in the past, Mr.

Malloy. And I'm sure there are other secrets you still are holding on to. You didn't tell anyone else about this for days. So why are you bringing this up now when you don't have to? Why not just forget about it and pretend it never happened, like you've done so many times in the past?"

"It was probably a mistake to even mention it. No big deal really."

"Why are you telling me about this now, Mr. Malloy?" she repeated. "I'm going to keep asking you that question until I get an answer."

I sighed.

"Okay, it's because in the past I always kind of understood why I was having the anxiety attacks. I was under a lot of stress. In my professional life, my personal life—you name it, I was stressed out with problems. But now everything's going great for me. I'm back on top at the *News*, I'm an ace reporter and a TV star. Everyone loves me there, even my two crazy female bosses. Plus, I'm back with Susan again, or at least I've got a shot at having a relationship with her for the first time since our marriage ended. I'm on a roll, Dr. Landis. My life is perfect right now. So why did I have another one of those damn anxiety attacks?"

Dr. Landis nodded sympathetically. Like she could relate to the confusion and distress I was going through over this. I wondered if they taught you how to do that in psychiatrist school. The empathy nod. Probably a whole class devoted to learning that nod, right between Mental Health 101 and Dealing with Schizophrenics.

"I think the fact that your life is going so well now is exactly the reason you had the anxiety attack," Landis said.

"That doesn't make any sense."

"Sure it does."

I thought about what she was saying for a moment, and then I realized where she was going with this.

"I'm worried that it won't last. That everything is too good to be true. Something will happen—or I'll do something—to screw it all up. Like I did with the original Houston story and my marriage to Susan and all the rest. I'm waiting for something bad to happen. The anxiety attack stemmed from my fears that this was all going to fall apart for me again."

"That's right," Landis said. "You already told me about how you've still kept secrets about Houston from your editors at the paper. That could jeopardize your position there if it ever came out, right? And you still don't know what's going to happen between you and Susan. I think on some level you don't believe she will ever really come back and marry you. The brain is a complex thing. When all the insecurities and doubts come together—even in your subconscious, they are overwhelming to you. The anxiety attack was the result of this." Landis shrugged. "Anyway, that's my theory. What do you think?"

I groaned and shook my head in frustration.

"You don't agree with me?" she said

"Actually, it's a pretty good theory."

"That's what they pay us hotshot shrinks to do, Mr. Malloy."

She almost smiled when she said that. And Dr. Landis hardly ever smiled during a session.

"What can I do about it?" I asked her.

"Well, I noticed you said it happened while you were sitting alone in your apartment watching TV. We've talked in the past about your propensity for sitting in front of the TV and brooding about things. How this is very . . ."

"Immature?"

"Yes, immature. You still live like someone in their early twenties—with no stability, no structure to your life outside the office. I've said before that you're a popular guy, but you don't really seem to have any close friends. You retreat back into that apartment—and use that TV—like it's some kind of a cave to hide from the rest of the world."

"You're saying I should get out more?"

"I'm saying you need to start establishing a more mature lifestyle for yourself than you have now."

I thought about how to respond to that. There were a lot of ways. But I didn't want to go with any of them. I was tired of talking about myself, and there were only a few minutes left in our session anyway.

"Did you ever hear this one?" I asked Landis. "A guy walks into a psychiatrist's office and says he's obsessed with sex. The psychiatrist shows him an inkblot and asks what he sees. 'That's a man and a woman making love,' the guy says. The psychiatrist shows him a series of other inkblots, but his answer is always the same: 'That's a man and a woman making love.' The psychiatrist says: 'Well, you really do seem to be obsessed with sex.' The guy answers: 'Me? You're the one who keeps showing me all the dirty pictures.'"

Landis smiled again. Really. Two times in one session, that was a record for her. "I look forward to exploring these topics further at our next appointment, Mr. Malloy."

"Right back at you, Doc," I said.

CHAPTER 35

HAD a date with Susan. Well, not just a date. More like a romantic evening all planned out. And—if things went the way I hoped— our evening together wouldn't end until the sun came up.

Susan had never been to my new apartment since we split up. Any of my new apartments. And I'd only been to her new place once. We always met at restaurants, parks, ball games, or movies when we got together now. I guess it had something to do with us living together for those years in our own place. It just seemed strange for us to be in each other's home now.

But I had decided to change all that.

I invited her over to my apartment on 36th Street for dinner. We'd have cocktails in my living room overlooking Lexington Avenue. Dinner in my dining area after that. And then . . . well, it was only a few steps to the bedroom, where I planned to rectify the decision I'd made in the bar that night to turn down Susan's suggestion of sex.

It was the perfect plan.

Flawless. Foolproof. Fail-safe.

And—if I might add—I thought it was awfully mature. How about that, Dr. Landis?

Susan arrived a little after 6:30. She seemed impressed by my apartment and the fact that I had actually invited her to a sit-down meal there.

"You're really going to make dinner for me?" she said as we sat with drinks on my couch.

"That I am."

"What are we having?"

"Roast chicken. Scalloped potatoes. Green beans. Salad."

"You cooked all this?"

"Ordered out."

"Oh."

"Well, that takes some work too."

I glanced over at the TV.

"Later, I thought we could watch something together on television like we used to."

"You're not going to make me watch another *Three Stooges* marathon, are you?"

"The Stooges were a very underrated comic act. No, I DVR'd a movie. An old one I remember you like. *An Affair to Remember*."

"Wow! Cary Grant, Deborah Kerr. That's a very romantic movie, Gil," Susan shook her head. "This is quite the little seduction scenario you seem to have worked out for tonight. Think it will work?"

"I'm giving it my best shot," I smiled.

———

While we ate, I went through everything I'd found out about Melissa Ross and her bizarre connection with Bob Wylie. I told Susan about my conversation with Houston too, involving Wylie.

"Are you going to print any of this?"

"Not at the moment."

"Ask Wylie about it?"

"My next step."

"That should be interesting."

"There's still no indication the guy did anything wrong here. Unless you think patronizing a prostitute is wrong. Well, it is technically illegal. But you know what I'm saying. Wylie is involved somehow in this. But for the life of me I can't figure out how or why."

"So Wylie is connected in at least three separate ways to the Blonde Ice killings," Susan said. "The Houston relationship and the fact that her husband was the first victim. The murder of Tim Hammacher. And now all this about Melissa Ross being the daughter of the woman he once dated—and how Ross died in the same way and the same place as her mother."

"Thanks for the recap. Any theories?

"Not a one."

"Me either."

Later she told me about her divorce. How she and her husband were going to fast-track it through the court system. How they agreed to remain friends even though the marriage was a mistake. How she thought he was a really great guy who would make some woman very happy.

I listened patiently.

I even pretended like I really cared.

I thought that was pretty mature of me too.

"The bottom line is I'm a free woman," Susan said.

"And I'm a free man."

She smiled.

"So here we are," she said.

"Here we are," I repeated.

Everything was going according to plan. I have no doubt that it would have continued that way too. Except something happened. My cell phone rang. I looked down at the number. I didn't recognize it. But I had a bad feeling. This was the same thing that had happened the last time the woman I thought then was Melissa Ross had called.

I hit the answer button on my phone.

"Hello again, Gil," the now-familiar woman's voice on the other end said. "I've got another dumb blonde joke for you:

"Q: What did the blonde say when she found out she was pregnant?

"A: She said: 'Are you sure it's mine?'"

I had promised myself I would be ready when the next phone call came. But I wasn't. This woman scared me on all kinds of different levels.

"Who are you?" I said.

"Well, I'm sure not Melissa Ross," she laughed.

I gestured to Susan who it was. She looked shocked too. I wrote down the number showing up on my phone and handed it to her. She took out her phone and called her own office and the police with it while I tried to keep the woman talking on the phone for as long as possible.

"Tell me about you and Melissa."

"Melissa was a great disappointment to me in the end."

"Because she found out what you were really doing—and didn't want to help you anymore? Melissa was the one who took the first victim, Walter Issacs, up to the hotel room. She had sex with him. But you killed him. And then killed her too. Why? Was revenge fine with her, but not murder? I guess maybe Melissa just wasn't as crazy as you, huh? I'll bet you got really jealous when you found out she'd actually slept with Issacs. How and why exactly did you kill her? And, after she was dead, why go to all the trouble of taking her body out to that lake in Ohio?"

"Poor Melissa Ross," she laughed. "Killing herself would have been an appropriate ending to all this, don't you think? She kills all those men. She's been beaten down and hurt by men so many times in her life, so she carries out her revenge. And then, just as the police finally close in around her, she commits suicide—ending her own tragic life on this planet. Kind of a nice touch, huh? I figured I might be able to fool people for a while. But not you. You're smart, Gil. Just not smart enough to keep up with me. For instance, I know you're trying to keep me on the line now while you check out the number I'm calling from. But I'm afraid that won't be of much help."

"I'm not doing that."

"Sure, you are."

"No, wait . . ."

"Don't worry, Gil. We'll talk again very soon. But until then, here's another dumb blonde joke for you.

"Q: Why do men like dumb-blonde jokes?

"A: Because they can understand them."

She laughed loudly.

"And now, just to make sure no one forgets about me, I've got two new victims for you. One is a gift to my old pal, Melissa. A last good deed in her memory. A little payback to her ex-husband. I just didn't think it was right that he should live when she couldn't. The other one is . . . well, he just pissed me off. You'll find them both at Joe Delvecchio's apartment. Bay Ridge. Brooklyn."

CHAPTER 36

T HE police found two bodies in the apartment of Joe Delvecchio, Melissa Ross's ex-husband.

Just like the woman on the phone had said.

Delvecchio was tied down to the bed, spread-eagled with his
hands and feet handcuffed to the corners, a gag in his mouth—just
like the encounter he'd described with his then-wife Melissa Ross.
The rest was the same as the other victims. Evidence of severe beat-
ings. Stab wounds. And it appeared he'd been strangled.

The second body was in the bathroom. He looked like he'd
died the same way. He was a young guy, in his early twenties, good-
looking, with a body that looked like he worked out a lot. Probably
thought of himself as a real ladies' man. Same as with the earlier
victims, I couldn't help but imagine what these two men's final moments were like—the agony they suffered at the hands of this crazy
woman, whoever she was.

"It looks like she killed the guy in the bathroom first," Wohlers
said to me at the scene. I'd gotten there ahead of the police and
waited until they broke down the door. Then I'd put a piece up
on the Web even before the rest of the media heard anything
about it. It's easy to be first when the killer calls you up at home
with her latest body count. "Probably out here in the bedroom.
Then she dragged him into the bathtub, went out and picked up

Delvecchio, brought him here, and did it all over again with him. A two-fer."

"She kills one guy while the other body is still in the other room? Wouldn't Delvecchio have seen the other guy's body?"

"Probably not until it was too late. Hell, she might have gotten off by bragging to him about the first killing."

"Who is the first guy?" I asked.

"His name is Mike Jacobson. He's a fireman, lives around here in Bay Ridge. Hangs out in a bar called Finnegan's, people there say. Known to flirt with women at the bar. That's where she must have picked him up. The owner says he remembers him talking to a woman there that night. He thinks he left with her."

"Any other description of the woman?"

"Just that she was . . ."

"A sexy blonde?"

"Yes."

It still didn't make much sense to me. "This guy Jacobson was a fireman, Lieutenant. He must have been in good shape. He had to know how to take care of himself. How does a woman put a man that physically strong in this kind of position? How exactly does she accomplish that?"

"Sex is a powerful weapon against a man," Wohlers said.

"So you think she somehow uses her sexuality to lure these men into some kind of a situation where she can control them—with restraints or some other way—that leaves them at her mercy?"

"It looks that way."

The crime lab people said a preliminary check showed no fingerprints, hair, or evidence of any kind left behind by the killer. That didn't surprise me. The woman hadn't made that kind of mistake before; there was no reason to think she'd start now.

"What about semen?" I asked.

"None that we could find," Wohlers said. "Which is strange. There was semen at the scenes of all the other killings."

"But it was all from the first guy, Issacs," I said.

"Still, it might mean something . . ."

"Probably just that she ran out of Issacs's semen."

"And she didn't want to get any from these guys here?"

"This isn't about sex," I said. "At least not the kind of sex that would make sense to any of us."

"There's one more thing," a lab guy said. "It was underneath the body of the guy on the bed. Someone taped it to his buttocks. We found it when we turned him over."

It was a picture. A wedding picture of Melissa Ross and Joe Delvecchio. Smiling and looking happily at the camera as they sliced their wedding cake. A typical wedding picture. Except someone had torn this one right down the middle, splitting Delvecchio and Ross up into two separate pieces.

"She told me she wanted to kill him as a final favor to Melissa Ross," I said, looking at the pieces of the wedding picture. "Damn, this is one sick woman."

"Tell me something I don't know," Wohlers grunted.

———

There was a big press conference later outside the crime scene. Wylie showed up for this one. It would have been hard for him not to be there for something so big. He went through the details of what happened inside Delvecchio's apartment. I listened with everyone else and filed new updates to the office with Wylie quotes. He mentioned me as the one who got the phone call from the killer alerting police to the new victims.

Some of the reporters and media outlets wanted to interview me afterward.

Like it or not, I wasn't just covering this story.

I was a part of it.

Of course, the cops wanted to interrogate me too about everything I could tell them from the phone call. I did the best I could. But I was pretty sure it wasn't going to help much. Even the phone number that had shown up on my cell turned out to be a dead end. It was Delvecchio's phone. She'd used it to make the call after she killed him. They were still hoping to find some fingerprints or other forensic evidence off of it, but that seemed to be wishful thinking too. When it was all over, I managed to intercept Wylie on the way to his car.

"I need to talk to you about something," I said. "In private."

There were a number of Wylie aides and police officers standing around us. He paused as the driver held the car door open.

"You can make an appointment with my office and—"

"We need to talk now."

"What's the urgency?"

"What I have to tell you is very important."

Wylie nodded and motioned for me to get into the backseat of the car with him. Then he closed the door so we were alone while the others waited outside. I think at first he thought I wanted to talk about the job offer. He started saying how everything was in flux with the loss of Hammacher, so all staff appointments were on hold for the moment. He seemed rattled again—even more than he had at the press conference after Hammacher's body was found. I told him I wasn't here to talk about a job in his office.

"I've uncovered things that are somewhat . . . well, somewhat sensitive," I said.

"Sensitive to who?"

"You."

"I don't understand."

"Did you ever know a girl named Patty Tagliarini?" I asked him. He looked at me blankly.

"This would have been a very long time ago. Back when you were in high school."

"Yes, I believe so," Wylie said slowly. "I remember a girl by that name when I was in high school."

"Did you have a relationship with this Tagliarini girl?"

"What kind of a question is that?"

"I think it might be relevant to the case. I know it sounds improbable and way out of left field. But I need to have the answer to that question."

Wylie sighed. "Yes, I had a relationship—as you call it—with Patty Tagliarini when I was in high school. I had relationships with several girls while I was in high school. The one with this girl was very brief. I only saw her a couple of times. She died in a car accident not long after I stopped seeing her. It was very tragic. But why are you asking me all of this?"

"Patty Tagliarini was Melissa Ross's biological mother," I said. "And she died in the exact same lake where Melissa Ross's body was found thirty years later. Put there by the real Blonde Ice killer. What do you make of all that?"

I'm not sure what I expected to happen next. Wylie gasping in shock? Breaking down and telling me something that would blow the lid off this story? Awarding me an official Dick Tracy Crimestopper ring for my exemplary investigative work? But he didn't do any of these things. He just listened intently as if I was talking about some other story that didn't involve him.

I told him how I'd found out from Melissa Ross's mother about the adoption, that I'd learned the name of the biological mother from the adoption agency, and the details I had come up with from Ohio about the accident and the Tagliarini girl.

I did not bring up anything about Houston. I'd discussed that with Marilyn. We figured that the Tagliarini stuff was based on facts that couldn't be denied. Whether or not he patronized Houston when she was a prostitute would simply be her word against his. So, for now, I was keeping that juicy tidbit a secret. For now.

"I really don't understand," Wylie said when I finished talking about Munson Lake. "I mean I recognized the name Munson Lake when I heard where Melissa Ross's body was found. But I assumed it was just a coincidence that it happened close to where I grew up."

"And now that you know Ross was the daughter of the woman you were dating for a while back then—and died in the same place?"

"But what could any of that have to do with this case?"

"I'm not sure either. But I think the killer murdered Melissa Ross here in New York, then drove the body out to Ohio and dumped her into that lake—just the way her mother died in 1986—to send some kind of message. I have no specific theories beyond this. But there's too much here for it all to just be a coincidence. It's part of her game. And somehow that game now involves you."

CHAPTER 37

WYLIE wants us to print the story about him and Melissa Ross's biological mother," I said at the morning news meeting.

"What did he say to you?" Marilyn wanted to know.

"His exact words were"—I looked down at my notes from the interview with Wylie and began reading from them—" 'I want to find out the answers to these troubling questions as much as you and your paper do. Please publish this story as soon as possible in the hope that someone may read it and come forward with more information. I am totally committed to doing whatever is needed to bring this Blonde Ice case to a successful conclusion.' "

"Jeez, that doesn't make much political sense for him," one of the editors muttered.

"Actually, it does," I said.

I'd thought about this a lot since the Wylie interview. Before I came in and laid it all out for everyone at the news meeting. I didn't mention that I'd told Marilyn all the Tagliarini stuff earlier and she'd given me the go-ahead to confront Wylie. She didn't let on that she knew about it beforehand either. Which was kind of a shame because that would have driven Stacy crazy. But I wanted them both on my side, and that was a delicate balancing act.

"Wylie's smart," I said. "And cool under pressure. He never

batted an eye when I brought up the Patty Tagliarini connection, even though he had to have been shocked to find out I knew about it. He must have weighed all his options very quickly and decided this was the best one. If he denied it, he'd just look foolish when the facts came out. If he tried to get me not to print the story, that would look like he had something to hide. He knew I was going to publish the story—one way or another—so he went with this approach. Full disclosure. Let the truth come out no matter what it is, he says to us. He's on the same side as us, he just wants answers. Pretty smart, it seems to me."

"It's still going to be politically embarrassing to him," Stacy said.

"Embarrassing yes, at first. But only by association. He didn't do anything wrong here, he just got dragged into the case personally. He's kind of a victim too, you might say. At least as far as we know."

"Is there any possibility at all he could have had anything to do with the Tagliarini woman's death?" an editor asked.

"Or that he's the father of the baby who turned out to be Melissa Ross?" another one said, bringing up the same obvious points Marilyn had earlier. "That would explain a lot."

I shook my head no.

"Wylie didn't even know the Tagliarini girl until a year after she had the baby. Plus, she was alone in the car and there was no evidence of foul play. She just got drunk and drove off the road into that lake. The police ruled definitively at the time that her death was accidental."

There was some more discussion about the political fallout for Wylie and speculation about what the Blonde Ice case might have to do with all this, but in the end there wasn't much more to say.

"Okay," Marilyn said finally, "this is the easiest decision I've had all month. Let's do what Wylie wants us to do. Print the story."

———

This story—more than the others—really made a big media splash when we ran it. Maybe it was because the story had so many questions with no answers. Maybe because it was so wacky and unexpected how a high school romance was somehow linked to these serial killer murders. Or maybe it was just because there was so much interest in the Blonde Ice case that any new exclusive was going to get huge play. Everyone—the other newspapers, the TV stations, the cable news networks, and the whole damn Internet—blanketed it with coverage, commentary, and speculation.

There's a tradition at the paper that when a reporter breaks a big story like this, he gets taken out for drinks at a place called Headliners to celebrate his scoop.

Which is what happened to me that night.

Hey, who am I to buck tradition?

Headliners is a newspaper bar that has been around for years—long before I was a reporter at the *News*. The walls are lined with pictures of great reporters, great editors, and great front page stories. Sitting in the middle of the place there's even an old-fashioned linotype machine from the composing room of a New York City newspaper in the fifties. Walking into Headliners is sort of like going back in time. I loved it.

Once we were all there, Marilyn stood up and made a speech about how my story had beaten everyone else in town again. She also, of course, tried to grab a bit of the glory—making a big point of emphasizing that she was my editor for this wonderful piece of journalistic work. Then Stacy stood up and did pretty much the same thing. It was uncomfortable watching the two of them competing for attention like this, but also compelling in a way. Sort of like rubbernecking at a car accident. You just couldn't look away.

At some point, Stacy came over and dragged me into a corner for a personal conversation.

"Have you thought much about your future, Gil?" she asked.

"You mean like retirement? Social Security? Medicare? Shuffleboard and checkers in Florida?"

She laughed—a little too loudly—at that. I wondered how much she'd had to drink.

"No, I'm talking about your future at the paper. There are big changes coming, Gil, and you can be a part of them. There's the TV thing, of course, I can really make you a star. And there's so many exciting opportunities ahead on the website. The print edition of the paper will continue to shrink in importance, maybe even disappear altogether. But that's going to just open up even more possibilities for you. For you and me together."

"You figure you're going to be in charge of all this?" I asked.

"Yes."

"Not Marilyn?"

She looked over at Marilyn Staley on the other side of the room, then back at me.

"Marilyn is yesterday's journalist," she said to me. "I'm the journalist of today—and tomorrow. You're going to have to make a choice between me and Marilyn very soon. Whose team do you want to be on? I hope that you're going to be on my side. The winning side. What do you think about all of that?"

"I think I want another beer," I said.

As I made my way to the bar, Marilyn intercepted me.

"What were you and Stacy talking about over there?" she asked.

"Oh, she was just asking my advice on some social media questions. She wanted to know if I preferred Instagram, Google plus, or Twitter. I said I generally went with AOL dial-up service, it seemed to me to be the way of the future. I also said I thought the Internet was a passing fad like hula hoops or the pet rock. She thanked me for my keen insights and that was pretty much it."

"Who do you like better, Stacy or me?" Marilyn suddenly asked.

"What are we—in high school?"

"Answer the question."

"Well, you did fire me once," I pointed out.

I was afraid that Marilyn was really going to push for my support in her war with Stacy, just like Stacy had done a few minutes earlier. And I didn't want to be a part of that discusson with her. I liked Marilyn. I really did. But Stacy was right about one thing. There was going to be a winner and a loser in all this, and I needed to stay on the side of the winner—whoever that might be. The longer I could put off picking sides in this battle the better it was for me.

But it turned out that at the moment Marilyn had something else in mind to talk with me about.

She was an old-time editor, and old-time editors are always the same when it comes to big stories. They'll praise you for a big front page exclusive, take you out for drinks to celebrate, but—in the end—they always come back to you with that age-old editors' question.

Which is what Marilyn did with me now.

"So what have you got for tomorrow?" she asked.

CHAPTER 38

DID have an idea for where to go next on the story. Sort of.

I had been thinking about that college class.

The one on women's empowerment.

Karen Faris attended it. So did Janet Creighton, one of the other women in Melissa Ross's files. And both of them said that's how they found out about Melissa Ross and her investigative agency specializing in wayward spouses. Somehow there was a connection between that class and Melissa Ross. And that connection could be the key to how the victims, or at least some of them, were selected. And to how Ross herself was involved. Someone in that class must have had a connection to her.

Except it wasn't that easy.

Faris didn't know the answer, and she said they didn't even know one another's names in the class. Neither did Creighton. And Dr. Kate Lyon, the instructor, refused to cooperate because of the doctor-patient confidentiality thing.

So where did that leave me? Where else could I try to find out the information I needed?

The college itself.

That's where the classes were held.

Maybe they could help.

———

I never particularly liked going back to college campuses as a reporter.

For one thing, it brought back some bad memories. College wasn't a particularly happy experience for me. My father died while I was in college, and I'd already lost my mother several years earlier. I thought too many of the journalism professors were idiots living in ivory towers who couldn't cover a simple fire story if their lives depended on it. And all I wanted to do was get out of school and work at a newspaper, which I did for much of my time there, as an intern at the *News*.

Also, being around college students always made me feel old. It really didn't seem like that long ago that I'd been a student just like them. But seeing all the young faces on a campus now made me remember that I wasn't a kid anymore, I was pushing forty.

Finally—and I know this probably comes across as a bit vain— I'd never really had much luck with college coeds. I do okay with most women. But every female college student I ever tried to hook up with always seemed more interested in saving the environment or something than being impressed by Gil Malloy and his reporting credentials.

The student sitting at the reception desk outside the office of the university president was no exception.

She had been openly unfriendly to me ever since I told her I wanted to talk to Jackie Dowling, the head of the college.

"Who are you again?" she asked.

I told her and showed her my *Daily News* press credentials.

"A reporter, huh?"

"Do you read the *News*?"

"I hate newspapers."

"A free press is the cornerstone of democracy," I said.

"Is that why you people spend most of your time ignoring serious issues and writing about the size of Kim Kardashian's butt?"

"The size of Kim's butt is a pretty serious issue."

"I'm afraid President Dowling has no time in her schedule today for unannounced appointments," she said haughtily.

"How about if I do my Ben Bradlee impression from *All the President's Men* for the two of you?"

"There's no way President Dowling can see you today," she repeated.

"Perry White from *Superman*?"

She didn't even crack a smile.

"Do me a favor and just ask President Dowling if she'll see me," I said. "If you do that, I promise not to write any more Kim Kardashian stories this week."

She still didn't smile back, but stood up, walked into the office behind her, and closed the door.

She came out a few minutes later, walking stiffly over to her desk.

"President Dowling says she will see you," she said.

Terrific, I thought. Dowling would probably turn out to be another goddamned snooty academic who'd do anything to avoid helping me catch a killer.

———

Except it wasn't like that.

Jackie Dowling was an attractive woman, in her fifties, with a warm smile and a friendly manner. When I came into the office, she strode quickly over to me from behind her desk and put her hand out to shake mine. I remembered reading somewhere that she had been in politics—working for the previous administration—before being appointed president of the college. So this cordiality could be political grandstanding. But, grandstanding or not, I was still glad to have it after the frosty reception I'd gotten outside.

"I'm so sorry you had to wait out there that long," she said after I introduced myself and told her what I was looking for. "The minute Nicole told me, I said to bring you in here. I'll do anything that I can to help you."

I relaxed a bit. I liked Jackie Dowling. I told her what I was looking for.

"Have you talked to our adult education office?" Dowling asked after I finished.

"They say they don't have records of the people in the classes. That it was handled completely by Dr. Kate Lyon, the instructor."

Dowling nodded. "Yes, that's the way many of those adult education classes work. We only provide the space and a few other logistics for the class. The instructor is in charge of everything else. There's no college credit involved, so we don't have to uphold any particular academic standards the way we would with regular courses. Have you spoken to Dr. Lyon about this?"

"She won't reveal the names of the people in her class."

"An academic freedom issue?"

"She actually used the doctor-patient confidentiality reason."

Dowling sighed. "I'm not really sure that would stand up in an academic situation like this."

"I was hoping you might be able to get her to change her mind."

"I can try. But I'm not sure how much good I will do. Like I said, it's not technically a patient-doctor relationship in a class-room. But Dr. Lyon's not really a part of the college and doesn't answer directly to me. Normally, I would say I could be persuasive enough to get her to do that based on her relationship with us here at the school. Presumably, she wants to maintain that good relationship—and I could threaten to not allow her to conduct classes here anymore. But I'm not sure that will work with Dr.

Lyon. I met her at a reception not long ago and I must say that she came across to me as a very strong-willed woman. When she talks about the importance of doctor-patient confidentiality with you, I am sure she feels very strongly about the issue. I'm not confident that she's going to change her mind for anyone. Even me."

"I understand that," I smiled. "But let's give it a try, huh?"

"Sure."

She started to pick up a phone. "I'll have to get her number from the Adult Education Department. It'll probably take a little while for Nicole to do that for me. Do you want to wait? Or can I contact you later after I've talked to Dr. Lyon?"

"Actually I found her number on the Web," I said. "You can just look it up there."

She clicked on a computer by her desk. I walked around her desk, looked at the computer screen, and then gave her the URL for the website where I had gotten the information and phone number for Dr. Lyon.

Dowling punched it into the computer, waited for the website to load, and then began to read the data on it.

Suddenly she looked confused.

"This can't be right."

"What do you mean?"

"You must have given me the wrong Web address."

I looked over her shoulder at the website on the screen.

The name Dr. Kate Lyon was at the top, along with a picture of Lyon and a few lines of bio on her education and professional credentials. The bio said she had practiced in Philadelphia for a number of years and then moved to New York City, where she set up an office on Central Park West.

"That's it," I said.

"Then this must be a different Kate Lyon, not the one who taught here."

"No, I spoke to Dr. Lyon when I called the number on this site. She said she taught the class here, she just refused to give me any details about the people who attended it."

Dowling stared at the picture of Kate Lyon at the top of the page.

"Mr. Malloy, I told you I met Dr. Lyon at a reception," she said. "Talked to her for several minutes. And this is not the Kate Lyon I met. It doesn't look anything at all like her."

"What did the Kate Lyon you met look like?"

"She was a very attractive blonde woman."

Part V

DEADLIER THAN THE MALE

WAS there when police descended on the block of Central Park West where the office of Dr. Kate Lyon was located.

There was an army of cops—heavily armed, decked out in riot gear, with sharpshooters on the roof. Flashing red lights from police cars and emergency vehicles lit up the block. The cops smashed down the door and stormed into Lyon's office. The only problem was there was no Kate Lyon inside. Just like Melissa Ross a few weeks earlier, she was gone.

Dr. Kate Lyon—or whoever she really was—must have somehow figured out the cops were onto her.

Once the building was clear, I went inside with Wohlers. Lyon's office consisted of several rooms. A waiting area. A private office for the doctor. And a larger area—informal-looking, almost like a living room—where she apparently met with her patients. There were degrees on the walls in her office, similar to the way most doctors' offices were decorated. They said that Kate Lyon had graduated from Temple University Medical School in Philadelphia, with a specialty in psychiatric guidance for women, and practiced in that city for a number of years.

"What do you think?" I asked Wohlers as he studied the certificates on the wall. "Fakes?"

"I bet they're real."

"You figure the killer really is this Dr. Lyon?"

He shook his head no. "I think the real Dr. Lyon is probably at the bottom of a lake or something somewhere, just like Melissa Ross was."

There were no pictures of the woman who called herself Dr. Kate Lyon anywhere in the office. Besides the diplomas, there were just some paintings and decorations on the wall that looked as if they had come from a Holiday Inn. It was a blank, nondescript office. No clues about its occupant.

Other residents in the building said she had moved in several months earlier. They had seen clients going in and out of the office to see her. All of them seemed to be women. Dr. Lyon herself was rarely seen. And, when she was, no one had any major interplay with her. She kept to herself. Maybe trying to not draw any attention to herself. Which made sense. Except for one thing. She was so damned good-looking.

"I tried to talk to her," a dentist with an office on the ground floor told me when I did a series of interviews with people in the building. "I used to see her coming and going sometimes from the window of my office near the front entrance. I tried to keep an eye out for her. She was a real looker. I figured if I started up a conversation with her, maybe I could ask her out or something. Maybe something could happen between us."

"So what did happen?"

"Nothing at all."

"You never talked to her?"

"Oh, I talked to her. Once. After that, I never tried again. In fact, I made sure to stay away from her."

"Why?"

"I asked her if she wanted to have a drink sometime. Suggested it would be fun to get to know her better. Hell, I was hitting on her, sure. But I've hit on plenty of women before. Never got a reaction like this one before."

"She said no?"

He nodded. "It wasn't just her turning me down. It was the way she said it. And the way she looked at me. The anger. The hatred. I could feel it practically burning into me from her stare. Scared the hell out of me, I gotta say. It wasn't simply that she wasn't interested. It was more like . . . well, like she wanted to kill me."

It was in Dr. Kate Lyon's private office that Wohlers and the cops finally struck pay dirt.

There were files there on her patients. All of them were women. Most of the cases were similar. Abusive husbands. Harassment and claims of discrimination at work. Women's empowerment was the topic of many of the patient profiles—the same way it was in the class that Lyon taught at the college.

The name on one of the files was Melissa Ross.

Things started to get a bit sticky for me at this point. I'd been sending tweets, texts, and emails back to the office on everything I'd found out so far. But now Wohlers was having second thoughts about me being there when they opened up the Melissa Ross file. I pointed out to him that the only reason he knew about Kate Lyon was me. And that I'd gone directly to him with the information instead of reporting it to someone else in the department or just going ahead and printing it first. I told him he owed me this exclusive. The whole exclusive. He made another halfhearted effort to argue about it, but eventually let me stay.

According to the file, Melissa Ross had been seeing the woman who called herself Kate Lyon for regular sessions. She talked extensively about all the problems she'd had with men in her life. Her abusive adoptive father. The men she had dated. Her marriage to Joe Delvecchio—and how it fell apart because she couldn't trust him any more than she'd ever been able to trust any of the men in her life. The problems with male coworkers and superiors on the police force, which culminated in her attack on the commanding officer of her unit and her subsequent dismissal from the NYPD.

She talked in the sessions about the satisfaction she got from starting her own private investigation agency which exposed cheating husbands and boyfriends for what they really were to the women who had trusted them.

"The patient has a deep-seated need to hurt men," Lyon wrote at the bottom of one of the session files. "To make them pay for the injustices and the indignities that she believes she has suffered from men in her own life. She has transferred her own anger at the specific men in her life who have hurt her to an overriding rage against all men—and this has consumed her to the point where it is the only thing that now matters to her and the only thing that gives her satisfaction. Her investigative agency is her true therapy. Even more than me. And yet the more revenge she gains by exposing the cheating and lies of the men she is investigating, the more her own hatred and distrust of men grows."

The entries were all very professional-sounding like that. There was very little emotion in them. Just a fact-filled account of the activities taking place during the psychiatric sessions with the patient and a medical evaluation of the causes and possible treatments for her. And all of the things Melissa Ross was telling Dr. Lyon so far were the kinds of things you'd expect her to be talking about to a professional therapist—the abusive adoptive father, the ex-husband, the problems with her superiors at work, etc.

I wondered if the writing had been done by the real Dr. Kate Lyon—or by the woman who we now believed had taken over her identity.

But then, after searching through most of the files, Wohlers found something that jumped right off of the page.

"Melissa Ross told me today that she had begun looking for

information about her birth parents," the entry said. "More specifically, she wants to know about her birth father. She felt that all of the men so far in her life had been abusive and harmful to her. Except for him. Because she didn't even know who he was. But she needs to find out why he abandoned her and gave her up for adoption. She believes that if she can find out the answer to that, maybe she can figure out the answers for other things in her life too. She seems quite determined about this. She has thrown all of her investigative skills—the things she has used in the past to help other women—into this mission. I wonder what the outcome will be for her if she does not find out the information she is looking for, or if it somehow is not what she wants to hear."

Melissa Ross was looking for information about her birth mother and birth father. She was a private investigator. So presumably at some point she was able to find out about her mother's death at Munson Lake. Maybe she even found out about her mother's brief relationship with Wylie, the same way I had.

But what did that have to do with Wylie now or the murders or anything else?

At some point after that in the Lyon files, the Melissa Ross entries stopped. Maybe she had stopped coming to the doctor's office after that. Maybe their relationship had gone from being professional to something beyond. Or maybe the blonde woman simply stopped adding the details of the visits into the files because something was going on between the two of them.

The last entry we found was the only one that had the hint of anything personal—anything beyond the normal doctor-patient relationship.

"Melissa Ross has invited me for a drink outside the office," the entry read. "I generally make it a policy not to have any interaction with my patients outside the office. I will make an exception this time. Melissa is too interesting a patient to ignore. She wants me to help her, and I think I can. More importantly, I think she can help me. . . ."

It was somewhere around this time that someone in Lyon's class began to partner with Melissa to investigate the husbands of women in the class. Obviously, this was the connection. Lyon, or whoever she really was, steered the women to Ross. Maybe to help Ross's business. Maybe to help Lyon accomplish her own goals, whatever those might be. Maybe Lyon did it for personal reasons. Or maybe it was a combination of all of the above.

So what happened then?

Did the two of them become kindred spirits out to avenge the wrongs that men had done to them and to other women? Was there a sexual element involved? Did they have some kind of a lesbian relationship? Did Melissa Ross somehow betray that relationship when she slept with the first victim, Walter Issacs?

I'd always been bothered by the fact that Issacs's was the only murder in which the victim seemingly had sex before his own death. Maybe that made the real blonde killer jealous. Or maybe Melissa had just gotten cold feet, when people actually started dying, and tried to back out of the bizarre relationship, whatever that relationship was. So she wound up dead too.

Sure, there were a lot of unanswered questions. But it was a sensational story, and I had it first. The *News* was all over the Internet with the story, and media outlets everywhere were picking it up from us. Meanwhile, *Live from New York* was ready to do a live remote with me at Lyon's office. And I'd be the lead story on the front page the next day.

Yep, all in all, it was a pretty good day for me.

All I had to do now was find out where the woman who called herself Dr. Kate Lyon really was.

And, of course, who she was.

CHAPTER 40

JACKIE Dowling told me that the fund-raising event at the college where she had been introduced to Dr. Kate Lyon had happened a few months earlier.

"It was to promote our adult education program," Dowling said when I went back to the college to do follow-up interviews. "That's why all the instructors were required to attend."

"So Lyon might not have shown up otherwise?"

"I don't remember her coming to any other events."

"But she had to come to this one to keep her position as an adjunct professor or whatever in the adult education program?"

Dowling nodded.

"What did she seem like to you?" I asked.

"Very beautiful. I mean really beautiful. I felt like an ugly duckling standing next to her. Men didn't seem to notice me or any other woman when she was around."

"And she talked to you at some point that night?"

"Nothing memorable. It was all very professional. We talked a bit about the college, her class. She was very passionate about the class, I remember that. Talked about how most women needed to be empowered to realize how much they could accomplish. She said women didn't realize how strong they were, the kind of impact they could really make. She said she had been that way once, but no more. And now she was trying to help other women. It was very convincing, although I've heard variations of it before."

"Anything else you remember?"

"Just this weird thing she said at the end. She asked me if I was married. I said yes. To the same man for twenty-five years. I told her how great my husband was, and she seemed . . . well, she seemed almost disappointed by that. Like I was somehow invalidating her theory about the ways men hold women back or something. Finally, she just looked at me strangely and said: 'Hold on to him then. A good man is hard to find.' "

"That's all?"

"That's all. I mean we only talked for a few minutes. There were a lot of people at the event that night."

"Could I question some of them? Also any other people here who might have had contact with her?"

"I'll see what I can do."

———

Everyone I talked to at the college told me pretty much the same story. The woman that they knew as Dr. Kate Lyon had kept a very low profile. She showed up to conduct her evening class, but that was about the only time anyone ever saw her. Except for the night at that fund-raising event.

The description of her was always the same. Blonde. Drop-dead gorgeous. Friendly enough to women during the few exchanges anyone had with her, but not to men. If there was a way for a super-sexy blonde like her to make herself virtually invisible, this woman seemed to have somehow accomplished that.

I thought again about the fund-raising party. The only event she had attended. The one time she was exposed to the people at the college. Maybe she'd made a mistake that night and let her guard down in a way that could give me a clue to her real identity.

"What exactly are you looking for?" one faculty member asked me.

"I'm just hoping I can find someone who had a meaningful contact with her. I'm trying to get some kind of picture of her and interviewing people who've actually been in contact with her might help me to compile that picture."

"Well, if you're looking for a picture, you should ask the photographer."

"What photographer?"

"There was a photographer at the event. Most of the events here that Dowling attends are covered by a photographer. It helps fund-raising efforts to publish the pictures in the alumni newsletter—so potential donors can see all the exciting activities going on at their old college. The alumni people always have a photographer on call."

I got Dowling to take me to the office of the school's alumni newsletter.

"I should've thought of that myself," Dowling said.

"That's why I always talk to as many people as possible on a story," I told her. "You never know what you're going to find out."

"You're very good at your job, Mr. Malloy. Any way I could convince you to teach a course on being a reporter here next semester?"

I shook my head no. "Those who can do, those who can't teach," I said. "And those who can't do either teach journalism."

———

The editor of the alumni newsletter went through his back files for us and found the pictures from the night of the fund-raiser.

"There's maybe a couple hundred of them," the editor said, clicking on a computer file that opened up to rows and rows of pictures.

"Why so many?" I asked.

"We just like to have a lot of choices. We only use a few in the alumni newsletter. But the others are all here in this file, if you want to go through them."

"President Dowling says she was talking to the woman we're looking for at one point."

"Okay, that helps."

"Would you have taken a picture of everyone I talked to that night?" Dowling asked.

"Maybe not everyone, but most of them."

"So the woman should be in here?"

"Hopefully."

As it turned out, there was no picture of Dr. Kate Lyon talking to President Dowling. We went through pictures of Dowling talking to a lot of people. Faculty members. Alumni. College officials. Students. None of them was the woman we were looking for.

But her picture did turn out to be there.

Dowling spotted it. She pointed to a blonde woman standing in the background of one of the shots. The woman was next to the refreshments table. Alone. There was a man not far from her. Eying her up. I could almost imagine the man approaching her, trying to hit on the attractive guest. Probably got shot down. If so, he didn't know how lucky he was.

The woman was staring out at the crowd of people. Icily. Coldly. I wondered what the hell she was thinking at that moment.

"That's the woman I know as Dr. Kate Lyon," Dowling said.

The editor clicked the zoom button on the computer we were viewing to get a closer look at her. The face jumped into clearer focus now. Blonde. Sexy. A real fox. Just like Melissa Ross used to be. Even more so . . . if that was possible.

I felt a sense of exhilaration. The feeling I got on a story whenever I made a big breakthrough. This was one of those times. I'd finally found out who we were really looking for.

I didn't know her name.

And I didn't know anything more about her yet.

But I had a face for Blonde Ice now.

CHAPTER 41

I WENT to see Susan at the Manhattan District Attorney's Office in Foley Square.

"This is a surprise," Susan said when I sat down in front of her desk. "The last time we were together, you ran out in the middle of our date to find two more murder victims."

"The pursuit of justice is a relentless task," I said.

I showed her the picture from the college reception and told her all about it.

"Didn't you tell me once there was some sophisticated computer technology now that can use a picture of someone's face to identify that person?"

"Face recognition pattern," she said. "The computer identifies characteristics and features in the picture and matches them up against similar characteristics and features in a criminal database. Of course, the person you're looking for has to be in the database. But most criminals are. Have you shown this picture to the police?"

"Not yet."

"Because you want to find out who she is and break the story yourself. Only you need my help to do that."

"C'mon, Susan, it would be fun. You and I working together to find out who this woman is. Solving the case and all that. Kind of romantic too. We'd be this cool couple of crime-solvers like Nick and Nora Charles from *The Thin Man*."

"Before my time."

"Okay, *Hart to Hart* then. Robert Wagner and Stefanie Powers. Solving crimes, kissing and making out between cases. I actually think I look a bit like Robert Wagner. The younger version, of course. And to tell you the truth, I've always really had this thing for Stefanie Powers. What do you think?"

"I think *Remington Steele* would be a better example of what you want us to do here. I do the investigative work and then this big handsome hunk gets all the credit. Although, just for the record, I don't think you really look at all like Pierce Brosnan."

I laughed. It was good to be able to banter with Susan like this. It felt so comfortable, so natural. She looked really good too. Her hair hung long again, the way she used to wear it. She was wearing a dark blue pantsuit, with a pink blouse, that made her look both businesslike and sexy at the same time. And when I handed her the picture, I smelled a slight whiff of her perfume—the same perfume she always wore back when we were together. I wondered again to myself how I had ever managed to let her get away. But, of course, I knew the answer to that. I screwed up, just like I had screwed up a lot of things in my life. But now I was getting a second chance with Susan, just like I'd gotten a second chance with my newspaper reporting career. I couldn't screw either of them up again.

"Will you help me?" I asked Susan.

She looked down at the picture, then back at me.

"Yeah, I'm in," she sighed.

———

She took me to a guy named Danny Jamieson at a technology lab they worked with. Jamieson would try to match the photo of Dr. Lyon to someone in the criminal database.

"We don't usually allow non–law enforcement personnel in here to observe the investigative process," Jamieson said to me.

"I can vouch for Gil, Danny," Susan said.

"Have you known him long?"

"He's an old friend."

"Actually, we used to be married," I said.

"And you're still friends?" Jamieson asked.

"It's kind of a fluid situation," I told him.

Jamieson explained how the facial recognition technology worked.

"In some ways, it's as simple as it sounds. It analyzes all of the basic visual features of the person and comes out with a list of people from a data bank with similar characteristics. Even ranks them by percentage of matches. Anything from a small percentage of similarity to an ultimate 100 percent perfect score."

He said that the best thing about it was that the computer wasn't confused or distracted by efforts from a suspect to change his or her identity. Hair color, mustaches, beards, even plastic surgery wouldn't hide the basics of that person's identity from the computer.

The technology had been around for a while, even though now it was much more sophisticated.

"One of the first uses of this was for war criminals. Nazis who fled, changed their identity, etc. The Israelis, human rights groups, and all sorts of others who tried to track them down found all these SS officers, concentration camp guards, and the like who had created new lives for themselves. Looked different, different names, sometimes they had remained undetected for years and years. No one suspected that the old man living next to them had been a Nazi butcher as a youth. But there are some things you can't change about your identity. A picture of the person as a young Nazi in Germany is submitted to this computer. It compares it to a present day picture of the person suspected of being the Nazi. A lot of war criminals were finally tracked down this way.

"Then there's the casinos. Las Vegas. Atlantic City. Whenever they used to try to bar someone who had been cheating—a con man or a card counter or anyone else who had a system to make big money there illegally—it was very difficult to enforce. These people frequently could slip back into the Taj or the Borgata or the Sands, even if they were on this casino blacklist. All they had to do was change the way they looked enough to get past any security that had a picture of them. Not anymore. There's a spy in the sky camera in every casino that watches everyone in the place. The casino security people have files of the blackballed people fed into the computer for that—and it automatically checks if any of the gamblers have any of the telltale characteristics of the people that have been barred. It's pretty amazing really, when you think about it.

"All of this is somewhat basic, though, compared to what we do here. This data we have takes in everyone who has ever been in the criminal justice system for whatever reason. Anything from armed robbery to DUI to a simple arrest at a protest. It will go through them all to find a potential match for the person you're looking for. If she's in there, we'll find her. No matter how hard she's tried to hide her old identity."

"What if she's never been in the criminal justice system?"

"Then you're screwed."

"But if she is . . . ?"

"This will find her for you."

The time it took to complete the process varied, Jamieson explained. Depending on the number of possible similarities and matches the machine needed to detect and check out between this picture and all of the endless data it was comparing it with in the system. The computer first came up with a large number of possible matches, then gradually whittled them down to a smaller number as it compared the matching characteristics against one another. I listened to it all from Jamieson, nodded like I understood—but really just wanted to get on with it and hoped the damn thing worked.

It took about a half hour to get something. Several candidates popped up as possibilities, but nothing for sure. Finally, though, Jamieson looked down at the screen and smiled broadly.

"We struck pay dirt, my friends," he said. "We've got a match."

There was a photo on the screen of a young blonde girl. She looked like a teenager. Susan and I looked down at the name below the picture.

Claudia Borrell.

"Who is Claudia Borrell?" I asked.

"Arrested on suspicion of murder in Belleville, Illinois, in 2000," Jamieson said, reading from the screen.

"Who was she suspected of murdering?" Susan wanted to know.

Jamieson looked through the rest of the data.

"Jesus Christ!" he said.

"What?"

"She killed her whole family."

CHAPTER 42

CLAUDIA Borrell was fifteen years old when it happened," Danny Jamieson told Susan and me after he'd gone back and accumulated more information on the woman we'd identified in the picture. "Lived with her family in Belleville, Illinois. Two brothers, one was twelve and the other was a baby that had just been born ten months earlier. Father was a doctor, a highly regarded heart specialist; mother was a business executive. A grandmother, the father's mother, lived with them too. Expensive place called Carlton Street Estates. Sounds like Claudia Borrell's family was living the American dream. Until they wound up dead. All of them except for Claudia."

Jamieson called up a newspaper front page on a computer screen. The date was June 12, 2000. The headline said: FIVE DEAD IN FAMILY MASSACRE; DAUGHTER MISSING.

"When the mother and father didn't show up for work, the cops eventually went to the house to investigate," he said. "They found her father and mother dead in their bedroom. Their throats had been cut while they slept. The twelve-year-old's throat was cut too. The baby had been suffocated with a pillow. The worst was the grandmother. The killer had beaten her to death with some kind of a blunt object. Turned out to be one of the father's golf clubs. They found the bloody club in his golf bag, where it had apparently been returned by the killer after the fatal deed was done."

"What about the fifteen-year-old girl?" Susan asked.

"At first, the cops assumed she'd been kidnapped. The killer—or killers—had wiped out the family for some reason, and then taken their pretty teenage daughter. A missing person alert was sent out for her. But it soon became apparent to the authorities there that she wasn't missing at all, she was on the run."

Jamieson clicked to bring up another newspaper clipping. This headline said: MISSING TEEN IN MASSACRE HAD TALKED OF KILLING.

It described Claudia Borrell as a brilliant but troubled student. She had gotten straight A's and won every academic honor possible in school. Her IQ had been measured at a phenomenal 181, which made her a genius almost on the Einstein level. She had even been accepted for early college enrollment for a pre-med course at Stanford University the following semester. And she was gorgeous, people said. A beautiful girl. Claudia Borrell seemed to have it all.

But there were problems, everyone who knew her said. Big problems. She was a loner, seemed to have no friends. And there was a lot of anger there. A violent side of this girl who seemed to have everything, but never looked or acted happy. The school, and her family, had forced her to undergo counseling. But it didn't seem to help. In fact, at the last session she had with the school counselor, she said she hated her family and that every day she thought about how much she "wanted to kill them all."

Also, there was no sign of any forced entry into the house. No fingerprints or other evidence of anyone except the victims and their fifteen-year-old daughter anywhere, including the bloody golf club and the pillow used to suffocate the baby. Eventually, the police realized that the unthinkable had happened. This pretty, brilliant fifteen-year-old girl was the cold-blooded mass murderer they were looking for.

"So when did they arrest her?" I asked Jamieson.

"A couple of days later. She just walked into the police station and confessed to the murders. Confessed to killing her family. Confessed to another death too."

"Who?"

"A teenage boy she went to school with. Kid named Bobby Jenkins. Jenkins had been found dead in his family's swimming pool a week or so earlier. No sign of any violence. The police had ruled it an accidental drowning. But the girl said she did it. Said she'd flirted with the Jenkins kid, got him to invite her over to his house when his parents were away, and brought some beer for them to drink. She'd worn a skimpy bikini to keep him distracted, and then drowned him in the pool when she got the chance."

"Why did she kill him?"

"That's the scary thing. There was no reason. She said she did it 'just to see what it felt like.' She wanted to kill someone, to experience that feeling of power—and she chose him. She said it was everything she'd hoped for and more."

I looked down at the screen where he'd now called up a picture of fifteen-year-old Claudia Borrell that the newspaper had run with the article. It was from a professional photo shoot of some sort. She looked beautiful, all dressed up for the occasion. Blonde hair, gorgeous face, beautiful eyes—even as a teenager she'd been a real fox.

"She sure doesn't look like a killer," I said. "But I guess that's the most dangerous kind of killer. The one who doesn't look like a killer at all to anyone until it's too late."

"The police psychologist who interviewed her after she was in custody diagnosed her as a cold-blooded, emotionless murderer," Jamieson said. "Someone who just enjoyed watching people die. And reveling in the power of life and death she held over them. A murderer who killed for no other reason than the satisfaction she got out of it. A true thrill killer. There's not a whole lot of them. And certainly not many of them who are fifteen-year-old girls. She was brilliant, everyone said. A brilliant killer who was barely in her teens."

"If she was so smart, how come she just walked in and confessed to everything?" Susan asked.

"She wanted the police to know what she did. That was part of the satisfaction she got out of the murders, she told them. She wanted them to know what she did, how she did it, why she did it—but not be able to do anything about it."

"But you said she was arrested and charged with murder?"

"She escaped. Flirted with one of the guards who was supposed to be watching her in her holding cell. No one is sure exactly what happened after that. But they found him dead in the cell, with his keys missing along with his security ID badge that would've let him in and out. No one ever saw Claudia Borrell again."

"Until she turned up now as Dr. Kate Lyon," Susan said.

"How long do you think she's been Kate Lyon?" Jamieson asked.

"Not clear," I said. "I checked on Lyon's background. People who knew her in Philadelphia describe her as the plain-looking woman I saw in that first photo, not the one that was operating out of Central Park West and the college here. But she had a blonde woman assistant working for her. A very attractive blonde woman. I'm betting it was Claudia Borrell. Then Borrell must have assumed the Kate Lyon identity soon after moving to New York City."

"That leaves lots of missing time between 2000 and now," Susan pointed out.

"Yes, it does."

"She probably was using someone else's identity then."

"Maybe more than one identity," I said. "Maybe she switched around who she was every few years—or even more than that—in order to make sure that no one ever figured out who she really was."

Susan looked down at the picture of the fifteen-year-old Claudia Borrell from the old newspaper. Then she said the words we were both thinking at the same time.

"All those years," she said, "you figure there were more murders?"

"Don't you?" I said.

———

Wohlers was as mad as I'd ever seen him. I'd brought along a corned beef sandwich from his favorite deli to try to placate him. But I hadn't even had a chance to give it to him yet because he was too busy yelling at me.

"You should have come to me with that picture from the college as soon as you found it," he screamed at me. "But instead you run off on your own with it because you wanted to get a big exclusive."

"It's called freedom of the press, Lieutenant."

"I could have you thrown in jail, Malloy."

"On what charges?"

"Uh, well . . . obstruction of justice, tampering with evidence, and . . . oh, just being an all-around jerk in general."

"I'm pretty sure I can beat those first two raps," I said.

"I'm not fooling around, Malloy."

"Well, I've got a pretty lawyer on my side."

"You mean that high-powered woman from the DA's office you somehow got to go in on this with you?"

"Her name is Susan Endicott."

"Okay."

"The once and possibly future Mrs. Gil Malloy."

"How did you wind up with her again? I thought she decided to divorce you."

"I'm appealing that decision."

Wohlers shook his head.

"Look on the bright side, Lieutenant—I identified the Blonde Ice killer for you. You know who you're looking for now. The way

I see it you should be thanking me. I came to you with a critical bit of information to assist your investigation."

"Yes, only after you made sure you timed it so you could break the story first in the *News*, before we got a chance to tell anyone else."

"Well, that was the point, wasn't it?" I said.

I figured I had nothing to do at that moment but give him the corned beef, which is what I did.

"Does that help at all?" I asked him.

"Couldn't hurt."

———

After Wohlers consumed most of the corned beef and calmed down a bit, I told him about a theory I'd been pursuing ever since my Claudia Borrell exclusive broke.

"Claudia Borrell assumed the identity—and presumably killed—a psychiatrist named Kate Lyon, who graduated from Temple University and then set up her practice in Philadelphia. In order to do that, Borrell must have been in Philadelphia. Probably living there for a while too."

"So you think she was killing people in Philadelphia?"

"That's my theory. I went through a lot of unsolved homicides in the Philadelphia area over the past few years. I eliminated from consideration any cases in which the victims were shot to death. None of Claudia Borrell's victims had been killed with a gun. It was always stabbing, beating to death, strangulation, or some combination of all of those things. A gun seemed too impersonal for her. She wanted to feel them die, not just watch them. I pinpointed three murders."

I went through them with Wohlers. One was a twenty-one-year-old college football star and self-admitted ladies' man found beaten and strangled in his car after leaving a Center City club where he'd been seen hitting on a sexy blonde. Another was a Princeton professor beaten to death with a baseball bat at his home while his wife was out of town—and he was seen running around with another woman. Then there was a family in Langhorne—about fifteen miles outside Philadelphia—that was brutally murdered in their home. The husband, wife, and their two sons were all found with their throats slit—apparently while they slept. Nothing was taken from the home, and there was no sign of any personal disputes between members of the family and people who knew them. The more likely scenario was that an intruder had done it, for some unknown reason.

"The Princeton professor and the college football player in Center City definitely fit the criteria—guys fooling around with other women," I said to Wohlers. "The family in Langhorne was just too similar to what happened to Claudia Borrell's own family years ago to ignore. Was there something about this family that reminded her of her own family? Or was there something else at work here, some other reason, she might have decided to kill them? They all died in their sleep, just like the Borrell family. And the makeup of the family was the same—a husband, wife, and two sons who died. That seems like more than just a coincidence."

He looked down at the list and shook his head. "You might be onto something," he said.

"There could be even more in other parts of the country," I told him. "Any unsolved murder of a man who was killed this way after fooling around with other women, we've got to look at Borrell now as a possible suspect. There's no telling how many men she might have killed."

CHAPTER 43

NOTHING about Claudia Borrell fits the pattern of a serial killer," Vincent D'Nolfo said.

"When did you suddenly become an expert on serial killers?"

"I took a college course on serial killers."

"Really?"

"Bernard Baruch School of Criminal Justice. I've been going there at night while I've been in the academy. They've got some interesting courses there. This one was called: Serial Killer Syndrome: Motivation, Causes, and Answers."

We were sitting at a coffee shop in Greenwich Village. The same coffee shop where I'd first gone with Abbie Kincaid, the TV star D'Nolfo had been a bodyguard for before she was murdered. Sometimes I went back there to eat. Why? I wasn't sure. But it had become a kind of ritual for me. I guess because it brought back nice memories about Abbie. I'd mentioned it to D'Nolfo, who said he'd like to join me.

"First off," D'Nolfo said, "we have a serial killer who's a woman. That's almost unheard of. Ted Bundy, Son of Sam, Jack the Ripper—almost all the famous serial killers were men who killed women. This is a woman who kills men."

"I am woman, hear me roar," I smiled.

"I'm not sure that's exactly what the feminist movement has in mind when they demand equality with men."

"So what could have set her off on the path to become a cold-blooded female serial killer of men?"

"Well, the first—and most obvious—possibility is that she was abused in some way by her father as a child, developed a hatred for all men, and now gets satisfaction—possibly even sexual satisfaction—out of killing men. Every time she kills a man, she kills her father all over again. And that makes her feel good. The father was the motivation."

"Except there's no evidence that the father ever did anything to her. Everyone said he was a good guy. A good dad. No one really knows what goes on inside a house, but still there's no indication whatsoever that Claudia Borrell had anything other than a happy, normal home environment as a child."

"And so that brings us to the second possibility."

"Which is?"

"There was no specific motivation for her actions."

"C'mon, people don't kill other people for no reason at all."

"Actually they do. In this case, we could be talking about someone who has no sense of right or wrong; no moral compass; no conscience. Someone who kills simply for the sake of killing. A thrill so powerful, so overpowering that it probably even surpassed the thrill of sex for her. There's historically been a sexual component to most serial killers. What's happened here is we have a woman serial killer displaying these same behavioral traits. A serial killer with a tremendous intellect. A genius. She was so far ahead of anyone in her class back in Illinois that she didn't belong in that school. She could have gone to college right then. She could have used her enormous intelligence capacity for anything. Instead, she used it to become a cold-blooded killing machine."

"What about the first victim—the boy from her school?" I asked.

"I think that was a practice kill," D'Nolfo said. "To see if she could do it. To make sure the reality lived up to the fantasy. So she killed Bobby Jenkins. He was a test. After that, she was ready for her next goal. To wipe out her own family."

"Then why did she walk into a police station afterward and confess? A brief bit of remorse?"

"Hardly. Like I said, this is probably a woman without remorse or conscience or any of the traits that stop most of us from doing terrible things. She liked the killings that she did. She was proud of them. That's why she confessed and gave herself up back then. She wanted everyone to know that she did it. More importantly, she wanted everyone to know she could get away with it. She knew she could escape afterward."

"How could she be so sure of that?"

"My theory? Because she believes she can do anything. She believes she's smarter and more resourceful than anyone. And she'll keep on believing that until the day we finally catch her."

"A cold-blooded serial killer who doesn't fit the pattern of any other serial killer," I grunted. "So we can't figure out what the hell she might do next or why. That's just great. . . ."

"There is one thing about this particular serial killer that does run according to form. Serial killers generally kill in sprees. Sometimes they'll go months, even years without killing. Then, unless they're caught, they start up again. That's what Claudia Borrell has done. There was the spree early when she was young in Illinois. And now the spree here in New York. In between, not so much."

"We think there were more killings, we just don't know about them yet," I pointed out.

"Probably were. But still that would not be the same kind of murder spree. She would have carried out those murders quietly, without drawing any attention to herself. Now, for some reason, she's upping her profile. She's turned herself into front page news. She's taunting us, playing games with us and the press, practically daring us to try to catch her. The same way the most infamous male serial killers have done in the past."

"So what do we do next?"

"Try to find out why she started the killing spree again. That might be the best chance to catch her."

———

On that first night I'd come to this coffee shop with Abbie, D'Nolfo had waited outside in his car. I was glad of that at the time. I didn't like D'Nolfo very much then. I reminded him of that now.

"I didn't like you either. I thought you were a wiseass with a big mouth who was very annoying."

"And now you realize you were wrong, huh?"

"No, I've just gotten used to it. Besides, I realized you had some pretty good qualities underneath all that crap. And, well . . . most of all, you did right by Abbie."

We sat there silently for a while, lost in our own thoughts about Abbie Kincaid—who had played such a big role in our lives before her own was cut tragically short. She'd been murdered by her ex-boyfriend in a senseless slaying that happened while she was pursuing a sensational story. I'd finished the story after her death and found out who murdered her.

The whole thing had hit D'Nolfo particularly hard because he felt guilty for allowing her to be killed, even though there was nothing he could have done to stop it. He drifted from one security job to another after that until the police academy opportunity came along. I hoped it would work out for him.

"So do you think they'll catch this Blonde Ice woman?" I asked.

"Yes. She'll make a mistake sooner or later. No matter how brilliant she is."

We stood up to leave.

"By the way," I asked D'Nolfo, "this course you took on serial killers—what kind of a grade did you get on it?"

"I got an A," he said.

"That's good," I smiled. "I'm glad to hear it."

CHAPTER 44

LIKE D'Nolfo had said, the big question was "Why?" Why did Claudia Borrell suddenly go public with this killing spree now? There had to be a reason—some common denominator that tied everything together.

Well, there was me—she'd sought me out to talk to the media about the murders.

Then there was Bob Wylie, who was with me on *Live from New York* when she came on the air to announce to him a new murder; who'd gone out with Melissa Ross's biological mother back in Munson Lake, Ohio; and whose closest friend and ally, Tim Hammacher, had been one of the victims.

But there was something else too.

Another thread running through all this.

Houston.

The first victim was Houston's husband. I was the reporter who became famous—or infamous—for writing about Houston. And Wylie used to be a client of Houston. So Houston must have some significance—had to be some kind of a trigger—to the Blonde Ice killings.

———

Victoria Issacs—the woman who used to be Houston—was still living at the Sutton Place townhouse.

Her children were both with her this time. Two little girls—eleven and seven. The eleven-year-old had blonde hair and looked like a young version of her mother. The seven-year-old's hair was darker, but she was very cute too. Both of them were going to grow up to be real beauties. The older one was playing a game on a tablet while the younger one watched a cartoon show on TV.

She introduced me to them. They greeted me with the kind of bored indifference kids that age have to adults they don't know or particularly care about. Of course, they'd lost their father. And gone through a lot more with the sudden notoriety of their mother and the battle with the grandparents over custody. I wondered how much impact this had on kids that young. My assumption was a lot. And it might be emotional baggage they'd have to carry with them through the rest of their lives.

She told the kids to go upstairs to their rooms so she could talk to me.

"Walter's parents gave up on the custody fight," she told me when they were gone. "In the end, I think they realized that a mother's right to be with her children trumped theirs—no matter what they thought of me and no matter what scandalous things they say that I might have done."

"That's good," I said.

"But they're selling this house, so I'll have to move."

"That's bad."

"Not really. I found a nice place on the West Side for us to live. My attorney was able to get me some substantial money from Walter's estate. So we'll be good financially."

She also told me how the Houston name—which she had tried to hide for a long time—was helping her again now. She said a fashion company wanted to make a Houston line of sexy lingerie and sleepwear. Plus, she had an offer to appear as Houston on a TV reality show in the fall.

As she talked, I couldn't help but notice how great she looked. She was wearing a pair of shorts and a skimpy white halter top that showed off a lot of her body. I tried to keep my mind on the conversation, but I kept drifting back to her. I had a feeling she knew that and enjoyed the effect she had on me.

So why not push for a little more with Houston? She was a single woman now. I wasn't married. Except I knew that was not going to happen. No, that wasn't why I had come to see her.

"I've got a problem," I said.

"What's that?"

"You."

"I don't understand."

"Your story doesn't make sense."

"What do you mean?"

"How did Claudia Borrell find out you were Houston?"

"Someone must have told her."

"Who?"

"Well, I said I ran into some of my former clients from time to time. I suppose one of them could have said something to someone . . ."

I shook my head no.

"They had as much to lose as you being connected with Houston. All of them, especially Wylie. So that doesn't work as an explanation of how Borrell knew about you."

She looked at me impassively, as if she had no idea what I was going to say next. But she knew. She'd probably known I was going to show up at her door again ever since she read my story about Claudia Borrell, aka Dr. Kate Lyon.

"Nevertheless, there was no way she could have known you were Houston unless someone told her. You were the only person besides me that knew. You insisted that you had never told anyone. And I didn't tell anybody. Or at least I didn't think I did. Then I realized that I did tell someone. I shared that information with my psychiatrist, the woman I'm seeing for therapy. Did you share it with your therapist too, Mrs. Issacs?"

She sat there for a long time without saying anything, then nodded almost imperceptibly.

"Yes."

"And that therapist was Dr. Kate Lyon?"

Another nod.

"The real one or Claudia Borrell?"

"The real one."

She told me the story then. I like to think she would have done that anyway. She said she wanted to do that from the minute she read my article about Claudia Borrell assuming the identity of Kate Lyon. Maybe that was true. But, in the end, I had to do what I do as a reporter in order to find the connection between Houston and Claudia Borrell. Follow the trail of evidence until it gave me the answers I needed.

"Taking that money from Bob Wylie made me realize how much I missed being Houston. Having a man pay me because he thought I was desirable. I was having difficulties adjusting to being a wife, adjusting to being a mother, just adjusting in general to leaving my Houston persona behind. It was a dramatic readjustment from the life I had lived. I know that I made it all sound like a fairy tale when I told it to you that first day you tracked me down here. But it wasn't. I was unhappy. So I started seeing Dr. Lyon."

"Here in New York?"

"No, she was in Philadelphia."

"Why would you go to Philadelphia to see a therapist?"

"She was a specialist in women's empowerment. And that was what I wanted to feel again—empowered. I felt powerful when I was Houston. But now I was simply Mrs. Walter Issacs. I looked around at therapists and she seemed to be the one that could help me the most. So I went to Philadelphia to see her. Every week I took the Acela train down there. It was nice actually, a pleasant ride and it felt good to get away from New York. Plus, I liked the idea of seeing a therapist in another city. I didn't want to take a chance on any of my friends finding out what I was doing. There was always the possibility I could run into someone I knew by going to a therapist's office here in New York City."

"What was the original Dr. Lyon like?"

"She was very supportive, insightful, she had a lot of empathy for me and my situation. We delved into my life and my past to talk about reasons for my discontent."

"So you told her about being Houston?"

"Yes."

"About your life as Houston?"

"That's right."

"Even the stuff you told me about your relationship with Bob Wylie in New York?"

"I told her everything."

"And your husband knew nothing about your past?"

"No."

"No one else either?"

"Just Dr. Lyon."

I wanted to be mad at her for lying to me when she assured me she'd never told anyone else about being Houston. But, like I said, I'd done the same thing. I claimed I hadn't told anyone else either, but I'd certainly divulged it during my sessions with Dr. Landis. I guess you never think about your shrink when you promise to keep a secret. You're supposed to tell them everything.

"Why did you stop seeing Dr. Lyon?"

"I thought she'd given me as much help as she could. I mean

I talked about everything with her and—after a while—it seemed like we were going over the same stuff. Besides, Walter was asking me about where I was going during the week. I made up some story, but I was afraid I'd eventually get exposed. So I just stopped seeing her."

Kate Lyon was still Kate Lyon then. It was at some point much more recently that she was replaced—and probably killed—by Claudia Borrell, who moved the practice to New York. Patients in Philadelphia knew Dr. Lyon, no one in New York did. Except for Victoria Issacs, but she'd stopped seeing her by then.

"It's not hard to figure out what happened next," I said. "Psychiatrists and therapists write everything down. I'm sure Dr. Lyon did that with you. It would have all been in her files. At some point, Claudia Borrell goes through Lyon's back files and reads yours. That's how she knew you were Houston. I have no idea why, but that must be why she picked your husband as her first victim. She sent Melissa Ross to that show of yours at the art gallery. Melissa wasn't really interested in your art—she was just there to meet you and get you to confide in her about your troubles with your husband. Just like Borrell hooked up Melissa with those women in the class at the college. Except you were special, because she knew you were Houston and she knew all about that life and about your marital problems from the Lyon files. She used Melissa Ross to lure your husband to that hotel and murder him because he was married to you."

"So Walter might be dead because of me."

She said it matter-of-factly, as if she were talking about someone else's husband who had been brutally murdered. It was almost as if she'd come to peace with her husband's death and embraced her new identity as Houston again.

I remembered sitting with her that day on Houston Street when she talked about channeling some of the old Houston back into her life. "She was a tough lady, that Houston," Victoria Issacs had said to me. "Sometimes I miss her."

This made me wonder if she had ever been truly comfortable all those years being the wife of a wealthy corporate lawyer, along with her art shows and community projects and country clubs. Maybe Victoria Issacs really was Houston all along. And now that Houston—legendary queen of New York City hookers—was back with a sexy fashion line, a reality TV show, and who knows what else in the future.

Oh, she talked about staying in touch when she walked me to her door. And I said that sounded like a good idea. But I think we both knew that this visit to her was an act of closure on my part. Houston had played a very big role in my life. Changed it dramatically on both a professional and personal level. But now it was time for both of us to move on.

She leaned up and kissed me on the cheek.

I kissed her back on her cheek.

Then I closed her door behind me and said goodbye to Houston for the last time.

CHAPTER **45**

HERE was a huge gap in Claudia Borrell's life that still remained unaccounted for.

I sat at my desk the next morning and made notes about what I
knew and what I didn't know about her.

Well, I knew she was in Belleville, Illinois, in 2000. That was
a hard fact. I was pretty sure she was in Philadelphia when she
assumed the identity of the psychiatrist named Kate Lyon. I
presumed she had killed Dr. Lyon—and very likely other people
too—before she left Philadelphia. She may well have killed people
in other places too, but that was only speculation at this point. And
she had definitely been in Manhattan, working out of the Central
Park office and teaching the class at the college, when the New
York murders began.

Still that left a lot of years—and a lot of places—where she
could have been between Belleville and Philadelphia/New York.

What was she doing then?

And where?

I remembered the *News* had LexisNexis software that provided
detailed data on criminal and legal cases around the country.

I decided to try the Gil Malloy charm on Zeena to see if I could
get her to use the software to help me.

"Did you change your hairdo, Zeena?" I said when I approached her at the reception desk. "It looks nice."

"No, I just didn't have time to wash my hair before I came to work this morning," she said.

"Still looks nice."

"What do you want from me?"

"I need you to use LexisNexis to look up some cases for me."

"I'm the receptionist, not your secretary."

"Just this one favor for all the good times we had in the past."

"What good times?"

"Well, I bought you dinner once."

"You gave me a leftover slice of pizza that you were too full to eat, after you put away the first five pieces."

"Exactly. Good times, Zeena."

"Why don't you do your own research?"

"You're so much better at this stuff."

"Here's a log-in and password for LexisNexis," she said, writing them down on a slip of paper and handing them to me. "The computer it's installed on is next to Marilyn's office. Have a nice day."

I deduced by this point that the Malloy charm offensive wasn't working too well on her, so I went to the computer and logged on myself, eventually figuring out how to maneuver through the system to find what I wanted.

Belleville was in Illinois. The biggest city in Illinois was Chicago. So I first looked up unsolved murders in the Chicago area over the past fifteen years, looking for anything that might look like a link to Claudia Borrell. I found a few possibilities, but nothing clearly jumped out at me as an obvious match.

I moved on to Springfield, the capital city of Illinois and one of the other biggest cities in the state. No reason to be certain that the teenaged Claudia Borrell had gone to a big city, of course. But it made more sense that a teenager wanted for murder could disappear more easily into a large urban environment than a small town where she would stick out more.

After several hours of checking, I was more frustrated than ever. I came up with nothing. And I realized that the Borrell girl could have fled anywhere after breaking out of jail in Belleville—not just Chicago or Springfield.

Still . . .

I called up a map of the state of Illinois. I began looking for any big city within a reasonable distance of Belleville. Someplace else where I could look for a series of unsolved murders of men, presumably men who had cheated on or somehow otherwise mistreated women. I studied the map intently. And that's when I realized my mistake.

Chicago was in the northernmost part of Illinois, on the shores of Lake Michigan; Belleville was in the southern part of the state, several hundred miles away. I'd been operating under the assumption that the state of Illinois was the key, not the geography around the town of Belleville itself.

I studied the map on the screen some more, looking for any big cities within a reasonable distance of Belleville, no matter what state they were in.

Suddenly I saw it.

Hell, it practically jumped off the map at me.

St. Louis.

St. Louis was across the Mississippi River from Illinois. Less than twenty miles from Belleville. You just had to cross over to the next state.

And I remembered something else.

Before coming to New York City, Bob Wylie had once been the police commissioner of St. Louis.

I went back now and checked the dates. Wylie was police commissioner of St. Louis from 1998 to 2000. Claudia Borrell had committed the murders of her family and Bobby Jenkins in Belleville in 2000. Of course, they didn't happen in Wylie's jurisdiction. But it was only twenty miles away,

Just like with Ohio, Bob Wylie kept turning up everywhere I looked.

CHAPTER 46

OKAY, there were two things about the Blonde Ice story I didn't understand. Actually, there were plenty of things about it I didn't understand. But two of them that really bothered me. And both involved Bob Wylie.

First had been the link with Munson Lake—the area where Wylie had grown up and dated Patty Tagliarini.

Now there was the fact that he'd been the police chief of St. Louis at the same time Claudia Borrell murdered her family just twenty miles across the river, in Belleville.

I needed more answers about what might have happened in the past at Munson Lake and in Belleville.

And so I did what any good reporter does who's looking for answers on a story.

I picked up the phone and made a lot of calls to a lot of people....

——

"The Belleville Police Department is pretty small," I told Marilyn and Stacy later. "They weren't really equipped to deal with a crime this big. So they got advice—and some personnel support—from large police forces in the area. The most obvious of these was St. Louis, just across the river. Where the police commissioner at the time was none other than our old friend Bob Wylie."

"Is this in the official records about him being involved in the Borrell murder case back then?" Marilyn asked.

"Nothing I can find."

"Then how did you get this information?" Stacy wanted to know.

"I talked to a lot of people in Belleville."

"Did any of them specifically tie Wylie to the investigation?"

"Not officially, no. But I found one old-timer—retired from the force now—who remembered Wylie being there. He said Wylie showed up at their police headquarters soon after Borrell was arrested. Told me Wylie actually went into the interrogation room and talked to Borrell. Questioned her for more than an hour."

"So why was none of this ever made public?"

"Probably because the case went bad, and the Borrell girl escaped. After she got away, the police handling of Borrell came under all sorts of criticism for letting her get away. Wylie didn't want to be connected with the case anymore. So he made sure his visit to see her was kept quiet and out of the media. He's always been smart at manipulating the media to make him look good and, more importantly, to not look bad."

"But Wylie must have recognized her name when she was identified as the Blonde Ice killer," Marilyn said.

"That's right."

"Except he never said anything about meeting her back then."

"He's still trying to keep his involvement in that snafu a secret."

"Jeez," Stacy muttered.

"What she just said," Marilyn added.

It was the first time I'd ever heard them both agree on anything.

"There's more," I said.

I handed them a printout of an article I'd found in an Ohio newspaper about the Patty Tagliarini death. It was a recent piece. A reporter from the local paper had gone back and done a big feature about the thirty-year-old drowning at Munson Lake because of all the publicity over the discovery of Melissa Ross's car and body there.

Most of the details were the same as we already knew. The Tagliarini girl was driving drunk and lost control of her car—plunging into the lake. She managed to get out of the car, but couldn't swim—and drowned. The police said it was clearly an accident, with no possibility of foul play.

But there was something else in the article. It said someone in a boat nearby that night saw her thrashing around in the water from a distance. By the time he got to the spot where she was, Tagliarini had slipped back beneath the water. Another few minutes, he could have saved her. But it was too late.

The guy in the boat thought he saw two people in the water at first. But when he got closer, he just saw Tagliarini desperately struggling until she went underneath the water and died. It was dark out there, and the guy figured he must have just been mistaken about someone else in the water.

"What if someone else was in the car with her that night?" I said to Marilyn and Stacy.

"Wylie?" Stacy asked.

"That's my guess."

"He survived and she died," Marilyn said. "He could have saved her, but he didn't."

I nodded.

"Think about it. Wylie's girlfriend in high school was from a rich family, an influential family. The father was a big shot alumni and contributor to Cornell University. He told Wylie he could get him into Cornell. Get him a scholarship too. It was the key to his future. He just had to make sure he didn't mess up the relationship with the daughter. Except he did. He was sneaking out again behind his girlfriend's back with Tagliarini. He probably could have saved her, but he saved himself instead. He did that to insure his future. If anyone ever found out he was with her, the rich girlfriend with the powerful father would dump Wylie and the scholarship to Cornell and everything else would be gone. Maybe he didn't realize she couldn't swim at first. But, even when he heard her screams for help and saw the boat in the distance trying to reach her, he knew he couldn't take a chance on being there, so he fled. Leaving her to die. He ran to save his own life and his own future. It's the only scenario that makes sense."

"My God," Marilyn said. "That's horrible."

"Yeah, ain't it?"

"But what does any of this have to do with Claudia Borrell? How did she find out about it? Why does she care so much about Wylie who, as far as we know, only met her briefly years ago when she was confessing to murdering her family? What does any of this stuff you found out have to do with the new victims here?"

"Like we keep saying, I guess we just have to wait for Claudia Borrell to tell us."

CHAPTER 47

CLAUDIA Borrell called me again, like I knew she would.

"I should have been more careful to not let anyone take my picture that night," said the now familiar voice on the end of the line. I realized she didn't sound anything like she had when I thought she was Dr. Kate Lyon—she must have disguised her voice with me on the phone then. "To tell you the truth, I was getting tired of being Kate Lyon anyway. She kinda cramped my style. It was time to move on from her. Just like it was time to move on from Melissa Ross."

"Hello, Claudia," I said, trying to keep any anger or emotion of any kind out of my voice so she'd continue talking to me.

"Well, at least we're on a first name basis now."

"Did you call me to give up?"

"Ha! That's funny. You're a pretty funny guy, Gil. I like a sense of humor in a man. But only to a point."

"So tell me about Belleville."

"Oh, I still remember those first murders in Belleville. I remember them like they happened yesterday. I'd dreamed of that moment for so long, fantasized about it, planned for it—all of which made the final culmination of the deed so especially exciting and fulfilling for me. My only concern had been that it would be a singular thrill, one that I could never hope to repeat again. That I would never again feel that level of indescribable ecstasy I had felt that first time I took a human life. At least not the same way. That the first time would always be the best. Like a first kiss. It was so different, so exciting, so thrilling the first time you kissed someone new. After that, the thrill eventually wore off. Like the thrill I'd felt the first time I'd kissed Melissa Ross. But I got tired of those kisses after a while, just like I got tired of Melissa and her whining and complaining.

"The amazing thing that I discovered about killing, though, was that the first wasn't necessarily the best. It kept getting better and better each time I did it. Oh, killing Bobby Jenkins had been great, no question about it. But killing my entire family—watching them die one by one as I moved through the house on that memorable night—well, that was even more satisfying than poor Bobby. Didn't you ever fantasize about killing someone, Gil?"

"No."

"Sure you have. Everyone does."

I didn't say anything.

"With me, the fantasy became more and more powerful. My father would hug me and say how much he loved me. And all I could think about was how great it would be to slit his throat and watch him bleed to death."

"Did your father abuse you in some way as a little girl? Is that what you're doing when you kill all of these men? Killing your father over and over again because of things he did to you?"

Borrell laughed. "It wasn't like that. My father never did anything bad to me. The truth is he was a good father. Almost a perfect father. The whole family was perfect. I was growing up in the perfect house in the perfect community with the perfect family. My whole damned life was perfect."

"So then why did you murder your family?"

"Because I wanted to see what it felt like."

"And you enjoyed it?"

"More than I could have ever imagined."

"And you just kept on killing people . . ."

"That's what God put me on this planet to do. We all have a purpose. Killing is my purpose. I'm already looking forward to my next victim. The anticipation of it is almost as good as the actual killing. Maybe better."

"Why do you hate men so much?" I asked, just trying to keep her talking. "Why kill them?"

"Did anyone ask Speck and Bundy and Son of Sam why they only killed women? Of course not. When men kill women for the sexual thrill of it, no one thinks that's unusual at all. Well, I do it for the same reason as Speck and Bundy and Son of Sam. I'm just like all the other serial killers you ever heard about or read about. Except I'm smarter than any of those men ever were."

There was a ping in the email inbox on my computer.

"Another message from you?"

"Of course. You knew it was coming."

"More killings?"

"Killing is what I do."

"Who is it this time?" I asked, fearing the worst.

"Read the message, Gil," she said. "I decided I needed to make as big a media splash as possible with my next victim. So how do I do that? Well, it's really pretty simple when you think about it. . . ."

"Who is it?" I repeated.

There was a click on the phone and she was gone.

I opened up the email from Claudia Borrell and read it:

No dumb blonde jokes this time, Gil. No time for that now. People always assume blondes are dumb, don't they?

Think about Marilyn Monroe. She was the biggest movie star in the world, the most famous movie star in history. But she was a joke too. Just a blonde joke.

And remember Jayne Mansfield? How she played the part of the airhead bimbo in all those '50s (and very sexist) movies like "The Girl Can't Help It." Everyone figured that was the way she was in real life too. She wasn't, but no one cared about the truth. She wound up losing her head (literally) in a car crash, which seems slightly ironic for the woman everyone called a blonde airhead. Well, at least she wasn't a blonde anymore. Ha! Ha!

The list goes on and on.

Farrah Fawcett. A great actress, a great talent. Did you ever see her dramatic performance in "The Burning Bed"? But people remember her as silly Jill from "Charlie's Angels" and the ultimate poster girl with that big blonde hairdo from the '70s.

Jessica Simpson. Loni Anderson. Pamela Anderson. Well, you get the idea. . . .

So I'm here to teach a lesson to all of you men out there. Not all blondes are dumb. Some of us, believe it or not, are just as smart as you. Or, in my case, smarter. A lot smarter.

Ask Walter Issacs, Rick Faris, Tim Hammacher, Joe Delvecchio, and Mike Jacobson about that!

And so now the game goes on.

Except with a difference.

You see, I'm going to change the rules a bit.

Up the ante.

Raise the stakes for you. . . .

And so I've been following my next victim, recording

his every move—waiting for the right moment to move in for the kill.

Enjoy the pictures, Gil!

There was a photo attachment to the email. I opened it and found a series of pictures. They were pictures of me. Me on the way to work. Me going into my apartment. Me at the grocery store. Me walking down the street. And most shocking of all was a picture of me hugging Susan outside a restaurant before she got into a cab.

At the bottom of all these pictures, Claudia Borrell had written:

Looking forward to meeting you in person, Gil. I'm going to show you this time firsthand how much fun blondes can be—although I'm afraid it won't be much fun for you. Walter Issacs, Rick Faris, Tim Hammacher, Mark Jacobson, Joe Delvecchio—and now Gil Malloy. See you real soon!

Part VI

BLONDE ICE

CHAPTER 48

DON'T need police protection," I said to Marilyn. "I can't do my job that way."

"This woman wants to kill you."

"A lot of women have said they want to kill me."

No one laughed. It was a big meeting in Marilyn's office, and everyone was very serious. Marilyn. Stacy. Other editors. Wohlers was there too. Also the *Daily News* attorney, the head of HR, and a public relations person.

"She's stalking you," Marilyn said.

"Okay, she has some pictures."

"Pictures of you doing everything you do all day," Wohlers said. "She put them in the letter to tell us that she's got you in her sights next, Malloy."

"You need police protection, Gil," Stacy said. "We want to make sure you're safe."

Stacy, of all people, was worried about me. I didn't figure she had human compassion for anyone. I guess putting up those big Web traffic numbers like I'd been doing was the key to a girl like Stacy's heart.

In the end, it was the chance to play a role in the killer's eventual capture—and be on the inside of the big story —that convinced me to go along with the police protection plan.

Wohlers laid it all out for us.

"It's not just protection," he said. "It's a stakeout. A trap. And you're the bait. We never knew where she was going to strike before. But now she's made a mistake. She tipped us off that you're her next target. My men will always be around you. Not close enough that she sees them, but close enough to see her if she comes anywhere near you. So, when she does make her move, we'll be there. Then we've got her."

"And what happens to me?"

"We catch her before she does anything to you."

"Ideally."

I looked around the room at everyone waiting for me to say whether I'd cooperate or not.

"How about I just get out of town for a while?" I asked. "The paper could put me up, all expenses paid, at some remote beachside hotel—like in Tahiti or the Caribbean somewhere—until this all blows over. Or what's the situation with the witness protection program these days? That could be fun too. Just disappear into that. New name, new identity, new life—just say goodbye to Gil Malloy forever. Of course, I realize you would all miss me terribly, but . . ."

"Will you help us, Malloy?" Wohlers asked.

"Sure, I'll do it," I said.

But, for the first time, I admitted something to myself at that moment. The quips were just my defense mechanism to cover up what a serious business all this really was. Despite my bravado, there was a part of me that wished I'd never gotten involved so personally in this story. All of the excitement, all the thrill of being part of the big exclusives that I had felt at the beginning—that was gone now. I just wanted the Blonde Ice story to be over. I'd seen enough of Claudia Borrell to know what she was capable of doing.

The stakeout of me would be a tricky one to pull off.

On the one hand, the cops had to make sure I stayed safe. Wohlers, before he left, talked about it with everyone in the room. "This man is sitting out there with a target on his back," he said. "He's depending on us to protect him. And that's what we're going to do. No matter what happens, we need to make certain that Gil Malloy is not killed, that Gil Malloy is not hurt, that Gil Malloy doesn't even get a scratch out of all this."

I was sure all aboard with that concept.

On the other hand, they couldn't let Borrell know they were protecting me. They had to stay back, out of sight, until she made her move. Then they'd swoop in before she could claim another victim. That was the plan, Wohlers said, and he expressed great confidence that it would work. It sure sounded like a good plan. But, as that great philosopher Mike Tyson used to say, "Everyone's got a plan until they get punched in the face."

The basics were that a team of cops would be tailing me at all times. At home. At work. On the street, in restaurants. Whatever I did during the day or night, there would be cops watching and protecting me from Borrell. It wasn't like she was a sniper pinpointing a target afar from a window or passing car. This woman worked up close. Lured her targets somewhere else to kill them. That's what she'd done with all of her victims. Only this time they'd be ready for her.

At least I hoped they would be.

Wohlers was certainly taking no chances though. He had double teams of detectives and cops assigned to me at all times. One primary team, plus a backup team in case anything went wrong with the primary squad. No way they could miss her, I told myself. Not a chick that looked like that.

There was plenty more security too. They even decided to put listening equipment in my apartment in case anything happened there while I was out of their sight.

"They'll hear everything that goes on in my apartment?" I said when they told me about that.

"Everything," Wohlers said.

"Even in the bedroom?"

"Yes."

"What if I take a girl home and you know, get lucky . . ."

"Then we'll hear that too."

"Wow, I always said that if those walls could ever talk . . ."

"They'd probably yawn," Wohlers grunted.

But, like I said, the quips were just my defense mechanism—maybe they were Wohlers's too—to cover up how serious of a business this all was. Sure, we were acting like it was a game. Except we both knew it was no game.

No matter how many precautions everyone took, I wouldn't rest easy until Claudia Borrell was finally in custody.

CHAPTER 49

THINK I know how she overpowered her victims," Susan said.

We were sitting in her office at the district attorney's building in Foley Square. All the awards and plaques honoring her were still up on her desk and the wall behind her. But I noticed that the picture of her ex-husband Dan or Dale or whatever was now gone. There was a big space on the desk where it had been sitting. I took this as a good sign for me. Of course, it would have been better if she'd had a big picture of Gil Malloy there. I thought about suggesting that to her, but decided it might be a tad pushy.

"Karate or some other kind of martial arts?" I asked.

She shook her head no.

"It's gotta be more than that. Even if she were an expert in martial arts, she couldn't be sure she'd overpower every man she chose as one of her victims. Most of them were pretty big and in relatively good shape. Plus, any of them could have been into judo or some other kind of fighting thing too. She couldn't depend on that. So I started going through all of the possible alternative scenarios she might have used to gain control over them. Kinky sex. A gun, even though she never used one that we're aware of. Even hypnosis. But, in the end, there was only one thing that made sense. She drugged them."

Susan picked up a computer printout from her desk and

handed it to me. There was data from a lot of medical websites. The title at the top of the page said: "Date Rape Drugs."

"We always hear about date rape drugs," Susan said. "It's usually men using them against women. A guy slips one into a woman's drink. The date rape drug knocks her out, makes her vulnerable to be raped while she's in that condition. Sometimes she might not even remember what happened afterward. That's how powerful these drugs are.

"There are three different date rape drugs that are the most common. Rohypnol. GHB. And Ketamine. There's street names for them too. Liquid Ecstasy. Trip and Fall. Roofies. Mind Erasers. Super Acid. Psychedelic Heroin.

"All of these drugs are very powerful. They knock you out quickly without you even realizing what happened. Alcohol makes them even stronger. So putting them in someone's drink is the most efficient way of delivering the drug.

"Once a victim was drugged, he would become weak and confused. Even if he were aware of what was happening, he'd be unable to defend himself. After she gave them that date rape drug, she would definitely be able to gain control of the victims."

I scanned the document quickly.

"Except there was no sign of any drugs in the systems of the victims," I pointed out. "They checked that during the autopsies."

"That's another thing about these drugs," Susan said. "They disappear from the body very quickly. As quickly as a few hours. At most, twelve hours from the time the drug is given to the victim. She held all of these men for hours after she took control of them—and the police found them. Starting with spending the night with Walter Issacs's body in the hotel room. Any date rape drug wouldn't show up in blood or tissue samples from the autopsies."

"So you can't be sure about the date rape drug theory?"

"There was alcohol found in the systems of all of the men," she said. "And alcohol is the most likely way she would have given the date rape drug to them."

"Still, that's not proof. Most guys have a drink when they're out trying to bed a woman like this."

"Ah, but there's something else. Even though the date rape drug leaves the body within a few hours, it does remain longer in the victim's urine."

"So do we have any of the victims' urine?"

"Tim Hammacher."

I suddenly understood where she was going. "He pissed his pants."

"That's right. I asked the lab people to check the urine stains on his underwear, which was still being kept in the evidence storage area. Guess what they found? A trace of Rohypnol, one of the date rape drugs. And Borrell was posing as a shrink. She probably had some knowledge of different kinds of drugs and access to them. It wouldn't have been hard for her to obtain Rohypnol, drop it into the drinks of her victims once they got back to the hotel room or wherever she did it—and then, when the man lost consciousness, she'd tie him up so he couldn't get away."

I looked down again at the computer printouts in front of me. Rohypnol. A date rape drug. Damn.

"I think you've done it," I said.

"We've done it."

"Because we're a team?"

"Like you said before. Nick and Nora Charles. Hart to Hart. Remington Steele. You and me."

"You know, I always heard that those couples celebrated finding a break in a big case like this by having wild, passionate sex together."

"They didn't have sex on TV or in the movies back then."

"Well, we would be breaking new ground here then."

"Give it some time, Gil."

I handed the computer printout back to her. The open space where her husband's picture had been was still there. It took away from the otherwise overall impeccable décor of the office. She really needed to do something about that.

"Would you like a four-by-six or an eight-by-ten glossy print?" I asked.

"Of what?"

"Me."

I pointed to the empty space on her desk.

"I'll give you a picture of myself to replace the one you used to have there of Duane."

"Dale."

"Right, him."

"Why would I want to stare at a picture of you all day while I'm at work?"

"To bask in the memory of the sensual pleasures we enjoyed in the bedroom the night before."

Susan sighed.

"Like I said, Gil, let's just give it all some time."

Then we went off to tell the cops that we'd figured out how Blonde Ice was able to subdue her victims.

CHAPTER 50

G OD, I hate stakeouts," Wohlers said. "They're boring."

We were sitting in Wohlers's unmarked police car outside my building. I'd been inside the car with him there for a few hours. I'd had a big day at the office—filing the latest Blonde Ice story, talking about it on TV, and then doing interviews with other media. But, when I got home, I was still revved up from all the adrenaline and didn't want to just sit up there alone in my apartment. I knew Wohlers was part of the evening-shift stakeout outside my building, so I went down and joined him undercover. Nothing like being part of a police stakeout team for yourself.

Wohlers belched softly. He'd gone out for food twice so far, while I stayed in the car with the rest of the stakeout team. The first time was for a few slices of pizza, and that hadn't been too bad. But the last time he'd gone to a McDonald's and brought back a box of cheeseburgers—figuring he and the rest of us could share them. But we ate only a couple, leaving the rest for Wohlers. He'd littered the floor of the car with the yellow burger wrappers. He'd also had too much coffee, which necessitated several bathroom runs.

"Being on a stakeout alone is the worst," he said. "You can't get anything to eat. You can't get anything to drink. You can't go to the bathroom. You can't shut your eyes for even a second. You can't leave your stakeout post for anything. My old partner used to talk about the worst stakeout he was ever on. Watching a house for a murder suspect. After a few hours, he had to go the bathroom. He had only two choices. Go right there in his pants or find a bathroom. He opted for the latter. He'd been sitting in front of that house for seven hours. He was gone for maybe five minutes, tops. But that was the five minutes when the guy showed up. And he wasn't there, he missed him."

"What did he do?"

"He went out and caught the guy."

"No, I mean what did he do about the blown stakeout?"

"That's what I mean too. He spent the next forty-eight hours searching everywhere for this guy. Didn't eat. Didn't sleep. Finally tracked him down to a motel on the West Side, broke the door down while he was sleeping and got handcuffs on the guy. Brought him back to the precinct. That's when he finally told everyone what happened on the stakeout. Not before. I remember him telling me, 'No way I was going back without that guy in custody. No way I was going to live with that for the rest of my career. I didn't want to be known as the cop who let a suspect get away because he was taking a crap.'"

Wohlers reached into the backseat for the empty pizza box. There were still a few crusts and tiny bits of cheese stuck to the cardboard. He eyed them hungrily.

"There's something wrong here," I said to him.

"What do you mean?"

"Why would Borrell tell us in advance who she had targeted as her next victim?"

"She made a mistake."

"She never made that mistake before."

"Okay, if Borrell didn't make a mistake telling us you would be her next target, then why did she do it?"

"I don't know. But it just seems too easy. She tells us who she's coming after. Me. She never did that before. Why change the pattern? Or did she change the pattern? The pattern of this woman has always been to do the unexpected. Like with Melissa Ross. Or with the doctor, Kate Lyon. And even back when she was a teen-ager . . . she just walked into the police station and confessed. Why? Because she knew she could escape. It was all part of her plan. So what's her plan now?"

Wohlers shrugged and scraped some of the cheese off the pizza box and licked it with his finger. He asked me if I wanted any of that or the leftover remains of the crust. I politely declined.

"So what exactly is it that you think is wrong?" he asked me again.

"I don't know. I just have this bad feeling. Like we're missing something. Like she's still playing a game with us. A game where she makes all of the rules and we don't even know what they are."

"We know now who she is and how she managed to immobilize her men victims. That's something."

"There's still too much we don't know. Stuff that doesn't make any sense."

A woman got out of a cab in front of my apartment house now. She had blonde hair and looked attractive. We both sat up straight and stared at her. It was difficult to tell much in the dark.

"We got something here," Wohlers said into the police radio. "Woman getting out of a cab in front of the building."

"Description?"

"Can't tell yet."

"But she could be the suspect?"

"Could be, if . . ."

Suddenly another door of the cab opened. A man got out, along with two small children. They all walked together up to the front door of the building, where the doorman gave them a big greeting. He obviously knew who they were. The lights of the building were on the family now, and we could see the woman clearly.

It wasn't Claudia Borrell.

"What's going on?" a voice on the police radio crackled.

"Nothing, we're good here," Wohlers replied.

"Not her?"

"Not her."

Wohlers reached over now and rummaged around through some of the empty McDonald's wrappers on the floor of the car to see if there was anything left to eat. There wasn't. All he could find was some cold coffee. He grimaced, took a big gulp, and then belched loudly.

"God, I hate stakeouts," Wohlers said. "They're so boring."

CHAPTER 51

WAS sitting at my desk in the newsroom when the call came.

"I've got him," Claudia Borrell said on the other end.

"Who?"

"I've got him," she repeated.

"Well, this is Malloy you're talking to and you don't have me."

She laughed loudly.

"Oh, I never wanted you, Gil. I just needed you to get my message out through the media. As long as you keep doing that so well, I won't harm a hair on your pretty little head. I must say, though, I got a real kick out of that police stakeout contingent they put up around you. But, you see, they were watching the wrong person. Did you really think I was going to walk into a police trap? Did you actually think I was that stupid?"

"Who do you have?" I asked.

"Bob Wylie."

Wylie. Of course. He was the one constant in all of this. The picture and warning to me were just more misdirection on her part. Wylie had been her next target all along. Somehow this was all about Wylie.

"How do I know you're telling the truth?"

"I'll let Wylie tell you himself." There was a brief pause on the line. Then another voice came on. Faint. Weak. It was difficult for me to hear at first. But, when I did, I realized that it was definitely Bob Wylie.

"Help me," he said in a pleading voice. "Help me."

Borrell came back on the line.

"Convinced?" she asked.

"Yes," I said, wondering what she had done to him but afraid to ask.

"I will call back later," Borrell said. "And when I call back, I want whoever is in charge of law enforcement to be there with you. Also, that fat cop, Wohlers. Plus the people shooting that TV show you're on. And, of course, I want you, Gil. Then I'll tell all of you my demands."

"Demands? Is this about money?"

"No, this about something far more important than money. It's about Wylie finally paying the price for things he did a long time ago."

"Do you mean Munson Lake?"

She laughed loudly. "Munson Lake was Melissa's grudge against Wylie, not mine. He was with her mother that night, you know. He left her to die in the water. Melissa was angry at Wylie when she found out. I convinced Melissa that I would help her get revenge against Wylie and against a lot of other men too. We would be a team. A devastating team against the men who had hurt women like her and me."

"She helped you with the first killing, didn't she?"

"Actually she didn't know it was going to be a killing."

"And when she found out what you did, she wanted out. Maybe threatened to go to the police. She wanted no part of murder. And so you killed her. Then you drove her body all the way to Munson Lake in Ohio. The same lake where her mother died."

"I thought it was such a nice touch—a perfect bit of symmetry—to have Melissa's body found the same way as her mother's body had been found years ago in that lake. I like things to be perfect, Gil. I guess I'm kind of compulsive that way."

"I still don't understand," I said. "Why do you care so much about what Wylie did at Munson Lake? You said that was Melissa's grudge against him, not yours."

"Let's just say I have my own score to settle with Bob Wylie."

"From back in Belleville when you met Wylie at the police station?"

"I vowed then that one day Wylie would pay for what he did to me, and now I will finally get my revenge."

I tried to ask her what it was that Wylie had done to her, but she had already hung up.

——

By the time Borrell called back, my desk was surrounded by people. Police Commissioner Eaton was there. So were Wohlers, Marilyn, and Stacy. Along with lots of other law enforcement officers and *Daily News* execs and TV people from *Live from New York*.

The cops had rigged my phone again to try to track Borrell's call when it came in. Eaton had an entire team of technicians there in hopes of getting some kind of location where she was holding Wylie.

I pointed out that they were probably wasting their time. "She made a big point of telling me she's not stupid. And she's not. She won't give anything away that she doesn't want us to know about."

"All you need to do is hold her on the phone long enough so that maybe we can at least pinpoint her general location," Eaton said.

The phone rang. I picked it up and nodded to everyone. It was Borrell again. I put the call on speaker.

"Is the whole gang there?" Borrell asked.

"This is Police Commissioner William Eaton. I am now in charge here. And I'm warning you that we will hold you personally responsible for Deputy Mayor Wylie's safety. We demand you release him immediately. It will be easier for you if you do as exactly as I say."

"No, Police Commissioner William Eaton," Borrell said, laying on the sarcasm as she repeated the title he'd just given her. "You better do exactly as *I* say. That is, if you ever want to see Wylie alive again."

"How do we know for sure you have him?"

"Can you find him?"

"No."

"That's because he's here with me."

"Where's here?"

"In due time, Commissioner."

"Let us talk to him," Eaton said.

"He already talked to my friend Gil."

"So put him on the phone again."

"I don't think that's possible," she laughed. "He's kind of, well . . . unconscious at the moment."

"What do you want us to do?" Wohlers asked.

"Ah, finally a reasonable question. I like that. The practical and straightforward approach."

"What do you want?" Wohlers repeated.

"I want to do a TV show."

"Is that why you asked for the people from *Live from New York* to be here?" Stacy asked.

"Exactly. You do live breaking stories that are being covered by the *Daily News* on the show. Well, I'm going to give you your biggest story ever. And it will all be happening live on the air. With me and Bob Wylie as the stars."

"How's that exactly going to work?" Stacy asked.

"I want you to bring a TV camera to where Wylie and I are now," she said. "And then we will put on a live performance for

Live from New York. Send a reporter to interview him. But no one is getting in here except the reporter and someone with the camera to televise it. If I see a cop, I'll kill Wylie. You already know that I'm capable of that, don't you? Send a TV camera here, let me broadcast something on *Live from New York*—and I'll let Wylie go. That's all I want."

No one said anything right away.

"Oh, one more thing," Borrell said. "I want Gil Malloy here. Gil needs to be the reporter asking the questions. I insist on that. That's a nonnegotiable demand. He has been such a big part of this since it started. He really should be here to see how it all ends."

"What's the location?" Eaton asked.

"I'll get back to you on that," she said, and then the line went dead again.

———

"How the hell could she have snatched Wylie?" Eaton asked.

"This woman is brilliant," I said. "She can do pretty much anything she wants to do."

"What are you, president of her fan club?" he snapped.

"No, he's just telling the truth," Wohlers said. "Which is what we all need to do. She's got Wylie. How she got him doesn't really matter at this point. We need to figure out what to do next to save him."

"Well, we're not sending a goddamned TV show in there just so she can become famous," Eaton said.

"Why not?" Marilyn asked.

"This isn't about the media," Eaton told her. "This is about a law enforcement operation now. You're not a part of this."

"Yes, I am," Marilyn said. "She specifically asked for my reporter to interview her on TV. Like it or not, she's setting the agenda—not you."

Eaton looked like he was about to explode. He was a bureaucrat, not an experienced street cop like Wohlers. He was in over his head here. He'd never handled an operation like this before, and it was a helluva time to start.

"I think we should do the TV show with her," Wohlers said.

"Why?" Eaton asked.

"Maybe we save Wylie's life."

"Do you really think she won't kill him no matter what we do?" Eaton asked.

"I don't know, but it's our best chance to try to save him."

There were nods from all around.

"I say we send a TV cameraman in with Malloy to shoot the whole interview like she wants," Wohlers continued. "Only the cameraman won't really be a TV guy. He'll be a cop. Once they're in, he assesses the situation. Then he does whatever he can do—whatever he thinks is the right move—to try to end this."

Eaton nodded glumly. He still didn't like the idea. But he had no alternative.

"Okay," he said. "Who goes in?"

"I will," Wohlers said.

I shook my head no. "Lieutenant, you can't. She knows what you look like. She talked about it on the phone. Besides, it can't just be any cop. It has to be a cop that has some knowledge of TV equipment so that he can convince Borrell he's for real. Someone who has a general working knowledge about how a TV show works. But is tough enough to do whatever has to be done. I think I know the perfect guy."

"Vincent D'Nolfo," Wohlers blurted out before I could say the name.

"Right."

"Is he a cop?" Eaton wanted to know.

"He is now," I said.

I explained to him about D'Nolfo's background on Abbie Kincaid's show and how he had just graduated from the police academy.

"A recruit? I don't know. You realize that your life may well rest in this guy's hands once you're in there. Are you comfortable with this D'Nolfo?"

"I can't think of anyone I'd trust more," I said.

———

Now all we could do was wait until Claudia Borrell called back with the location.

The cops were ready to descend on the spot and position themselves outside while the drama on live TV played out. D'Nolfo was ready too. The TV people had given him a quick course in handling a TV camera, but he pretty much knew how to do that from his days with Abbie.

D'Nolfo would have a gun hidden deep in the bag of television equipment he'd be carrying. That would make it harder for him to get at the weapon, but also more difficult for Borrell to find the gun if she did any kind of search when we got there. Our big dilemma was that we had no idea what kind of situation we were walking into.

"She's got to have something wherever she is to protect her when you go in, something that gives her the upper hand," Wohlers said. "We just won't know what that is until you get in there."

"A gun?" Eaton said.

"She's never used a gun yet."

"I think she'll somehow use Wylie as a hostage," D'Nolfo said. "Set it up so there's no way we can get at her without putting him in danger. That's got to be the plan of action she's working under."

"So what do we do?" I asked.

"Wait for our chance," D'Nolfo said. "And, when it comes, I'll kill her."

More nods all around.

"Any other questions?" Eaton asked.

"I have one," I said. "How does she plan to get out? If this woman is so smart, why is she doing this? She has to realize the entire New York City police force will be outside waiting to take their best shot at her when this is over. What's her exit strategy? What's the end game for her?"

"Maybe it's a suicide strategy," Eaton said. "Maybe she has no exit plan."

I shook my head no. "She always has a plan. She boasts about how she's always one step ahead of us because she's so smart. So what's her plan here?"

No one had any answer for that.

She called back a short time after that. She still wouldn't tell us right off where she was. She wanted to know first if all of her demands had been met for the live TV broadcast. We explained the details to her. She asked some more questions, and we were able to give the right answers to satisfy her.

"Where are you with Wylie?" I asked finally.

"Funny you should ask that," Borrell laughed.

Suddenly one of the police tech team members frantically signaled to Eaton and Wohlers.

"We just pinpointed her location," he said.

"Where is she?" Wohlers asked.

"The address is 25 Waterview Terrace."

"That's Wylie's address," someone said.

"Jesus Christ," Eaton said, "she's inside Wylie's apartment!"

CHAPTER 52

CLAUDIA Borrell was waiting for us when we got to Wylie's apartment.

With a gun in her hand.

"I know what you're thinking," she said. "This woman never uses a gun. Except, as you can see, I do have one. You should know by now, I'm not predictable. And no matter how hard you try, you can never keep up with me. Because I'm smarter than any of you."

Wylie lived on the twenty-third floor of a big high-rise along the East River. We were standing in the living room, which had a sweeping view of the water and the Brooklyn skyline on the other side. I had no idea how Borrell found out where Wylie lived. Or how she'd managed to get inside. But, like she told us, she always seemed to be one step ahead of us.

In person, Borrell looked amazing. She was dressed in a tight miniskirt, a low-cut blouse, and high heels—with long blonde hair. Did she pick up Wylie by using sex as a lure like she did with the others? That made no sense at all. Wylie knew what she looked like and who she was. He never would have gone along willingly. She must have drugged him. But how?

"Gil Malloy, what a pleasure to finally meet you," she said. "I've admired you from afar for so long. I imagine you've admired me and my work too, right, Gil?"

"There's nothing to admire about killing innocent people."

"They're only men," Borrell shrugged.

She turned now and looked at D'Nolfo, the gun still pointing at both of us. "Who's this?" she asked.

"He's going to shoot this for *Live from New York*, like you wanted," I said.

"By himself?"

"Sure," D'Nolfo said.

Normally there's a video person and a sound person on a TV crew. But no one wanted to expose any of the TV people to the potential danger, and D'Nolfo said he could handle both jobs. I sure hoped he was right.

"Well, I'm going to have a TV on where we're going and I better see myself on that screen."

There was a pile of clothing lying nearby. Plain-looking clothes. Not the kind of clothes Borrell was wearing now. There was something else on the chair too. A brunette wig.

"Yes, I've been wearing all that," she said, noticing me looking at the wig. "The brunette wig and the drab clothes. Because everyone was looking for a sexy blonde, I had to blend in, not stand out or call attention to myself. So I wore the wig and those clothes. But I hate to look like that. So, as soon as I got here, I changed back into this outfit. I want to look really good. For the TV cameras. This is my big moment. I'm going to be famous now."

So far there was no sign of Bob Wylie.

"Where is he?" I asked.

"Oh, don't worry, Bob will be part of this too."

"Is he alive?"

"Of course. Let's go talk to him."

———

It was a big apartment, with five bedrooms and even a library. Wylie was in the one of the bedrooms—still alive, but barely.

He was tied by all sorts of restraints to a chair in the center of the room. He was hardly recognizable as the dynamic leader I'd seen before. There was blood all over his face and body. Lots of blood. I wasn't sure at first if Wylie was conscious or not. His eyes were open, but they looked dead and unseeing.

Borrell picked up something off a table and held it under Wylie's nose. His eyes jerked open wide now, filled with confusion and terror. Some kind of smelling salts, it seemed. And she definitely must have filled him with drugs. I don't think he even realized D'Nolfo and I were in the room.

D'Nolfo set up the video equipment and began shooting. As Borrell said, she had a TV set in there that she turned on. Sure enough, there we were in a few minutes broadcasting live to millions of people on *Live from New York*. So far, so good.

"It's showtime," Borrell said to Wylie in a taunting voice.

Wylie just nodded his head.

"Now you can interview him for the show," Borrell said to me.

"Interview him about what?"

"Why not start with Munson Lake?" she said. "Let's let him tell you what really happened at Munson Lake. I think the whole audience out there should know the kind of man he really is."

Then Wylie—slowly, almost mechanically—told the story of the long-ago date with Patty Tagliarini. Borrell had clearly drugged him and prepared him to do this bizarre presentation for the camera.

It was pretty much the same as I had already figured out. He took Patty Tagliarini to a place near Munson Lake, a good drive away from his hometown of Massillon, so that no one would recognize them and get word back to his girlfriend, Valerie. They ate, they danced, and then Tagliarini had a bottle that they shared while making out in her car. They both had too much to drink. On the way back, she lost control of the car and rolled down a hill into the lake.

"You were both able to get out of the car?" I asked Wylie, trying desperately to act as if this was a normal interview, even though I kept thinking about when D'Nolfo was going to go for his gun.

"Yes."

"What happened then?"

"I was underwater. I didn't think I'd make it to the surface."

"But you did. . . ."

Wylie nodded.

"What about Patty Tagliarini?"

"I heard her screaming for help."

"What did you do?"

"I wanted to save her. I really did."

"But that's when you saw a man in boat approaching, right?"

"He was just a short distance away."

"And you couldn't let him find out you were with Patty Tagliarini."

"I thought he'd save her."

"But he didn't make it to her in time."

"No, she couldn't swim."

"She drowned before he could get to her?"

"I didn't want her to die. . . . I didn't think she was going to die. . . . If I'd known, I would have . . . I would have . . ."

His voice had a pleading quality to it now.

"Patty Tagliarini left behind a one-year-old daughter," Borrell said. "Named Melissa. Melissa was given up for adoption after her mother died. Eventually, she grew up to be a private investigator. And one day she decided to investigate who her biological parents were and why she'd been adopted. So she went back to Ohio and to Munson Lake. She talked to everyone there who still remembered what happened. Kept digging until she finally figured out that Wylie had been with her mother that night. Now everyone will know the truth. Do you think people will still elect him mayor now? I don't. I think they'll see him now for the coward he really is."

Wylie seemed to be fading in and out of consciousness again. Moaning from pain and making unintelligible sounds.

"But why do you hate Wylie so much?" I asked. "That doesn't make sense. Melissa Ross, I guess I could understand because of what happened with her mother at Munson Lake. But you only met him once, for a very short time sixteen years ago, when you were still a teenager back in Belleville."

"Do you know what he did to me that day in Belleville?" she said as the cameras continued to roll.

She looked over at Wylie slumped down in the chair now.

"He laughed at me. He humiliated me. He rejected me. This was supposed to be my great victory day. I had killed my family, killed Bobby Jenkins, and now—after telling the police all that—I was going to walk out of their police station as my final moment of triumph. I knew I could do that because they were all men, and I could always get men to do what I wanted.

"It was all going according to plan until they brought Wylie in to talk to me. He was so arrogant, so full of himself. But he was a man, so I knew how to handle him. I flirted shamelessly with him after he came into the interrogation room. I unbuttoned the top of my blouse so he could get a glimpse of my breasts. I kept crossing and uncrossing my legs to give him a good show. Then I reached over, touched him, and moved closer to him. I whispered that he could have me if he wanted. I did all the things I've always done with men to get them to do what I want, to get them under my control. But nothing worked. Finally, I just leaned over the table where we were sitting and kissed him on the lips. That's when it happened. The moment that sealed his fate forever."

"What did he do?"

"He spit in my face. He just pulled away from me in surprise and then spit in my face. Like he was disgusted to touch me. Me? I mean look at me. I just sat there with his spittle dribbling down my face. He wouldn't even let me wipe it off. He just kept laughing at me and the way I looked with that spit all over my beautiful face. He brought in some of the guards and other people in the station and they all laughed at me too.

"Then he told me that I was nothing—just a silly little girl—and how much smarter than me he was. He boasted all about his future and how he was headed for big things—and that I was going to help him do that with all the publicity he'd get from me and how I killed my family. He said I was going to be his ticket to fame and fortune—and that I would rot away in prison for the rest of my life. I could still feel his spit all over my face. I was so humiliated. No one had ever talked to me like that. No one had ever laughed at me before. No man had ever rejected me until him. And that's when I vowed that I would get my revenge against Bob Wylie."

I looked over at D'Nolfo. He was still manning the TV equipment as if this was just another normal video. I knew he had to look like he was only doing his job, to avoid tipping off Borrell that anything was wrong. But it still seemed bizarre. When was D'Nolfo going to make a move against her?

"Why did you wait so long?" I asked, just trying to keep her talking.

"Oh, I got my first revenge a long time ago. Not long after we met. With the fire that killed his family. You see, that fire was no accident. I did that. He was supposed to be there with his wife and children. They were all supposed to die. I thought I'd made sure of that. But Wylie didn't. Just his wife and his family."

There was a sobbing. It was coming from Wylie. He was crying as she talked about the fire that killed his family.

"When I read in the newspapers and heard on TV about all the pain and suffering I'd caused Wylie by losing his family in that fire, I decided that I'd ruined his life with a fate worse than death. So I moved on. And I forgot about Bob Wylie and that day in Belleville. Or almost forgot about him.

"Then one day I saw his picture on the cover of *Time* magazine. I realized then that I hadn't destroyed his life at all. He was even more important now, just like he'd bragged to me he was going to be back in Belleville. I was so angry. I could have just killed him, of course. Like I did his family. But that would have been too easy. No, I wanted more. I wanted to dismantle his life. To take away everything that was important to him. I'd started that with his family. The next thing would be his future, the future greatness he boasted to me about.

"But I waited. I waited patiently for the right moment. I came to New York and began stalking his every move. Following him at public events and appearances. That's when I first saw him with that woman, Victoria Issacs. I watched him coming on to her at a big concert in Central Park. Then I trailed both of them back to his apartment. I couldn't understand it. He wasn't interested in me, but he was interested in this woman? That made me so mad at both of them. I watched her come and go from other meetings at his apartment. I began to become obsessed with her too. I followed her to Philadelphia one day, where she went to see the psychiatrist Kate Lyon. I managed to get a job with Lyon after that and read all of her files. That's how I found out about Houston and all the rest. I killed Lyon and moved to New York. Still waiting for the right moment to get my revenge against Wylie. And now I wanted revenge against Houston too because he had picked her over me. But I still waited for just the right moment to act."

"Then you heard about Wylie's candidacy for mayor," I said. She nodded.

"I wanted him to get close. So tantalizingly close to his dreams.

Then I would take it all away from him. Strip him of everything. His power. His reputation. His dignity. And now," she said, gesturing toward the commissioner, "it will all be on television for everyone to see.

"I believe that all of these things—Melissa Ross, Houston, Wylie and the election, even you, Gil—came together for me at this moment for a reason. Like a series of seemingly random entities moving through the eddies of the universe until they joined in a confluence of fate and destiny and divine intervention to bring us to this very place today.

"Wylie thought he was smarter than me. He thought Houston was more beautiful than me. Now everyone will know who is the smartest and the most beautiful. Everyone will know who Claudia Borrell is. I'm going to be the greatest serial killer of all time. And a woman serial killer too. Just one more thing that women can do better than men."

It was a preposterous motive for murder.

But then so was the killing of her family for no reason.

She was a psychopath—a dangerous, brilliant psychopath—who somehow got off on the idea of killing.

"If you're so smart, what happens now?" I asked. "You're trapped. No matter what you do, there's no way out for you. I might have thought someone as smart as you say you are would have taken that little fact into consideration before you pulled this whole stunt for the TV cameras. All for your silly little game."

"You really don't understand, do you? The game's over, Gil."

She turned and pointed the gun at Bob Wylie's head.

I knew D'Nolfo had to make his move now. I wasn't sure how he was going to do it. But he had to take the chance. And then something unexpected happened.

"Hello in there," someone outside the front door was saying

now. "This is Lieutenant Frank Wohlers. We have a hostage nego-
tiator here. We can talk about this. We . . ."

Borrell's head swiveled around in surprise. For just a second,
she was startled.

D'Nolfo had his opening, and he took it. He went for his gun.
Reached into the bag of equipment for it. Borrell turned her head
back at that moment. She saw the gun in D'Nolfo's hand and
fired. She was in a hurry though. The shot hit him in the right arm
and knocked the gun out of his hand. His gun clattered noisily to
the floor. I watched it skitter across the floor next to where I was
standing.

Reacting instinctively, I picked up the gun. In that blink of a
moment, I could hear D'Nolfo's voice in my head that day on the
gun range when he tried to teach me how to shoot: Aim. Steady.
Squeeze. I fired at Borrell. I wasn't sure whether or not I hit her.
But—either from the force of the blast or maybe just the shock of
being shot at by me—Borrell fell backward against a door of the
room. She somehow quickly got to her feet and tried to get out
the door.

I fired the gun again. Emptied it at the fleeing woman. Some of
the bullets hit the wall and the door, sending pieces of wood and
plaster flying around the room. But Borrell made it out the door
into another part of the apartment.

Suddenly the front door burst open and Wohlers and SWAT
team members were there. I pointed toward the direction where
Borrell had gone. The cops went after her, their guns drawn and
ready to finish the job. One of the bedroom doors was locked. She
had to be in there. They began smashing it down.

Wohlers stopped briefly to make sure D'Nolfo was all right.
He was holding his arm, but gave a thumbs-up sign. Wohlers then
raced into the next room, to be there when they finally caught
Borrell.

I ran after the cops to see what had happened. It was my story. No matter what, I had to get the story.

The cops were still banging on the locked door of the room.

But, when they finally burst their way in, the bedroom was empty.

Claudia Borrell wasn't there.

Just broken glass.

And an open window.

"It looks like she broke the window and jumped," one of the cops said.

"Damn," Wohlers said.

"At least she's dead," someone said.

"I just hope it was a painful death for her," Wohlers said, as he looked down at the water far below, where she had plummeted.

CHAPTER 53

I T was chaos inside the apartment. Cops everywhere. Guns drawn, but without anyone to shoot. Medical people there. Everyone trying to sort out everything that had just happened, not quite really believing yet that it was finally all over.

Wohlers and I knelt at D'Nolfo's side. There was blood coming from his shoulder, but he was conscious and alert.

"How does it look?" Wohlers asked the medic working on him.

"Not too bad," the medic replied as he worked. "Clean wound. Just hit the fleshy part of the shoulder. No bones, no organs involved. He's going to make it, Lieutenant."

There was a stretcher there now. The EMS guys lifted D'Nolfo gently onto it. One of them kept pressing on his wound to stop the bleeding.

"You take good care of this guy," Wohlers said. "He's a cop."

I reached down to clasp D'Nolfo's good hand. He squeezed it tightly. "We got her, Vincent."

D'Nolfo smiled weakly.

Another team of medical people was working on Wylie. Trying to determine how much damage had been done to him, how many injuries he'd suffered and the extent of those injuries. He was conscious too, but just barely. He had a blank, vacant stare in his eyes. They were open, but not really looking at anything.

"He's lost a lot of blood," one of the medical people said, looking down at the red stains that covered the floor underneath him. "We'll need transfusions right away. Not sure about the nature and extent of all the injuries yet. There's a lot of bruises and scars all over his body. They look pretty severe."

Once D'Nolfo and Wylie were in proper care, Wohlers went into the other bedroom where cops combed through the broken glass and the blood on the floor looking for evidence.

One of them talked to us about Borrell. "It looks like she made it into this room and then locked the door. Realized she had no way out and jumped out the window to make sure she died. She landed in the East River down there. Splashed down right next to a Circle Liner boat filled with tourists. Welcome to New York, huh?"

"And she's definitely dead?" Wohlers asked.

"No one survives a twenty-three-floor fall, Lieutenant."

———

Most of it had been broadcast live on TV. The dramatic confrontation when we first went into the apartment and met Borrell. Wylie talking about Patty Tagliarini and Munson Lake. Him crying and pleading. Then her turning the gun on him before D'Nolfo made his move. Even some of what happened afterward was captured, since D'Nolfo's video equipment was still running. There was screaming, sounds of shots—it was pretty amazing TV. That video would be broadcast later on every network and local news station, would go viral on social media, and later could still be clicked on in countless variations on YouTube.

Stacy Albright was there to direct everything at the scene immediately afterward. This was the high point of her career. She was the one who came up with the idea of the *Daily News* appearing on *Live from New York*, and now it had paid off big-time. Forget about the print editions, this was live TV and social media happening in real time. And, along with me, she was the one who would get all the credit for it.

Her plan now was for me to get right back on *Live from New York* and do a remote update from the scene outside the building, where Claudia Borrell's body had gone into the East River.

"Just tell your story when we get on the air. Exactly the way it happened. Don't leave anything out. Your fears, your emotions. Everything you did. Everything you can remember."

A few minutes later, *Live from New York* went to a special bulletin. Followed by a camera shot outside Wylie's building. Then a live picture of me standing at the spot on the East River where the killer fell to her death.

I began to talk:

"I'm standing here outside Deputy Mayor Bob Wylie's apartment house, where the Blonde Ice case today played out to a bloody and shocking conclusion. Wylie is in critical condition, but expected to survive, and a heroic police officer is wounded. But Claudia Borrell, the infamous woman serial killer, is finally dead.

"Here's what happened. . . ."

They found Claudia Borrell's body a few days later when it washed up near a Brooklyn pier. The obvious conclusion was that she was cornered with no way out and decided to commit suicide rather than be captured alive. It was pretty cut-and-dried. The twenty-three-floor fall into the water had done a lot of damage to her. Sea life had eaten away at much of her too before the body was recovered. You could tell from the remains they pulled out of the water that she was a woman and a blonde and that she'd probably been in her thirties. But that was about all.

Not that there was any doubt, but the authorities double-checked everything to make sure the body really was Claudia Borrell's.

They were able to get dental records of her teeth as a teenager in

Belleville to compare with the corpse. The same with fingerprints. They were still on file in Illinois from when she'd been arrested there. Everything came back a perfect match.

It was finally over, and cops could close the books on a serial murder case that had stretched over two decades and through countless cities and states.

In the days afterward, investigators filled in the missing pieces of the Claudia Borrell puzzle.

They found a room key she left behind in Wylie's apartment, for a hotel on the West Side. That was where she had apparently been hiding after her cover as Kate Lyon was blown. In the room, there were scrapbooks filled with newspaper clippings. All of them were about Bob Wylie. Covering his rise to fame and power and glory over the years. His days in St. Louis as police commissioner. His move to New York to set up a security consulting firm. His appointment as deputy mayor of New York City. And—most prominently of all—the picture of him on the cover of *Time* magazine that she said had convinced her to begin stalking him. She had the magazine cover posted on a wall. Along with all the more recent stories about him being the favorite candidate in the race for mayor.

She had clearly been obsessed with Wylie for a long time. Waiting for the right moment. And, for her, that moment had come at the confrontation she had orchestrated in front of TV cameras inside Wylie's apartment.

One of the doormen from Wylie's apartment was missing. They found his body stuffed inside an air-conditioning shaft in the basement. The working theory was that Borrell had flirted with him, seduced him, lured him down to the basement with the promise of sex, and then killed him so she could steal a key and get up to Wylie's apartment.

Then she must have confronted Wylie with the gun when he came home. Subdued him at first that way, tied him up, and then given him enough drugs to keep him totally under her control while she tortured him the way she had her other victims. It was all academic now, of course. The authorities were just filling in the blanks, connecting the dots to close the case.

In Borrell's hotel room, the closet was filled with her clothes. All of it very sexy stuff. There were low-cut blouses and sweaters. Short skirts. Spiked heels and boots. These were the tools of the trade for this killer—luring her victims into her trap before she killed them.

There was a picture of Melissa Ross in the drawer of a table next to her bed. Melissa was with Borrell in the picture. They were holding hands and kissing. They both looked very beautiful and very happy. There was a notation on the picture that said: "From the top of Rockefeller Center." They must have gone to visit there like any other tourists, and gotten their picture taken at the Top of the Rock. On the back of the picture was a notation. Two of them actually. The first one said: "Melissa and me. I have finally found my true kindred spirit. Someone just like me to share my life with." But that had been hastily crossed out at some point. Underneath it, in a different color ink and apparently written at a later time, a second notation said: "I thought Melissa was just like me. But she's not. There is no one just like me. I am unique. And I am truly alone in this world. I know that now. And so does Melissa."

Even though she was dead, authorities continued the search for something in Claudia Borrell's past that might explain what her motivation had been to kill so many people. But no one could come up with a simple answer. There were stories about the mother and father perhaps pushing her too hard to excel in school because of her genius IQ; about a neighbor who might or might not have molested her at some point when she was growing up and sparked her hatred of men; and about a fascination she had with violent video games that somehow could have had such a profound psychological effect on her that she started killing people for real. But none of it ever gave any hard answers as to why Claudia Borrell did what she did.

The bottom line seemed to be that there was no real motivation for all the horrible crimes she committed. That she was simply—as Danny Jamieson had once described her—"someone who just enjoyed watching people die. And reveling in the power of life and death she held over them. A murderer who killed for no other reason than the satisfaction she got out of it. A true thrill killer."

There was no evidence found—in the hotel room or in Wylie's apartment—of an escape plan for Borrell that day. No indication of how she expected it all to end. The conclusion was that her only goal was revenge on Bob Wylie. Her obsession with destroying Wylie's life had been more important to Borrell than her own life, and she was ready to sacrifice herself for this big final moment.

No one ever got a final body count for Claudia Borrell.

There were certainly the five men in New York. Melissa Ross. Probably Kate Lyon, even though the doctor's body was never found. Her own family. Bobby Jenkins, the kid she went to high school with in Illinois who became her first victim. Wylie's wife and children. Of course, there were likely even a lot more than that that we didn't know about yet.

If Borrell had been determined to show that a woman can be as horrific a serial killer as a man, she had accomplished that goal.

She would go down in history as the most deadly female serial killer ever—one who ranked right up there with Ted Bundy and Richard Speck and Son of Sam and all the others she had compared herself to. Like them, Claudia Borrell would live in infamy forever.

CHAPTER **54**

THERE were many repercussions from the Claudia Borrell story, starting with Bob Wylie.

Wylie recovered from his physical injuries, but his political career was over. That image of him on live TV pleading and crying to the woman who abducted him had left a lasting image with the public that erased any persona of a tough law enforcement official. His poll numbers plummeted, and he pulled out of the race.

The horrific incident seemed to have destroyed Wylie in other ways too. I met him at an event sometime later, and all the swagger, self-confidence, and charisma he'd had before were gone. I never thought he was a bad guy. On the contrary, he did a lot of good things. But he had done one bad thing—a terrible lapse in moral judgment on that long ago night at Munson Lake—that caught up with him in the end.

Claudia Borrell had succeeded in what she had set out to do—destroying the man she held a life-long grudge against, with a punishment maybe even worse than death.

———

Changes were happening at my paper too.

Marilyn Staley stopped by my desk and asked if I wanted to have a drink with her after work. I'd only gone out for drinks with

Marilyn a few times in all the years we'd worked at the *News*. So I figured she had something pretty important to tell me.

"I'm announcing my resignation tomorrow," she said after taking a few sips of wine.

"Why?"

"I see the writing on the wall. It says Stacy Albright. I can't work with her, and she can't work with me. So I need to leave."

"You're better than Stacy."

"As a newspaper editor I am."

"What else is there?"

She laughed. "Oh, Gil, you naive man."

"I'm serious. I've seen you in meetings with Stacy. You usually manage to one-up her. You're still in charge. You're the boss at the *News*, not Stacy."

"I've won some battles with her," Marilyn said. "But I'm losing the war. This business is changing rapidly, in case you hadn't noticed. It's not just about the best front page anymore, the kind of thing you and I do well. It's about new platforms and social media and interaction with the audience. Oh, there'll still be newspapers for the Internet and on tablets and smartphones. But that's not the kind of news I know. So I'm going to walk away. I have an opportunity to do some teaching. Maybe write a book. Spend more time raising my children. It's been a fun ride, but it's over now. Anyway, I wanted you to know before it became public. I figured I owed you that, Gil. After everything you and I have gone through over the years."

I sat there stunned. Marilyn and I were not exactly close friends. And we'd certainly had our differences and battles. But she was my ally at the paper. The one person there I felt comfortable going to for journalistic advice and support and guidance. And now she was leaving. I'd be left with Stacy, which meant there was no one I could trust as a journalist.

"It's something you might want to think about doing too, Gil," Marilyn said to me. "You're a good reporter. Hell, you're a great reporter. Even after you broke a big story, you always had an answer for me when I asked my favorite question: 'What have you got for tomorrow?' You never let me down. But how long are you going to be able to keep doing this job? What's your life going to be like in five years here? Ten years?"

I ordered another round, and we sat there for a long time swapping stories and reliving old memories.

But I couldn't escape the feeling that Marilyn's life wasn't the only one changing; mine was too, whether I wanted it to or not.

———

I met up with Wohlers for breakfast one morning after everything had started to calm down. We went to a diner near his precinct on the East Side. I watched in amazement as he consumed what was described on the menu as the "Hungry Man's Special"—consisting of three eggs, pancakes, toast, hash brown potatoes, bacon, and sausage.

"You think I need to go on a diet?" he asked.

"I never said that."

"My wife did."

Wohlers looked at a piece of bacon on his plate, picked it up, and then put it down—like he was thinking about the idea.

"Could stand to lose a few pounds though, I guess."

"Wouldn't hurt."

Eventually, of course, he snatched the bacon off the plate and popped it into his mouth.

"Some things about the whole Borrell story still don't make sense to me," I said.

"Like what?"

"The whole Melissa Ross connection. Borrell said Ross launched her own investigation to find out what happened to her biological parents. That's how Ross found out about Patty Tagliarini's car crash—and eventually discovered the Wylie connection, presumably from talking to people there just like I did. Then revealed it all to Borrell during one of her shrink sessions. Except there's no evidence Melissa Ross ever was in Ohio. No receipts in her files, no phone calls to Ohio in the months leading up to the murders, no record of any flight or train or bus reservations to Ohio. Nothing at all to indicate she had any connection with Ohio until she turned up dead in the same lake where her biological mother had died."

"Well, Borrell found out somehow," Wohlers said.

"I checked. There was a woman asking questions about the Tagliarini accident in Ohio a while back. I tracked down some people who remember her. She was a blonde woman, they said. An extraordinarily attractive blonde woman. But not Melissa Ross."

"You think it was Claudia Borrell?"

"That makes more sense than the story she told us about Melissa Ross coming to her with the information. All about how the eddies of time and the universe had brought her and Melissa Ross together in this grand design. I mean what are the odds that, to talk about her grudge against Wylie, Ross goes to the one psychiatrist who has her own grudge against Wylie? What makes more sense is Borrell found out the information herself, tracked down Tagliarini's biological daughter, and told Ross about it. Not the other way around."

"But we found Melissa Ross's files in her office."

"She could have faked those files. Knowing we'd find them sooner or later. This woman lied about everything. We can't believe anything she says she did."

Wohlers thought for a while about what I'd just said.

"Assuming you're right," he said finally, "how would Borrell have found Ross was the daughter of the woman Wylie dated in high school?"

"I did. And she's smarter than me."

"Good point."

That's when I brought up the big question I still had about Claudia Borrell.

"Why did she do it? Why did Borrell put herself in a situation like that at the end? Why did she let herself get cornered inside that apartment where there was no possible way out for her?"

"She wanted to go out in a blaze of glory," Wohlers said. "Make her statement on TV, become famous—or infamous—to the world before killing herself. She knew there was no way out for her. She didn't want to go to jail. So she committed suicide. She decided to end it on her terms. She was crazy."

"Crazy yes. But really smart. She was always one step ahead of everybody. That's why I don't understand what happened in Wylie's apartment. I kept waiting for some twist, some unexpected shock plan she was going to spring on us—like she'd always done in the past. But there was nothing. She just died."

"We got lucky," Wohlers said.

"Except nothing about what she did that last day makes sense. Especially the way she killed herself. She jumped out of a window and mangled her body and face in a twenty-three-floor fall. Borrell was extremely vain. She loved the way she looked, flaunted her beauty and sexiness at every occasion she could. Why would she mess herself up like that at the end? Even if she did want to die, wouldn't she plan it out in a different way? I don't think she was the suicidal type anyway. She loved herself too much."

"Maybe she didn't plan it that way. Maybe things just happened the way they did."

"Except things didn't 'just happen' for her. She always had a plan. Except for this time when she needed a plan the most, and there was no plan. Or maybe there was a plan, and we're just missing the plan."

I shook my head in frustration.

"Think about it, Lieutenant. Sixteen years ago in Illinois, she brazenly walked into a police station, gave herself up, and confessed. Why? Because she knew she could escape again anytime she wanted to. Which is exactly what she did. She had a plan. Now she does the same thing again. Brazenly summons us to the deputy mayor's home, confesses, and seemingly lets herself get trapped with no escape. Why? Because she had a plan to get away afterward just like she did in Illinois. That was part of the game for her. To prove that she could get away from us anytime she wanted. She had to have had some kind of goddamned escape plan for this."

"Then it didn't work," Wohlers said. "She underestimated us this time."

"Or maybe we're still underestimating her."

"The bottom line is Claudia Borrell is dead. Case closed."

"Is it?"

Wohlers put his coffee down and stared at me across the table. "What the hell are you saying?"

"How do we really know she's dead?"

"You were in that apartment," he said. "You saw the woman with the gun. That was Claudia Borrell, right?"

"Yes."

"Then she fled into another bedroom, locked the door behind her, and went out the window, right?"

"Maybe."

"Oh, c'mon . . ."

"What if there was another woman in the apartment? A dead woman, someone about Borrell's age and description, and with blonde hair, of course. Maybe someone she picked up, like she did with Melissa Ross or Kate Lyon. She kills the woman before we get there. Then later she throws the body out the window, hides somewhere until—in all of the confusion—she somehow manages to sneak out of the apartment."

"With all of the cops and CSI people and everyone else around?"

"No one was looking for her anymore. They assumed she was dead. Maybe she found some hiding place, or set one up beforehand, where she could wait until everyone was gone. Maybe that was her plan all along. Make us think we had her, while she somehow slips away to kill again someday. That's what the Claudia Borrell in Illinois did. That's the Claudia Borrell we knew too. Not someone who jumps out of a window to commit suicide."

"What about the dental records? The fingerprints?"

"Those were on file in Illinois. What if she switched them somehow? Got into the files and put the dental records and fingerprints of the dead woman there?"

"How would she get those?"

"She was a doctor, remember. Or at least pretended to be one. Maybe the dead woman was one of her patients. Maybe she got the records of this woman a while ago, went to Illinois, and made the switch. We're assuming that everything she did at the end was spontaneous. But what if she planned it? Spent weeks, months setting this up right down to the last detail. Like she did with the other murders. Doesn't that sound a lot more like the Claudia Borrell we knew than the one who conveniently killed herself?"

"This is all just speculation," Wohlers said. "All the evidence says that was Claudia Borrell's body we found in the water."

"Except for one other problem. I think I wounded her, Lieutenant. One of the shots I got off, it looked to me like it hit her, maybe in the shoulder or side. She jerked back against the wall before she ran out of the bedroom. I'm pretty sure she was wounded. Except there were no bullet wounds in the body."

"There's no evidence that you hit her with any of those shots."

"Then that bullet should be in the wall or the floor or somewhere else in that room."

"We dug several bullets out of the wall and floor in there afterward. They were all from D'Nolfo's gun. The ones you fired."

"How many bullets did you find?'

"Christ, I don't know."

"What if you counted the bullets you found? And compared them to how many shots I got off with the gun? And what if one bullet was missing? Wouldn't that mean something?"

Wohlers shrugged. "Bullets go missing at crime scenes all the time. They get lodged into a crevice or behind something and no one ever finds them. Or maybe the number of bullets does match the number of bullets fired from D'Nolfo's gun. Maybe you did hit her, and the bullet just grazed or passed through her—and went into the wall behind her. That's possible too. None of it really proves anything, none of it really matters. No investigation is perfect. But, at some point, you just need to put it behind you and move on to the next case."

"I guess you're probably right," I said.

———

"I keep having this dream," I told Dr. Landis. "I'm in a bar. I spot her the minute she walks into the place. A real knockout. A blonde fox. Wearing tight jeans, a low-cut top, and spike heels that put her on eye level with me. And, best of all, I love the blonde hair. Long yellow hair that cascades over her shoulders, falling loosely down her back.

"She just walks over to me in the crowded bar and starts talking. I buy her a drink. Then another.

" 'I've always loved blondes,' I tell her at one point as the alcohol starts to get to me.

" 'Most men do,' she says.

"Her face keeps changing in the dreams. Sometimes she looks like Houston. Sometimes she looks like Sherry DeConde or other women I went out with in the past. But most of the time her face is the same—Claudia Borrell.

"Then she kisses me. I kiss her back. And all I can think of is getting her into bed. Just the way Hammacher, Houston's husband, and all the rest of her victims might have felt. And I realize at that moment I'm just like them. I didn't survive her because I was better or smarter or better keeping it in my pants than them. I was just lucky. Lucky that she wanted me—needed me—to use as something other than just another victim. But she played me too. Just like she played all men. And that's when I wake up. . . ."

Landis had been taking notes while I talked about the dream. It used to annoy me when she took notes. Not anymore. We'd made a lot of progress together, Dr. Barbara Landis and I.

"This story really got to me," I told her. "In a way that none of the other big stories I worked on ever did. Seeing those victims that I knew or had some connection with this time—Tim Hammacher, Houston's husband, and then Wylie in his apartment at the end—all seemed too real. And I keep thinking about how it could have been me. Maybe the next time it will be me. Maybe I'm pushing my luck too much. I'm nearly forty now, and I think about stuff like that when I didn't before. The rest of my life and what I want to do with it. There's not a lot of old reporters running around the streets, it's really a young person's game. Is all of this really worth it—the danger, the stress, the upheaval of the rest of my life—just for another goddamned front page story? This story has made me consider all of that."

I looked over at Landis now. She had stopped taking notes and was listening intently.

"So what do you think?" I asked.

"Well, the first part is easy," Landis said. "The dream clearly illustrates your anxiety and insecurity and fears about all the things that have happened—and are happening now—in your life. Your obsession with Claudia Borrell, your identification with the men she killed, your guilt over being unfaithful to Susan in the past, and your concern that you could be tempted to be unfaithful again if a woman like Claudia Borrell provided the opportunity. But beyond that . . . well, I'm impressed, Mr. Malloy. Impressed that you're finally confronting some of these issues in your life. And openly admitting to me the impact that Claudia Borrell and this story have had on you. In the past, you would have covered those emotions up with some jokes or other devices to hide your true feelings from me. But instead you've opened up to me about Claudia Borrell and all the rest. Like I said, Mr. Malloy, I'm very impressed with your emotional growth since we started these sessions."

"I'm more mature now," I smiled.

Landis smiled back. She smiled a lot more during our sessions these days. I took that as a personal victory since she had been such a stone face when we started, my jokes and witty repartee having no impact on her. But clearly there was only so long she could remain impervious to the Malloy charm. Okay, so this was only a smile. But that was just a short step away from a chuckle or even a guffaw.

CHAPTER **55**

STACY called me into her office not long ago.

"Did you know Victoria Issacs was promoting a lingerie line and doing a reality TV show on Houston?" she asked.

"Sure," I said, remembering the last conversation I had with her at the Sutton Place townhouse. "She told me about that."

"Did she tell you that you were going to be a part of the reality show?"

Stacy handed me a printout from her computer. It was a Page Six item that had just gone up on the *New York Post* website. Page Six had gotten an exclusive sneak peek at plans for the reality show—and she would be revealing shocking new things about her life as Houston. Including "never-before-told details about her relationship with controversial *New York Daily News* reporter Gil Malloy."

"Is there more about Houston that you haven't told us?" Stacy asked.

It wasn't hard to figure out what was going on here. Victoria Issacs needed to make news—get publicity—for the Houston reality show and lingerie brand. What better way than to reveal secrets about her and Gil Malloy? Would one of those secrets be how I tracked her down as Mrs. Walter Issacs a long time earlier, but never told anyone about it? I wouldn't know until the reality show aired.

I suppose I should be angry at the possibility that Houston might betray me like that, but—even if she does—I will sort of understand.

I know now that I somehow romanticized Houston into more than she really was—a woman from the streets who would do anything to survive. Even if some people got hurt along the way. Like me—a reporter who had tried to do the right thing by her to make up for doing the wrong thing once, but just wound up making everything worse.

Stacy didn't question me any more that day. But I know she won't protect me if it all falls apart, like Marilyn once did. I am still useful to Stacy now because of all the publicity I've gotten from the Blonde Ice story. Still, no matter how hot a commodity I am, that could all disappear overnight if people find out I didn't really tell the whole truth about Houston. Just like last time.

I thought I'd finally gotten rid of Houston in my life, but I haven't. She is still there—and always will be for me. Like Sisyphus, I fear I am destined to keep pushing that rock up the hill in an eternal, fruitless quest for some sort of salvation.

I opened up a Pandora's Box when I wrote that first Houston story that damaged my career, my marriage, and my life.

And now somehow Houston is still turning my life upside down all over again—a curse from my past that will never leave me alone.

———

I spend a lot of time these days following new murder cases around the country. Murders of men. Men who might have been cheating on their wives with other women. Blonde women. I keep telling myself that there is no possibility Claudia Borrell is still out there playing her deadly game, but I check the new murder cases obsessively.

I suppose I'll never know the truth for sure.

It used to be that a big story was all I needed to be happy. A big story made me forget about all the problems in my life. A big story was the ultimate answer for me. A big story always made everything better.

But now, looking around the newsroom—this place that has been my home and my life for so many years—I see unfamiliar faces everywhere. Stacy is in charge now, and she's surrounded herself with young new people who talk and think like her. And I wonder how long I'll still be a reporter here; I wonder how long before I will be considered too old by Stacy; I wonder if Houston really will reveal the secret that could destroy my career as a reporter; and I wonder what might happen to me then.

It's a scary thought.

Even scarier than the possibility that Claudia Borrell is still out there somewhere.

And I remember Marilyn talking in the bar about the nightly newsroom ritual she and I always had when I left at the end of the day. "Even after you broke a big story, you always had an answer for me when I asked my favorite question," Marilyn had said. " 'So what have you got for tomorrow?' You never let me down."

So what have you got for tomorrow, Gil Malloy?

For the first time, I'm not sure of my answer.

———

But I guess I buried the lead here. The biggest news I have is about Susan and me. We're back together again. Sort of.

It happened after the dramatic scene that played out with Claudia Borrell. When it was over, Susan ran to me and grabbed me and hugged me tightly, telling me how worried she'd been something might have happened to me. And then we went back to her place and had sex together for the first time since we were married.

"This might just work out between us after all," Susan said as we lay in bed afterward.

"You think?"

"It's not going to be easy."

"Maybe we should practice some more," I said, starting to kiss her again.

"Not the sex. You've got the sex part down fine."

"I aim to please."

"I'm talking about outside the bedroom. That's where we've had our problems."

"So we never leave the bedroom. We order in, we've got like a thousand channels on cable TV and we've got each other. What more do we need?"

She laughed. I loved the way I could always make Susan laugh.

"Let's get married again now," I said.

"I'm not sure marriage is the right thing for us."

"Well, we did it once."

"Remember how that turned out?"

"Fair point. But I love you, Susan. I don't want to be with anyone else but you anymore."

"Same here."

"So what's the problem?"

"I don't want to marry you, Gil."

"Ever?"

"Right now. Marriage didn't work for us last time. But you and I work together. We always have. I don't understand that and neither do you. So why not just go with that for now. You and me. Together. Without marriage. We'll still be in love, but with our own arrangement."

"Does this arrangement include frequent sex?"

"I would hope so."

"Always a plus."

"What do you think?"

"About the frequent sex?"

"About everything."

"I just want to be with you, Susan."

Then I kissed her again to confirm the deal.